17 FEB 2018
11/18
Chipping Barnet Library
Stapylton Road
Barnet
Herts.
EN
Tel: 020 8359 4040
KT-430-591

Rowena Macdonald was bo
West Midlands and now liv
story collection, *Smoked Mea*
Hill Prize. *The Threat Level Ren*
the time of writing, she still works

30131 05610339 0
LONDON BOROUGH OF BARNET

The Threat Level Remains Severe

The Threat Level Remains Severe

Rowena Macdonald

Aardvark Bureau
London

An Aardvark Bureau Book
An imprint of Gallic Books

Copyright © Rowena Macdonald, 2017
The moral right of the author has been asserted.

First published in Great Britain in 2017 by
Aardvark Bureau, 59 Ebury Street, London SW1W 0NZ

This book is copyright under the Berne Convention
No reproduction without permission
All rights reserved

A CIP record for this book is available from the British Library
ISBN 978-1-910709-15-3

Typeset in Minion Pro & Calibri by Aardvark Bureau
Printed in the UK by CPI
(CR0 4YY)
2 4 6 8 10 9 7 5 3 1

Lyrics on p190 from 'Real Beauty Passed Through' by
The Band of Holy Joy (1990) Rough Trade;
on p209 from 'Suedehead' by Morrissey (1988) HMV;
on p276 from 'Silk Skin Paws' by Wire (1988) Mute.

This is a work of fiction. Names, characters, businesses, events and
incidents are the products of the author's imagination.
Any resemblance to actual persons, living or dead, or actual events
is purely coincidental.

For Mum and Dad

All institutions have the same soul.

Ivy Compton-Burnett
A Heritage and its History

Part One

A recent January

1

THE THREAT LEVEL REMAINS SEVERE.

The words flashed in the corner of Grace's eye as she padded through the carpeted hush of the corridor. The letters pulsed, white on green, from the small television screen above the portrait of Lloyd George. Small televisions were attached high up on the wall every few metres all the way down the corridor. They were known as annunciators, annunciating as they did the future business of the House and what was happening at that moment in the Chamber. Occasionally they announced the estimated terror threat to the House. In a blink the screen flicked back to THE FINANCIAL SERVICES BILL – MR THORPE (WYRE FOREST) 15.33 15.45, as if the threat level had been a subliminal message. The Honourable Member for Wyre Forest had been speaking for exactly twelve minutes. Grace pressed the brass lift button and wondered whether to take the stairs for the sake of her thighs but, before she had decided, the lift slid into view with a gentle creak and she slipped inside. The threat message had been flashing up for months. It always disturbed her although it was hard to believe that any threat could be severe enough to pierce the layers of protection here: the solid oak lift and the iron struts of its shaft, the labyrinth of warm corridors, the huge stone carapace of the Palace, guarded by policemen with machine guns. Somewhere in the world, faceless conspirators were plotting against Britain, against the symbols of British power. Somewhere in the world, faceless state servants were hunched at banks of computers, decoding the electronic whispers of these plots and sending them to police officers in Scotland Yard, who were sending them to managers in the House of Commons, who were sending them to the people who typed the messages into the annunciators, messages which reminded Grace every so often that someone who knew nothing about her wanted to kill her.

'Cup of tea?' asked Rosemary, as she sat back down at her desk.

'Yes, please. Lovely.' Grace passed Rosemary a tannin-stained mug with a teabag inside and immediately forgot the death threat.

While Rosemary was in the kitchen, Hugo shuffled through and stood wringing his hands and peering at the neon-pink stress ball balanced on Grace's disk drive.

'New committee specialist starting on Monday,' he said, without looking at Grace. 'On secondment from the Treasury.'

'Oh yes. I'd forgotten. Girl or boy?'

'Boy. Well, man … probably.'

'You're not sure?'

'No, no, of course I'm sure – I interviewed him the other week. Everyone looks so young these days though.'

'What's his name?'

'Brett Beamish.' Hugo's mouth, buried in his beard, twisted a little in amusement.

'Brett Beamish.'

'As in "Come to my arms, my beamish boy"', said Hugo.

'What's he like?' Grace hoped he was good-looking.

'Australian, I think. Some sort of Antipodean anyway.' There was a sniff of disapproval in Hugo's voice. Grace suspected that for him new countries were like new money: irredeemably vulgar.

'Australian … yeah, sounds like an Australian name … Is he very brash and loud?'

'I don't know. He didn't strike me as particularly brash and loud at the interview. However, I would say he's rather …' Hugo picked up and squeezed the stress ball as if testing its ripeness. 'What *is* this?'

'It's a stress ball.'

'A "stress ball". Are you stressed?'

'I was given it on that training day last week.'

Hugo placed the stress ball suspiciously back on the disk drive.

'So, the new specialist: you would say he's rather ...?'

'I would say he's rather ...' Hugo looked at the ceiling. '... rather pleased with himself.'

'Who's pleased with himself?' Rosemary pushed through the door backwards with her large bottom, a cup of tea sloshing in each hand. 'Sorry, Hugo, I would have made you one ...'

'Don't worry, I was on my way down to the Terrace ...'

'We were talking about the new committee specialist ...'

'Oh yes. Girl or boy?'

'A young man.'

'Australian,' said Grace. 'His name's Brett Beamish.'

'Brett Beamish. That's a funny name,' said Rosemary, without laughing. 'Why's he pleased with himself?'

'I suppose he's had rather a meteoric rise ... so I hear ...' said Hugo. 'He's been working at the Treasury, in some sort of advisory role, but he's looking for an "opportunity to broaden his perspective", he's ready for a "fresh challenge".' Hugo's mouth twisted again. 'I do wonder whether he'll find this place rather "slow lane".' He emphasised these two words as if they were a daring piece of modern slang. Big Ben's sixteen-note refrain rang out as the bell worked itself up to strike the hour. Hugo listened to the four bongs with a rapt expression and shuffled off in the direction of the Terrace Cafeteria. He always walked as if he was wearing slippers even when he wasn't.

Grace and Rosemary settled into the downturn towards home time. The hours between four and six were painfully long, even more so than the other hours in the day, which were long enough. Time taunted them with the imminent prospect of freedom by slowing to the pace of dripping treacle. It was January. The light was already fading, the sky growing purplish over the yellow turrets of the Palace. Their office overlooked other offices across a wide inner courtyard, where other people also sat at desks in front of computers, bathed in epileptic fluorescence. It was cosy peering into warm, bright offices from the vantage of another warm, bright office. They were all so protected, not only by the stone and the guns but by the sheer weight of tradition, the promise of their comfortable pensions and the knowledge that they could work here until their retirement and would never lose their jobs unless they did something truly terrible.

Rosemary opened her biscuit tin and offered Grace a chocolate chip cookie. They indulged in sniggering conjecture about Brett Beamish: 'I wonder if he'll be like Russell Crowe.' 'God, it'd be great if he is.' 'Who's that other Australian actor?' 'I don't know … Mel Gibson?' 'No. Is Mel Gibson Australian? I thought he was American.' 'Guy Pearce?' 'Who?' 'You know: Mike in *Neighbours*, and then he was in *Priscilla* …' 'No idea who you're talking about.' 'Nicole Kidman?' 'Don't be silly … Man! … I'm talking about a man!' 'Jason Donovan?' 'No!' 'I'll Google him.' 'Jason Donovan?' 'No, Brett Beamish …'

All that came up was the HM Treasury website, his email address there and his name attached to various reports: *Productivity in the UK 3: Progress and New Evidence*; *Debt and Reserves Management Report*; *Delivering Sustainable Development: HM Treasury Action Plan.*

'I suppose we'll find out what he looks like on Monday,' said Rosemary. 'Non-sitting Friday tomorrow. I think it's you, isn't it?' She and Grace took it in turns to have non-sitting Fridays off.

'I think it is,' said Grace, consulting the chart pinned to the noticeboard, though she knew full well it was her turn because she had been longing for Friday ever since Monday. She was desperate to be out of the place, to slough off the boredom and tension that clung to her. Full relaxation was impossible at work despite the easiness of her job because she couldn't totally slob out. Although, actually, Gail and Julia, her flatmates, were so pernickety it was hard to fully relax at home either.

At ten to six, after she had filed some papers, logged some memoranda on an Excel spreadsheet and was about to shut down her computer, Hugo shuffled in and asked if he could dictate a letter. He could type adequately with two fingers himself but she suspected it made him feel grand to pace back and forth beside her desk declaiming sonorously.

'Dear Sir Michael – comma – The Committee – capital C – is very grateful for your letter of 9th of January – comma – put in the little "t-h", Grace, and the "of"; we're not American yet – regarding the Committee's Report on The International Monetary Fund: A Blueprint for Parliamentary Accountability – capital C, capital R …'

Rosemary gathered her belongings and was out of the door before Big Ben had finished striking six. It was twenty past by the time Grace had worked out how to print Sir Michael's address onto an envelope and printed off the letter three times – first on the wrong side of the headed paper, the second because Hugo noticed she had put the previous year on the day's date. She threw the third printout onto Hugo's desk and rushed out of the office. At the exit from the Palace to Westminster Station she couldn't find her security pass and had to upend the contents of her handbag onto the floor under the impassive gaze of a policeman. At the Tube's ticket barrier she had to repeat the process to find her Oyster card. Passers-by peered at the items strewn around her crouched form – the book, the phone, the lipstick, the spare tampon, the screwed-up balls of chewing gum in silver foil, the unused condom with the worn silver wrapping – and tutted at her obstruction to the free flow of traffic. Had it been anyone else she would have done the same.

2

The first person Brett saw as he emerged from Westminster Tube was the BBC's chief political reporter in a dirty raincoat, scuttling towards the river with his head bent and shoulders hunched. Hard to believe the BBC employed such a dweeb as one of their main news guys. In Australia, in America, they'd have someone slick and tough, someone likely to scare the shit out of politicians and force them into answering hard questions. This guy looked like he would've got sand kicked in his face at school. But that was Brits for you. Always rooting for the underdog. Brett sometimes wondered how he had managed to be so successful in England, seeing as he looked like such a classic winner.

His résumé reeled through his head. Damn, it was good. Especially with this new job added to the list. Even his dad had been impressed when he told him, although obviously, being Dad, his admiration had been tempered: 'Reckon you should've screwed more money out of them, mate.' Whatever he achieved, Dad always moved the goalposts further away. He'd been doing it his whole life. One of the main reasons it was good to be in England and out of his orbit. Still, in Brett's own eyes, his career was progressing according to plan. The B-Man was moving on up. The House of Representatives, Canberra. Her Majesty's Treasury, Whitehall. The Economic Scrutiny Committee, House of Commons. What next? The White House?

He'd totally walked the interview. The three stooges on the panel hadn't known what had hit them. From the looks of them they hadn't seen anyone as sharp as him in a long while. If ever. He'd rocked his charcoal Paul Smith suit with the trippy silk lining – shame you couldn't see the lining unless you made a massive deal of taking off the jacket and swishing it round but it was nice to know it was there and, of course, if someone who knew about suits clocked it, someone in the cognoscenti, they would be able to tell where it was from.

With the suit he wore a new Thomas Pink shirt, a white Pink shirt, fresh out the packet, although he had ironed it first, of course, because there was nothing tackier than being able to see the fold marks in a new shirt. Details, details, details. Most people didn't pay enough attention to the details. With the shirt he wore a grey Armani tie: fifty quid from Heathrow duty-free last summer when he'd gone back to see his folks. Grey, white and charcoal. Keeping it subtle, keeping it simple. Don't want to blind people with too much pizzazz from the get-go. Of course, he also wore his silver cufflinks, the ones shaped like tennis racquets that Nadine had given him for his birthday. Brett wasn't entirely sure the whole novelty cufflink vibe was entirely him – it was verging on cartoon socks – but they were Dunhill, solid silver, hallmarked, so he guessed they were just about acceptable. Nadine had spent seventy-five quid on them – he'd checked the price in Selfridges. Shame it all ended two months later but when it was over, it was over. Nadine was loaded anyway. Fucking lawyers.

Anyway, he'd walked the interview. Firm handshake, lot of eye contact, a few key words thrown in – 'targets', 'outcomes', 'objectives', 'stakeholders', 'prioritise', 'challenges', 'opportunities'. Didn't really matter what you said so long as you said it with confidence and looked sharp. Presentation, presentation, presentation. The Brits were only just beginning to learn this. These days only tall, fit, sharp-suited guys with smooth charm got to be PM. Tall, fit, sharp, smooth and with hair. Hair was non-negotiable when it came to leadership. Unless you were like

Putin: a real hard bastard. The current leader of the Opposition had no chance at the upcoming election. Although he had hair, he was too short and his voice was too nasal. He might just about get away with his height if he got his voice fixed. Someone should tell him. Brett wondered if he should be a spin doctor. He'd make an excellent spin doctor. Brett Beamish: *the brains behind the scenes*. Brett Beamish: *where the real power lies*.

The Commons' working day started at 10 a.m. Slacker's start. Brett arrived at 8.45. The cop with the machine gun at the main entrance looked at his pass and nodded him in. How cool was it to work somewhere that needed armed guards?

Inside, everything was huge and echoey and smelt like a church. Though he walked purposefully up to Central Lobby he realised he had no idea how to get to the office. Humiliatingly, he had to get another cop to show him the way. He hated looking lost but the place was a maze. Anyone would get lost in it. When he finally got to his desk – he knew it was his because it had nothing on it – no one else was in. Not even the old dude with the beard from the interview panel.

The office was really old-school – the furniture looked literally antique, like it had been around since Queen Victoria or something. Really huge and heavy and wooden. Kind of depressing. Brett wondered why they didn't sell it, install some stuff that was more streamlined and funky. There was even a fax machine. What was this? The *eighties*?

There were two other desks in the office. One belonged to an animal lover, judging by all the animal-themed crap everywhere: chick, no doubt – did guys ever dig animals *that* much? The other desk was hideously messy and also occupied by a woman from the looks of it: art postcards on the pinboard, rainbow-coloured paperclips, little knick-knacks from training courses lined up around the monitor – stress balls, plastic puzzles, little foam-rubber stick men, et cetera et cetera. No boyfriend pics though. Brett hoped she was hot. He hoped at least one of them was hot. He got the computer geeks to log him in to his computer, checked his Gmail and flicked through his own copy of the *FT*, although he noticed a fresh copy on the sideboard, along with the other broadsheets. He'd have to see about getting a subscription to Bloomberg: keeping up to date with business news was vital.

At 9.30 he went down to get a coffee from the canteen on the ground floor. Yet another cop had to show him the way there, too, which made him feel like some sort of pathetic tourist. There were no suits down there, weirdly. Only a load of construction workers pigging out on fried breakfasts. What the hell were they constructing? Weren't the Houses of Parliament built already? Didn't they finish them in, like, the olden days? Back upstairs, he scanned the Order Paper and the previous Thursday's Hansard and waited for his co-workers to arrive.

3

Grace was twenty-five minutes late. As always she had cut her journey time too fine and on arriving at the underground entrance into the House she discovered her pass was missing. The policeman on duty insisted she go around the outside of the Palace to the pass office at Black Rod's Garden Entrance to get a temporary one. This would involve a half-mile walk through slow-moving tourists. 'But you see me every day. You know who I am. Can't I go through the building?' pleaded Grace.

'Rules are rules. I don't make them up. Orders from on high.'

Flushed and harried, wearing a temporary visitor's pass, she flitted past Hugo's office, the door of which was, thankfully, shut, though tendrils of classical music escaped from it, which meant he was in. Crashing into her own office, she was brought up short by the sight of a strange young man sitting at the desk opposite her own. She caught his infinitesimally brief glance at the clock above the door. Instantly, she hated him.

'Hi!' He stood up, shook her hand very firmly and bared white, even teeth. 'Brett. Brett Beamish. New committee specialist.'

'Oh yeah. Sorry, I forgot …'

'You must be …'

'Grace.'

'Grace. Good to meet you, Grace.'

His accent, in Australian terms, was posh, the tone deep and pompous. She was conscious of her wind-blown hair, cracked boots and the sweat gathering under her arms. Brett was incredibly clean. The kind of clean that made her feel dirty. He was wearing a pristine black suit and a grey tie. His teeth were as blazing white as his shirt and his hair was as black and polished as his shoes. She glanced at his hands. His nails looked as if they had been professionally manicured. He was so clean that her next immediate thought was: gay.

She switched on her computer, dumped her bags and unravelled her outdoor clothes while Brett sat back down and resumed typing as if he had been sitting at that particular desk and typing at that particular keyboard for years.

'Tube was delayed,' she muttered.

'Which line do you come in on?'

'Victoria. Finsbury Park.'

'Ah.'

'What about you?'

'Same line. Highbury and Islington.'

'Right. Just down the road from me.' Bastard: showing up her lie and trying to outdo her already with his punctuality and posh address. 'Although I'm the wrong side of the tracks.'

'Don't put yourself down: it's kinda cool, the F-Park.' Brett grinned. 'Kinda gritty.'

The *F-Park*? Grace fixed him with a cold stare. Brett did not look like he had ever been anywhere gritty in his life. 'Where's Rosemary?'

'Here I am ...' Rosemary bustled in, stirring a mug of tea with a plastic spoon. 'Sorry, Grace, I would have made you one if you'd been here ... Brett didn't want one ...'

Brett lifted a large takeaway coffee in explanation.

'... I've told him about the kitty, how we take it in turns to buy milk ...'

Grace forced a smile, embarrassed to be implicated in the pathetic office rituals. Rosemary had no self-consciousness.

'I'm more of a coffee drinker,' said Brett. 'Gotta have my latte.'

He dropped the 't's in 'gotta' and emphasised them in 'latte'. Grace gritted her teeth.

'I have got some Nescafé somewhere but I must admit I do like my tea, don't I, Grace?' Rosemary squeezed the teabag and threw it towards her bin.

'You certainly do,' said Grace. The wall behind Rosemary's bin had an abstract pattern of tea splatters accreted over many years.

'So, Brett, we hear you've come from the Treasury,' said Rosemary, as if it were an exotic foreign country.

'That's right.' Brett smiled. His tone and manner were entirely pleasant but Grace was sure that internally he was mocking them both.

'And you're originally from Australia?'

'That's right: Melbourne.'

'I've got a sister in Australia. In Sydney. Lovely place. Wonderful lifestyle, Australia. Can't imagine how you can bear our winters. I went to see my sister last recess. She lives in Clareville, just north of Sydney. Do you know it?'

Brett said he didn't but nodded politely as Rosemary continued a lengthy paean to his home country.

'How long have you been in Blighty?' she asked, finally. Grace's toes curled so much she thought she might get cramp. Next thing, Rosemary would be describing London as 'the Big Smoke'.

'Two years,' said Brett. 'Before that I worked for the Australian Parliament and before that I did an MBA.'

'Gosh, you don't look old enough to have done all that. He doesn't look old enough, does he, Grace?'

Grace shook her head. Brett looked as if he had been moulded out of flesh-coloured plastic like a Ken doll and just unpacked from his display box. She wondered about his genitals.

Rosemary was still talking: 'Do you mind me asking how old you are, Brett?'

‘Twenty-seven.’

‘Twenty-seven! Gosh!’ Rosemary eyed Grace significantly, so Brett could also not fail to read her meaning. Grace remained impassive. Brett was so far away from her type he might as well have been a woman. When he had turned back to his screen, she considered him further: his shiny hair, his sharp-shouldered suit, his cold, assessing eyes and carefully judged smile. He was charged with the assertive vigour you needed to get ahead these days. But she couldn’t help feeling that he was as out of place among the Pugin arcana as the computers and the fax machine and the annunciators with their terror threats. Brett had worked elsewhere and he was from Australia – he had outside-world, new-world ways. Already she knew he was going to show them all up with his briskness and efficiency. Even Hugo. Particularly Hugo.

As if on cue the door of Hugo’s office opened, followed by a burst of Beethoven and Hugo himself.

‘I see you three have already made each other’s acquaintance. Have Miss Ballard and Miss Ambrose been showing you the ropes, Mr Beamish?’

‘Absolutely, Mr Llewellyn,’ said Brett, which made Grace warm to him a little.

‘Good, good. Do call me Hugo, by the way. I’ll let you carry on settling in … If there’s anything else you need to know, you know where to find me. We’ll have a proper talk sometime after lunch, perhaps …’ Hugo picked up the *Telegraph* from the sideboard, squinted at the sports pages and shuffled back to his office.

‘Grace, do you want me to make you a cup of tea? I can do, it’s no trouble.’

‘Huh? What?’ Grace was transfixed by her computer screen. An involuntary gasp escaped from her, which she tried to disguise as a cough. Rosemary’s voice was a trapped bee suddenly bashing at the window of her consciousness again. She was staring at an email from a person she had never heard of before, a reubenswift@gmail.com:

—i know this will seem weird and i dont want to freak you out – i promise im genuine not spam so please dont delete this – but i just really have to tell you: i think you have amazing beauty

'Yeah, tea, thanks, please, whatever,' she said, as she typed back, 'Who is this??'

4

Hugo did not emerge from his office for the promised 'talk' all morning. There seemed to be no actual work so, to keep himself busy, Brett organised his desk drawers. They were full of junk, thrown in any which way. The previous occupant had obviously been a total slob. Brett extracted all the paperclips, treasury tags, drawing pins and pens and arranged them in size and colour order. He threw out all the unused ketchup and salt sachets, the pens that didn't work, the pens without lids, the lids without pens and the four crushed Remembrance Day poppies. The leather top of the desk was thick with dust, thick enough to write your name in if you were the kind of person who did that kind of thing, which he wasn't.

'Who sat here last?' he asked, as he wiped the dust away with a paper towel.

'Not sure,' said Rosemary. 'We haven't had a committee specialist for ages. Not since I've been on the Committee, at least. That desk is Georgian, you know. If you look on the lock you can see the GR on the brass.'

Brett saw the GR. Where the hell George came in the scheme of kings and queens he had no idea but from Rosemary's reverent tone, it had to be a while back.

'GR. George Rex. King George. The Third, I think,' said Rosemary. '"The Madness of" and all that. Gosh, haven't you made your drawers neat.'

'Yep: a place for everything, everything in its place,' said Brett. 'So you haven't had a committee specialist since Georgian times?'

Rosemary tittered. 'Hugo once told me that that desk's got a secret cupboard in the back with a bottle of brandy in it,' she said. 'There should be a key.'

The key, which looked like a cartoon of how a key should look, was threaded onto an ancient piece of string, which was stuck with cracked sticky tape to the inside of the bottom drawer.

'Are you going to open it?' asked Grace. It was the first time that morning she had spoken to him with anything other than disdain.

'OK.' He got down on his hands and knees and struggled with the blackened lock at the back of the desk. It opened to reveal a small compartment containing a bottle that looked like it had been there, if not since Georgian times, then at least since before Rosemary was born.

'House of Commons Whisky,' he read from the yellowing label. 'Looks gross.'

'It's fine. I tried it once. Whisky doesn't go off,' said Grace.

'You tried it?' Rosemary was gobsmacked. 'When?'

'On a non-sitting Friday when you weren't here.'

'It's for emergencies! For clerks, not admin staff.' Rosemary glanced towards the door, as if Hugo, or some higher power, might appear. 'It's for if the House sits beyond midnight and they're on night duty. That's what Hugo told me. He'd go mad if he knew you'd been at it.'

Brett reckoned Hugo was probably knocking back his own secret stash of whisky as they spoke but he replaced the bottle. 'I guess Monday mornings don't quite count as an emergency, right?'

'Hugo wouldn't give a toss.' Grace rolled her eyes as if she thought both he and Rosemary were a pair of saps. She immediately began typing again. The speedy slapdash sound of it suggested she was emailing a friend rather than doing work. Brett returned to his chair. The small flurry of excitement settled into torpid stillness like the dust he had just shifted. For the next hour he scanned the Committee's last four reports and the Order Paper and looked up each of the Committee members on the intranet. The Chairman looked improbably unlined and unbald in his photograph. Born 1952 in Norfolk of Mary Montague (née Delamere) and George Montague QC. Educated at Harrow, PPE at Oxford. Former lawyer. Old-school Tory. Recreations: point-to-point, polo and painting. Did he have any non-alliterative hobbies? Presumably painting as in art rather than painting and decorating. Brett's heart sank. He could foresee he and the Chairman would have a hard time finding common ground. He didn't even know what point-to-point was. Apart from Sheila Brenton, a garish blonde the wrong side of fifty, the other Committee members were also middle-aged white men, whom it was going to take a lot of effort to tell apart.

'Not sure whose responsibility this is' – Grace and Rosemary both started to attention, looking alarmed – 'but I think I'm going to need some business cards made up—'

'Business cards?' Grace stared at him as if he'd suggested something bizarre and faintly outrageous.

'For when I'm meeting with people on official business, schmoozing witnesses, et cetera et cetera.' He imagined himself flicking them out of the snakeskin monogrammed card holder Nadine had also bought him from Selfridges – sixty quid by Aspinal.

'Don't think there's usually much schmoozing involved with witnesses—'

'Schmoozing Members, then—'

'Witnesses don't have a choice about whether they come or not, eh, Rosemary?'

Rosemary shrugged and continued typing. 'Business cards are Grace's responsibility.'

'Hugo doesn't have business cards, does he?' said Grace. 'I'm sure I've never done any for him.'

'I'd find them useful,' said Brett. 'Please.' He aimed his most icy stare at Grace.

She gave him a sarcastically subservient smile. 'I'll get on to it right away.'

5

Schmoozing Members. God, the new guy really was a dick. He clearly had an inflated idea of what his job would involve. And why couldn't he sort out his own business cards? She wasn't his personal secretary. Grace flicked back and forth between Outlook and the stationery request form. It was so tedious of Brett to make her do something so trivial while she had this weird, exciting email conversation going on.

—im reuben swift

—Yes, but who are you exactly and where did you get my email address?

—why are you so suspicious?

—Why do you think? You can't send random emails out of the blue and then not explain yourself.

— it wasnt random. i think you have amazing beauty, very unusual beauty and i just wanted to tell you that. i reckon youre the kind of girl that doesnt think of yourself this way. dont be cross with me

—How do you know what I look like?

—ive seen you around

Amazing beauty? Though this was obviously just shameless flattery, a warmth unfurled inside Grace and she had to concentrate hard on not grinning at the computer, which would have given rise to demands from Rosemary to share the joke. She also fought the urge to get her pocket mirror out and examine her face for signs of unusual beauty.

—Where've you seen me?

—around

—Yeah, but where?

—just around

—All right, what do I look like?

—youve got long auburn hair, blue eyes and pale skin. you look like a bronte heroine.

—'bronte'?

—like ann bronte jane bronte whatever their names were.

—Oh, you mean the Bronte sisters: Anne, Emily and Charlotte. There wasn't a Jane Bronte. Charlotte Bronte wrote Jane Eyre.

—yeah yeah thats who i mean. theyre always on at christmas. middlemarch or whatever.

—That's George Eliot.

—oh well, whatever. i can imagine you on a moor with your hair flying about in the wind. the kate bush type.

—Kate Bush wasn't a Bronte heroine.

—yeah but she sang about one.

—I suppose so. Actually it should be Brontë. With an umlaut. But that is a bit of a hassle, I must admit.

—youre clever arent you? knowing how to spell bronte and who wrote middlemarch.

—If you say so. But I think these things are fairly common knowledge.

—not to a bit of rough like me.

—Are you a bit of rough?

—would you like me to be?

—Er. I don't know. Maybe.

—is that what you like?

A couple more messages and Grace knew they would plunge into pure filth. Amazing how easily you could start talking dirty with a stranger. The freeing anonymity of the Internet was extraordinary. Time to back-pedal. She was at work. In the office. She was supposed to be doing Brett's bloody business cards. If

Rosemary knew what she was up to she would be disgusted. Brett would probably think she was a bit sad. And, in any case, if she and this Reuben Swift did end up meeting in the flesh, it would be embarrassing to have kicked off on this note. He might not be someone she'd want to talk dirty with. Despite this, her crotch was flooded with heat.

—I'm not telling you what I like at this particular juncture.

—ha! fair enough. juncture. i like that. youre good with words arent you?

—I don't know. I'm OK with them, I guess.

—although its not an umlaut

—what?

—in bronte. i looked it up. its a diaeresis: a mark (¨) placed over a vowel to indicate that it is sounded separately, as in naïve, Brontë

—Oh well I'm not that good at words then. I've never heard of a diar— whatever it is ...

—even a bit of rough like me can teach you something eh?

—I guess so.

—can i just tell you something else?

—I'm not sure.

Grace braced herself for a sweaty revelation unconnected with obscure linguistic facts.

—youve got a very pretty name. both bits. your surname reminds me of rice pudding and heaven.

—Rice pudding?

—ambrosia creamed rice. you know: rice pudding in a tin.

—Oh right. Ha ha. You've got a nice name too.

—thanks

Reuben Swift was a wonderful name. Grace set great store by names and spent more time than most thinking about them. For as long as she could remember she had kept a running list of names for future babies. Reuben was, in fact, one of her current favourites, along with Silas, Freya and Roisin. She knew her own name was romantic and appealing and, for reasons of aesthetics more than feminism, she would never take on a husband's surname, unless it was even prettier than her own. For Grace, names held the characteristics of their owners. Rosemary was dependable and robust – like the herb – the delicacy of the two names within the one was cancelled out by their being conjoined. The first syllable of Hugo sounded like a noise you might make when yawning, while the second syllable made the name both pompous and clownish. She considered Brett. He was now wearing a pair of headphones and tapping languidly at his keyboard as if cruising along a freeway. Brett was a modern, sharp name with very little poetry: going by first impressions she suspected it suited him. He certainly beamed a lot too. In a rather false way.

But Reuben Swift. Reuben was old-fashioned, biblical probably, with an exotic Jewish/gypsy vibe, which made it also sound modern and slightly American. Swift implied graceful speed and flight. The Jonathan Swift connection added gravitas. It was a decisive, handsome, masculine name.

—Anyway, tell me properly, how do you know what I look like? I've never heard of you. You can't have seen me around. This is really weird.

He didn't reply. Until now he had replied within a minute of her replying to him. His first email had been sent at 01.45. Reuben Swift was a night owl.

Out of the corner of her eye, she suddenly noticed the voicemail light blinking on her phone. She picked it up and dialled. Eleven new messages. *Eleven*. Bloody hell. She'd never had eleven messages before. She hoped she hadn't done something wrong, that it wasn't a load of people ringing up and complaining about something. With a faint buzz of panic rising in her chest, she braced herself. But each message was blank. All she could hear was the click of a phone being put down eleven times. Puzzled but relieved, she continued filling in the stationery request form for Brett's business cards, saved it, then sent it as an attachment to the print unit. When she'd finished Reuben still hadn't replied. She supposed she'd have to get on with work in a normal way. If Brett hadn't been there she might have told Rosemary about her mystery admirer. Although Rosemary wouldn't understand the excitement of an unknown man emailing out of the blue. She'd put a dampener on the thing. Best not to tell anyone. Work was more bearable with a little secret fizzing away beneath the humdrum.

This was the thing with the Internet. Back in the day – though not any day Grace could remember because she had started her first job after the advent of the Internet – people probably talked to their colleagues more. Now, your colleagues could be emailing their illicit lover, in a neo-Nazi chat room, playing online poker or, if firewalls permitted, buying sex toys, and you would never know unless you tiptoed up behind them and peered over their shoulder. While they went through the blameless motions of work, they could be simultaneously living a far more intriguing virtual existence.

She Googled Reuben Swift. Up popped pictures of a middle-aged black man in Washington, DC, a young white man of unspecified location but with American teeth, a man rugby-tackling another man and a blurry sepia gent in a bow tie with the pale, staring eyes of all Victorians in photos. On Facebook the only Reuben Swift was a portly, cowboy-hatted man holding up a large fish. He lived in Idaho. There were no Reuben Swifts on Twitter. On 192.com there were three. One was 31 – 35: an ideal age for her, although his location in Derbyshire was not.

Also he lived with four other people, all surnamed Swift, which suggested he was married with kids.

She caught herself. She was being silly. Reuben Swift could be anyone. He could be a woman. He could be a complete weirdo. Or someone playing a prank. For a moment she wondered if he was someone in the IT Department, tasked by management to find out whether she was a good employee or not.

—ive written a poem for you:

eyes likc blue skies
hair a dying sunset
skin like the moon
your face is the promise
of a wide open space
where the wind blows free
lets roll and fall in green

This new email was squeezed between an invitation to a Symposium on Business and Economics in Times of Crisis and a request from someone who wanted to be put on their press list. Grace wasn't confident about what comprised a good or bad poem but 'blue skies' was obviously a total cliché, and the rhyme of 'face' and 'space' was clunky and old-fashioned. Comparing her skin to the moon was a bit odd as well; surely the moon was full of craters. The suave persona that radiated from the name Reuben Swift was now tempered a little by naive gaucherie. Even so, she smiled to herself, as she typed back,

—That's really sweet. Do you write a lot of poems?

6

In the small, sharp atmosphere that followed his demand for business cards, Brett printed out the floor plan for each of the three main layers of the House and pinned them to his green baize noticeboard with four matching red-topped pins selected from his newly tidied drawers. As he reached up to the pinboard he knew Grace was making an effort not to glare at him. Deliberately casual, he leafed through all the newspapers, even *The Guardian*, and suppressed his instinct to sneer at its comment pieces.

After lunch (which he thought he might as well take as there was nothing else to do), he ordered another plastic in-tray via email from Reg Doig, the office supplies guy, who, as Rosemary informed him, was 'responsible for in-trays'. Rosemary seemed affronted that he had assumed in-trays were her remit. She made out she was up to her eyeballs in work but, catching a glimpse of her screen on his way back from the toilet, he saw she was poring over a picture of Russell Crowe.

'Checking out some hot Aussie talent, eh, Rosemary?' He wanted to call her Rosie, butter her up with a friendly Aussie-style nickname but he held back: you never knew with Brits; sometimes they got offended if you were too familiar too soon.

Rosemary instantly reduced the screen with a giggle and a blush and even Grace looked startled and guilty, as if she was also browsing something embarrassing – there was no way of knowing as her screen faced the wall behind. Her hideously messy desk was boxed into a corner by shelves of green-bound, long-forgotten committee reports.

Silence resumed. Brett sensed Rosemary and Grace would have talked more if he hadn't been there. He footled through obscure pages of the parliamentary intranet and, as he clicked from one link to another, a weird feeling came over him. His limbs felt as if, with each small movement – skating the mouse over the mouse mat, picking up his cold cup of latte, adjusting the back of his swivel chair – they were dragging through the kind of custard served in the Terrace Cafeteria. He wanted to lay his head on his keyboard and close his eyes. The feeling, he realised, was tiredness. How could he be tired? He had gone to bed early in preparation for his first day and slept for eight hours solid before rising at 6.30 for a bracing run around Highbury Fields. At the Treasury he would have written half a report by now, briefed the Minister and conducted three or four conference calls, all on his usual five hours of sleep. He surveyed the dusty tomes on the shelves, the dark wood, the leaded windows in their stone surrounds with their view of other leaded windows leading into other offices filled with dark wood and dusty tomes. Rosemary sat, placid and immobile, like the nesting hen depicted on a postcard among her collection of animal memorabilia, her vast hips squeezed between the arms of her swivel chair. If she stood up, the chair would probably come with her. Grace's head was lolling on one hand. The place was dead. Like they were in a museum. Or a mausoleum. He needed to liven things up. Inject Grace and Rosemary with amphetamines. Brett often thought and spoke in drug references even though he had always been squeakily clean-living. He stood up.

'Anyone want anything from the café?'

'No, thank you, Brett. I'm still finishing my tea.'

Grace shook her lolling head.

As he was heading out the door, Rosemary said, 'Actually, Brett, I know it's very naughty and I promised myself I was going to be good today but could you possibly get me a—'

'Bottle of Jack Daniel's? Line of coke?'

Rosemary tittered. 'No! Some chocolate. Here's fifty p—'

'Don't worry. I got it. What kind of chocolate do you want?'

'Maybe a Twix? Do I want a Twix? Or do I want a KitKat?' Rosemary's plump face became dreamy and girlish. 'Maybe a Flake? Or perhaps an Aero? Less mess, more chocolate. Or … I wonder if they have Double Deckers down there? Haven't had a Double Decker in ages … What *do* I want?'

'I don't know, Rosemary. It's your call.' Rosemary had veered off down unknown avenues of confectionery. Brett, not a regular chocolate eater, was only really familiar with the more international brands.

'I just can't decide …'

'OK, Rosemary. You know what? I'm going to surprise you. You could be just about to enter a whole new realm of chocolate. I could be the guy who's gonna take you there.'

Rosemary tittered again and Brett bounced away. Once he was out of earshot he knew Rosemary would start enthusing about his niceness. He grinned.

He decided to check out the café in Portcullis House. The Refreshment Department web page called it 'Debate'. The lack of a definite article denoted its modernity and youth. Brett reckoned it would be more his style than the Terrace Cafeteria, where he had eaten a steak and kidney pie for lunch. The Terrace was so encased in dark wood panelling it was like being in a coffin.

His confident stroll to Debate – *the* Debate, he decided he would have to call it, as there were limits to how modern even he could be – was foiled by various wrong turns and backtrackings and two demeaning interrogations by old men in white ties and tails. Who was he and what was he looking for? He let them examine his pass and listened to their long-winded directions with outward patience, inwardly seething with irritation. Bringing the floor plans might have stopped him getting lost but would have looked uncool. There was an escalator at the end of the walkway, which swept him away from crumbling stone and dark oak into the shining glass and steel of Portcullis House: from darkness into light. Standing in the middle of the other side of the escalator with stately disregard for those behind him who were unable to get past was a blind MP with a black guide dog. He was talking loudly but indistinctly into a Dictaphone. What a bummer to be blind. Still, the bloke had done well for himself, considering.

The Debate was a total relief: reassuringly loud and bright and filled with chattering people, clattering plates and the dazzle of sunshine striking hard, modern surfaces. And the women. Forget the food, the Debate definitely had the tastiest talent. Researchers and interns, straight out of uni, some of them probably still at uni, some of them possibly still at school, teetering across the skiddy floor in their high heels and pencil-tight, so-called business suits. There were women everywhere. As shiny and new and expensive as Portcullis House itself. Hard to keep your mind on the job in hand: buying a latte and … what was it? Oh yeah, some chocolate for Rosemary. He selected a packet of Special Edition Rolos with Chocolate Orange-flavoured caramel centres – they sounded suitably absurd – and strode back through the pointless grove of indoor trees, aware of a few admiring glances in his wake. This was where he would hang out from now on. Why couldn't he have ended up sharing an office with one of these hotties? Rosemary and Grace were OK. Well, Rosemary was OK: an auntie type, easy to charm. But Grace was bloody unfriendly. Fair enough, he wasn't here to make friends but, still, it was nice to at least have a few laughs with your co-workers.

He didn't understand girls like Grace. Didn't understand why they didn't make more of themselves. OK, so she wasn't hot, she was kind of plain, had eaten a few too many pies, but she could have made herself passable at least. Her hair would have looked nice if she took more care styling it; it was reddish, not out-and-out ginger, luckily, but a darker, more brunette kind of red. A lot of guys would go for her. Not him, obviously, but other guys. Guys with lower standards. Why go around in weird op shop dresses and clumpy boots when it was obvious what guys liked? Yeah, yeah. Feminism. Women's Lib. *Yadda yadda yadda.* He knew some chicks didn't believe in pleasing guys or thought they wouldn't be taken seriously if they looked cute. But that was bullshit. Take Nadine. OK, Nadine was a bitch. *Is* a bitch. But the one thing you could say for Nadine was that she looked good. She knew how to dress for maximum impact. Short tight skirts. Tight tops. Heaps of cleavage. Super-high heels. Stockings. In no way stupid though: a first from Cambridge, top-flight City lawyer, earning megabucks. She knew that if she looked good she'd get ahead. She knew she'd get taken more seriously if she took care of herself than if she went round looking like Germaine Greer.

'Rolos. Haven't had a Rolo in years. And they're Special Edition too. How exciting,' said Rosemary. 'Let me give you some money.'

'No wuckin furries. Get me a latte sometime.'

'All right. Perhaps I'll give you my last Rolo instead.'

'Are you sure you love him enough?' said Grace.

Brett frowned but laughed along with Rosemary. Some kind of Pom joke obviously.

'Good to see you're all getting on so well,' said Hugo, materialising at the door with the bleary air of someone who had just woken from a deep sleep. 'Now, Mr Beamish, perhaps we ought to have that talk.'

7

The man on the pass-office desk tapped his keyboard a few times and said, 'We're going to have to cancel your pass. It is now officially missing.'

'Then what do I do?'

'You'll have to fill out another pass form and get your line manager to sign it, then get your head of department to sign it, then bring it back to me, then we'll issue you with another pass.' The man's plump, bland face was impassive but from the sing-song relish in his voice it was obvious he was enjoying this small moment of power. He was sitting beneath a youthful portrait of the Queen in a white sparkly evening dress.

'Can't you just print me off another pass right now?' For once, Grace was eager to get to work, eager to resume her correspondence with Reuben Swift.

'No.'

'Why not?'

'Because your pass might have actually expired and you might be trying to gain entry to the parliamentary estate under false pretences. You should have come to see me before. Anybody could be wandering around the Palace now using your old pass. Any old Tom, Dick or Harry …' The man was now gloating, his moment of power extending far beyond his expectations.

'I came to see you yesterday. If you think my pass has expired how would someone else have used it to get in? Anyway, can't you tell from the computer that my pass hasn't actually expired?'

The man consulted his screen. 'No.'

'What if I manage to find my pass today?'

'It won't work any more. I've cancelled it.'

'Right. OK. I suppose I'll have to fill out another pass form then. And could you give me another temporary pass for today … Please.'

The man typed a few words and printed out a new pass which he gave to Grace with sarcastically florid hand movements.

'I could be gaining entry to the parliamentary estate under false pretences right now,' she called over her shoulder as she left.

The big oak door into the first inner courtyard swung open before she'd even got to it. The Chancellor of the Exchequer was on the other side. He was a handsome silver fox in a sharp blue suit. His mouth twinkled into a smile as he gestured her through and murmured, 'After you.'

Grace returned the smile and slid past his outstretched arm. A frisson passed between them, a frisson of something she rarely felt as she passed other suited men in the dim corridors of the Palace: sexuality. With a spring in her step she swung through the echoing courtyards, past the big blue garbage crushers and the smokers loitering under an archway. One of the builders checked her out. She smiled at him, catching the guy next to him in her beam, and sashayed on, as much as you could sashay in a pair of heavy boots and a winter coat. She must be giving off something today, some sort of pheromone. Maybe Reuben Swift had triggered something in her. If only there was more flirting at work. More real-life rather than virtual flirting. If only there were more men she wanted to flirt with.

She never seemed to meet any men these days: in the past year or so her social life had been curtailed by many of her friends settling down into insular domesticity and the rest moving out of London or going travelling. The only men she encountered at work, apart from the Chancellor of the Exchequer and the occasional builder, were an utter disappointment. The few decent ones were married and the rest were either genuinely old or old before their time. Stiffs in suits. Some might have started off OK – Grace detected the palimpsest of long-suppressed sexuality in the odd one – but a few years fussing about with pedantic paperwork and acting as deferential apolitical adjuncts to Members drained the spunk out of them. Neutrality neutered them. Easy workloads, secure contracts, subsidised cafeterias and warm, cosy offices made them as plump and placid as eunuchs.

'The Chancellor of the Exchequer just held the door open for me,' she said, when she got to the office twenty minutes late. Rosemary and Brett appeared to have been tapping away for hours.

'Ooh, which door?' said Rosemary.

'Black Rod's Garden Entrance.'

'How very appropriate,' said Brett.

'I'm sure he was giving me the eye.'

'He bats for the other side,' said Brett.

'What?' Rosemary flinched.

'The Chancellor of the Exchequer is gay.'

'No, he's not. Is he?' said Rosemary. 'I thought he was married.'

'He is but she's a beard and he's a total flamer,' said Brett.

'What?' Rosemary blinked several times.

Brett caught Grace's disapproving expression. 'Yeah, it's an open secret in the Treasury. I'm amazed the tabloids haven't got onto it, to be honest. Not that there's anything wrong with being gay, obviously.'

'Obviously,' said Grace. 'Anyway, you're talking bollocks. He's not gay. The tabloids would have definitely got onto it by now if he was and he was definitely giving me the eye.'

'What did he do?' said Rosemary.

'I'd just been to the pass office, 'cos I still can't find my bloody pass, and I was just about to get a policeman to open the door at

Black Rod's but then he opened it … and he kind of went' – Grace demonstrated their positions, made the Chancellor's ushering gesture flamboyantly courteous – '"After you, my dear" …'

'He didn't say "my dear"!' Rosemary clapped her hand to her mouth.

'No, not exactly, but that was the general tone. He's got a lovely voice. Sort of deep and fruity but in a good way. And he looks quite athletic.' She squared her shoulders. 'Very fit for his age. Nice hair. Nice suit.'

Brett turned back to his screen, shaking his head. '"Deep and fruity in a good way."' He snorted.

Silence descended and was only broken by Windows' fanfare as Grace switched on her computer, reminding everyone yet again how late she was.

'I'll tell you who *is* gay.' For the first time ever she opened her parliamentary email address before her Hotmail.

Brett and Rosemary jerked their heads up.

'Not me,' said Brett. 'Straight as a die, me.'

'The man in the pass office,' said Grace. The thought crossed her mind that Reuben could be the man in the pass office. Maybe he wasn't gay after all. But the pass-office guy was totally unfriendly. And totally unattractive. The pass-office guy would be so disappointing.

'So many gay men in this place,' said Rosemary.

So many men that might as well be gay, Grace thought about adding but didn't, as it would reveal too much about her dismaying love life and she wanted to maintain the subtle upper hand that had presented itself. Brett was staring fixedly at his screen. Even though she had been late on his first two days and he obviously thought she was a scatty slacker, in his anxious eagerness to establish his heterosexuality he had unwittingly revealed a glitch in his androidy self-possession. It was almost endearing.

Her stomach churned as she searched through unread work emails, hoping for Reuben's latest missive. And there it was, the answer to her last question from the day before:

—im 6ft 3, slim, ive got brown hair, wavyish, and green eyes.

He sounded gorgeous. Definitely not the pass-office guy. Six foot three. He would tower over her in a deliciously dominating way. Brown hair and green eyes: a great colour combination. She wondered whether slim meant scrawny. Hopefully not. Yesterday he had told her he was thirty-two, that he was an aspiring musician, a 'singer-songwriter – though i hate that phrase, sounds really adele', he had a boring temp job – 'too boring to go into but it pays the bills' – and he lived in Essex, beside the sea but within commuting distance to London. He was 'massively into music – musics probably one of the most important things in my life' – and he listed some of the artists he liked: Leonard Cohen, Nick Cave, Nick Drake, Pavement, The Innocence Mission, Silver Jews, Bonnie 'Prince' Billy, Prince Buster, Grimes, Joy Division, Neu!, Can, Toy, The Fall, Wire, The Residents … 'i could go on but i wont'. Grace had only heard of about a third of them and worried her list was tediously mainstream by comparison. She didn't mention that she quite liked Adele.

—Why won't you tell me where you work? she had asked.

—because it doesnt mean anything to me, its only a temp job and i dont want you to define me by it. you dont like to be defined by yr job do you?

—No. BTW, you still haven't told me how you know what I look like.

—i saw you once in a committee evidence session. i was sitting in the public bit. i had to come cos of my previous temp job.

—Really?? When? Which evidence session? Where were you working?

After five heart-thumping minutes during which Grace scrolled through half-formed memories of unknown faces at various evidence sessions, Reuben replied:

—back in november. the pfi inquiry. i was temping at the cbi. the director general was giving evidence and i was temping as his assistant. i had to take notes. you were sitting at a table at the side of the room. in portcullis house.

Grace could barely recall the evidence session, let alone anyone in the public seats. The session did exist – she checked the Committee's web pages, even watched some of the video recording of it, but the camera was focused tightly on the director-general so she could see no one behind him.

—How did you know my name?

—i googled your committee and the contact details came up and i just reckoned you were grace ambrose. you looked more like a grace ambrose than a rosemary ballard. and then i googled you and your facebook photo came up so i knew it was you.

—I'm afraid I can't remember seeing you.

—well you probably wouldnt cos there were loads of people in the public gallery bit, whatever you call it.

—Why didn't you come over and talk to me after the session?

—im q shy. anyway i had to leave with my colleagues. it would have seemed weird me coming over to talk to you.

Not as weird as emailing out of the blue nearly two months later, but she decided to let it pass. Still, it was so frustrating not to be able to remember him. She doubted she had even paid any attention to the members of the public. She didn't usually. Usually she sat in a slough of despond, trying not to fall asleep.

—I wish I could remember you. I honestly can't. What do you look like?

That had been just before six o'clock yesterday. She'd hung on for quarter of an hour for his answer but he hadn't replied until long after she'd left – she checked the time on his email: 02.47. Now, today, seeing his reply, she racked her brains again. Surely a tall slim man with 'wavyish' brown hair and green eyes would have caught her eye during the evidence session.

—You sound nice, she wrote, and immediately deleted it.

Big Ben chimed eleven and she suddenly remembered she was at work and the post in the general office in-tray had to be sorted.

'Your cards have turned up.'

Grace placed the small plastic box on Brett's desk.

As she turned her back, Brett emitted a strangulated cry.

'What's the matter?' Rosemary stretched over to take a card and giggled as she read it. 'Oh dear. "*Bratt Beamish*." Oh dear …'

'Is this a deliberate joke?' Brett seemed confused and offended more than angry.

'No, of course not,' Grace said, sucking her lips in to stop laughter seeping out. 'The printers made the mistake. It's not deliberate. I'm really sorry, I'll get them done again.'

Brett forced a chuckle. His determination to seem a good sport was again almost endearing.

Back at her desk, with the cards placed on top of her wobbly to-do pile, she returned to contemplating her reply to Reuben.

—Maybe you could send me a photo of yourself, to jog my memory, she wrote, finally.

8

So far the new job was going great for Brett. He knew it would. He had never known a job not go great. In fact, reflecting on his life or, more specifically, his *goals* (as he did every morning while styling his hair and repeating positive affirmations to himself), Brett had never known many things *not* go great. True, the Nadine scenario had not been great and his current accommodation and money scenario were less than ideal, but, generally, he had a pretty brutal exclusion policy with anything that didn't go his way. As his dad always said, 'Show me a good loser, and I'll show you a loser.' His dad was obsessed with winning, used to go apeshit if he got anything less than top marks at school, and when he failed to make the district tennis league, his allowance got stopped for three months.

He'd got Hugo onside by talking about cricket and by offering to write the whole of the brief for the next evidence session. (The brief turned out great. Hugo was impressed. So was the Chairman.) He'd also offered to write the next one. Hugo was even more impressed. 'At this rate you'll be running the Committee and I can just put my feet up.'

Rosemary had been a cinch to charm by loading her up with chocolate and making out he was really into animals. She'd loved his semi-bullshit story about the tame kangaroo he used to feed as a kid. 'Don't you think he's got a lovely way about him?' he overheard her say to Grace one day as he snuck out to fetch her a KitKat. Dignity and a feeling he couldn't quite place stopped him from hanging around outside the office to wait for Grace's reply, even though, among his co-workers, Grace's opinion of him was the only one he was interested in, mainly because it was the only one he was unsure of.

In all honesty, Grace was the only part of his current job that wasn't great. He had a nagging suspicion she'd misspelt his name on the business cards on purpose; after all, she was always subtly dissing him, and they'd already had several small squabbles.

The first happened just before she went for lunch on his third day. She rifled through the newspapers on the sideboard and demanded to know what had happened to the G2.

'What's the G2?' he asked.

'You know: the arts bit of *The Guardian*.'

'I never read *The Guardian*.'

'Oh.'

'Actually, that's not strictly true. I do occasionally buy it on Saturdays along with *The Times* – to get a political overview, y'know. The Guide's quite useful as well. Once I've read the main news I chuck everything else away though. Definitely never read any arts bits.'

Grace looked at him like he'd committed a war crime. 'You chuck everything except the Guide away? That's so unecological.'

'I might have a quick flick through the Sport and Money. Maybe also Travel. But I dump the magazine, I dump the review section, I dump Family – I mean, what is *that* all about? – and, to be honest, I dump the news as soon as I've skimmed it because it's basically all politically correct, bleeding-heart liberal propaganda.'

'I hope you recycle it all.'

'Recycle!' He snorted. 'Recycling paper is a total waste of time. It only gets shipped off to China and causes an even bigger carbon footprint than if you don't bother.'

'Right.' Grace held up a section of newspaper between

finger and thumb. 'Thank you for enlightening us all with your fascinating opinions. I've found the G2. I'm going for lunch.' She stalked out as if she'd got a poker up her arse.

Two days later she shot down his idea to introduce a birthday chart. Even the wipe-clean whiteboard he ordered to write the chart on made her sneer.

'It doesn't fit in with the rest of the furniture. It looks really officey.'

'We are in an office, Grace.'

'And then what happens? Do we all have to sing "Happy Birthday" to each other or something?'

'In my previous office we brought in cakes when it was our birthday. I used to bring in champagne too, but obviously I'm not expecting you to do that.'

'I don't want to feel obliged to bring in cakes for my own birthday. It feels forced.'

'Nobody's forcing you.'

His plan to create a break-out area in the middle of the office with two comfy chairs and a coffee table was also mocked.

'So when do we use this "break-out area"?'

'Whenever we need a break.'

'If I'm having a break, I want to get away from the office. I don't want to feel compelled to "break out" in the office.'

'Nobody is compelling you, Grace. The break-out area is for when you want a short break: when you just need to take five, chillax for a minute.'

'I can "take five" at my desk.'

For the next week, she sauntered across the room once or twice a day, saying, 'Look at me, I'm breaking out, I'm breaking out,' before collapsing onto one of the chairs with a sigh. 'I've broken out.'

*

However, the worst spat came during an evidence session with various banking executives in Portcullis House. Brett was next to Grace at the table reserved for staff. Grace fidgeted throughout the first part of the session, checking her mobile, rustling her papers, sighing loudly and continually rearranging her feet. The foot business was particularly annoying. First she slipped her shoes off (totally inappropriate red sequinned ballet pumps, covered in damp dirt from puddles) and tucked her feet underneath herself, then she tucked one foot under and let the other dangle (revealing a hole in the toe of her tights), then she untucked her feet altogether and crossed her legs, then she crossed her legs the other way. After ten minutes of stillness, during which Brett finally was able to concentrate on what the guy from the CBI was saying about SME lending, she opened her large 'ethnic' handbag (which smelt of hot goat), dug around in it and produced a packet of what looked like birdseed. Noisily, she opened the packet, ignoring Brett's scowls, and began dropping pinches into her mouth with chipped black-polished nails. At one point she even offered him the packet but he shook his head furiously. Hugo, sensing the hubbub, glanced over from his seat beside the Chairman but was too short-sighted to see what Grace was up to. Rosemary, parked the other side of Brett, remained oblivious, staring straight ahead at the view of Big Ben beyond the plate-glass window. Brett reckoned she had mastered the trick of sleeping with her eyes open because when the session came to an end, she sat up with a jump and blinked rapidly, as if retuning her eyes to waking reality.

'God, I am absolutely starving,' said Grace, as they walked back to the office, carrying the Members' abandoned papers.

'Yeah, I noticed.'

Grace turned to him. Her eyes were wide. 'Do you think I

shouldn't have eaten that snack during the session?'

Brett paused. 'It's not something I'd've done, personally.'

The faintest line appeared on the bridge of her nose and her mouth narrowed. She said nothing more but her bitchy attitude shot up threefold.

He didn't know why Grace's unfriendliness bothered him. He wasn't someone who needed to be liked. He wasn't a needy person. Needy people were losers. That's what Nadine always said. *Stop being so fucking needy, Brett.* In any case, who the hell was Grace? She had no power. No influence. She acted like her opinions mattered but, really, when the shit hit the fan, they didn't. She was relatively intelligent, she'd got a degree – OK, it was in something pointless and artistic like flower-arranging or sock-designing from a second-rate uni: number 76 when he looked it up on the UK uni league table. But, still, her accent, her *Guardian*-reading and her patronising political correctness all told him that she was reasonably middle-class. So why was she doing such a dead-end job? When he told her he had a degree from Sydney University and an MBA from Melbourne Business School, she had looked at him coolly and said, 'What was your degree in?'

'Economics,' he replied, feeling weirdly defensive.

'I thought it probably would be.'

What was that supposed to mean? Everybody knew economics was the basis of everything.

Team spirit was important for … well, it was important for the team. He'd learned this at MBS and read it in a dozen business manuals. So far, Grace was the weak link in the team. He didn't trust her. If they didn't get on, she wouldn't do things for him, the team would be less efficient and, when it came to his annual report,

Hugo would canvass Grace and Rosemary for their opinion of him and if Grace was negative, it could affect his performance score and, ultimately, his pay. *Working effectively with others* was one of the core competencies of his job. As the manuals said, problems should always be viewed as challenges. If Grace could never be made to like him, she could at least be encouraged to treat him politely so that he was able, as the manuals also said, to *get her buy-in* on future team projects. Grace was Brett's next challenge.

To this end, he decided to invite her to lunch.

'What're you up to for lunch today?' he asked, when Rosemary had gone off to her Wednesday lunchtime Relaxation class at the Jubilee Gym. Frankly, Rosemary was relaxed enough and could have done with being a little more uptight, especially when it came to her work output, but at least the class meant he didn't have to invite her too; Brett knew it would be easier to break Grace down alone.

Grace looked up from her screen, apprehensively. 'Nothing. Why?'

'Fancy grabbing a bite to eat in the Debate?'

Grace's mouth dropped as if trying and failing to think of an excuse.

'Or should that be "Debate"?'

'What?'

'"Debate". No definite article.'

'What?'

'Forget it. So, you up for it?'

'All right. I suppose so.'

'Good to see you're a meat eater,' Brett said, when they were finally parked with their trays of turkey escalope.

'Why, do I not look like a meat eater?'

He'd started off on the wrong foot: she was doing that whole poker-up-the-arse thing again.

'I suppose you assumed that I'm some sort of politically correct, *Guardian*-reading, bleeding-heart liberal and therefore a vegetarian.'

'You do read *The Guardian*.'

'I sometimes read the *Daily Mail*. If it's lying around.'

'And you do like birdseed—'

'What?'

'And you do live in north London ...' If she was going to rip the piss, he would too.

'So do you.'

'I know but—'

'Islington, no less.'

'I know but ...' If she only knew how un-Islington his flat was. 'Anyway, all I meant was it's good to see you eat meat.'

'Good that I'm not a total cliché, eh?'

'You're not a cliché, Grace.'

'Thanks, Brett.'

She laughed – at rather than with him, he suspected. This whole 'getting an uncooperative co-worker onside' thing was harder than the manuals claimed. Stretching back in his chair to make out he was relaxed, he glanced around at the other diners and clocked a glossy researcher eating a yoghurt opposite some bloke two tables away. If only he was sitting in that bloke's place. He turned back to Grace. Time to try the earnest interested tack.

'So how long have you worked here, Grace?'

'Would you rather be sitting over there?'

'What?'

'With that girl you just checked out.'

'What girl? No!' Brett thanked God he was not a blusher, for if he had been this would've been a moment of red alert. Jeez,

Grace was tricky. He smoothed his tie and his hair. 'So, yes, tell me: how long have you worked here?'

Grace composed herself with fake prissiness. 'Seven years.'

'And do you like it?'

'It's OK. I mean, it's not my dream job. I can't believe I've been here so long, to be honest.'

'What would your dream job be?'

Grace contemplated the middle distance, apparently blind to all the good-looking girls in the intervening space. 'Probably no job.'

Brett was genuinely shocked. 'You mean you'd rather be unemployed?'

'No. I just mean that no job is my dream job because I don't find work a particularly dreamy thing to do. It's just work, isn't it? You have to do it to pay the bills. Is working as a committee specialist for the Economic Scrutiny Committee your dream job?'

Brett laughed. 'No.'

'I bet that's not what you told Hugo at your interview.'

'No, but that's not the kind of thing you say at interview anyway … "This is my dream job" …'

'I thought it was.'

'It's not the kind of thing I say. I tend to focus on my skills and my previous experience and what added value I can bring to the role.'

'"Added value".' Grace laughed, and again Brett sensed she was laughing at rather than with him. This lunch was going wrong. She was acting like she had the power. He needed to get back in the driving seat. More questions: that was the way to do it. Surprisingly, he was actually interested in her answers.

'So you've no ambitions to be a clerk, then?'

'God no!'

'I'm sure you could be – you're obviously smart enough. I'm surprised you haven't been promoted.'

'Thanks, Brett. You're really laying the compliments on thick today.' Again, the sarcasm, but this time there was something flirty in it. He smiled. He was getting somewhere. He'd read in the business section of *The Times* the other week that there was no harm in flirting at work: the most successful employees played on their erotic capital.

'No, honestly, you should do something that makes more use of your skill set. I've got the feeling you're a little wasted in your current role.'

'I try not to be. I've cut the lunchtime drinking down to a minimum.'

'What? … Oh … Ha! … No, seriously, there must be something you'd rather do … even if it's not your dream …'

'I don't know. I'd quite like to get into something a bit more creative. I don't really know what though. Something to do with art maybe, or books.'

'You like books?'

'Yes, I'm a big reader. Do you read much?'

'Only non-fiction. Work stuff.'

'You never read novels?'

'No.' Brett shifted uncomfortably under Grace's amazed stare. Usually he didn't give a rat's arse if people thought he was a philistine. 'I mean, I sometimes do. I like James Patterson, John Grisham, that kind of thing. Generally though, no. Fiction doesn't really interest me. I'm more into real life.'

'God, I think I'm more into fiction.' She returned her gaze to the middle distance and Brett thought again that she could be OK-looking if she stopped wearing such daggy clothes and smartened up. Today she had on some sort of washed-out flowered dress that had probably come from an op shop. True, it was shortish, but it was slightly too tight, and not in a good way, plus she was wearing totally unsexy thick grey tights and flat boots that made her legs look stumpy. He wondered when she'd last had a boyfriend. He got the impression she'd been single for a while. She probably went for real pasty, limp-wristed geeks: what his dad would describe as classic Pom blokes.

The rest of the lunch they talked about work. Or, rather, Brett talked about work: his plans for future evidence sessions; his assessments of previous evidence sessions; the thrust of what he planned to write in the final report. Grace listened, quite politely and with some interest, it seemed.

'So what's your dream job?' she asked eventually.

'I want to get closer to the heart of power. That's my goal.' He waited for an expression of intrigue, but she stared at him like he had something stuck between his teeth.

'What do you mean? You want to be a *Member*?' She said it like a double-entendre.

'No. This place isn't the heart of power.'

'It isn't?'

'Of course not. I used to think it was. But I've come to realise that the real power lies elsewhere.'

'Where's that then?'

'In the City, of course. Where do you think?'

'Really?' She looked blank. Brett wasn't sure if she was having him on.

'Bankers are the real decision-makers in this country. They've got the real power. Why d'you think the Prime Minister spends so much time hanging out with them?'

'Does he?'

'Of course he does. Don't you read the papers?'

'Only really the arts bits, to be honest … Anyway, I thought it was the bankers that got us into this recession.'

'No … You can't believe everything you read in *The Guardian*.'

Grace seemed kind of awestruck from the way she was staring at him. He was sure she was impressed. As Kissinger had once said, 'Power is the ultimate aphrodisiac.' Even if you were invoking a level of power you hadn't yet achieved, apparently. He didn't want to get off with Grace but if she was in his power, she'd be on his side.

'So why don't you get a bank job now?'

'I'm working on it. I'm building up my résumé, scoping out the lay of the land. Once the right opportunity presents itself I'm going to grab it.'

She recoiled and looked slightly troubled. He wondered if he'd revealed too much. 'I'm going to have a latte,' he said. 'You want one?'

'Yes, please. Do you want some money?'

He pushed back her outstretched pound with his palm. 'No worries. It's on me.'

On the way back from getting them both a latte, he noticed the bloke who had been sitting opposite the hot researcher staring straight at him. His stare was unsettling. It was as if the bloke had witnessed his attempts to charm Grace and thought he was a schmoozy bullshitter. The hot researcher had gone. The guy glanced away when Brett caught his eye and Brett wondered if he'd imagined his hostility but, no, when he glanced back the bloke was staring at him again with cold intensity.

9

'How was your lunch with Brett?' asked Rosemary.

'How do you know I had lunch with Brett?' said Grace.

'A little bird.' Rosemary tapped her finger against her nose in a gesture that Grace found both inexplicable and irritating.

It was four o'clock in the afternoon the day after her lunch with Brett. At work it always seemed to be four o'clock in the afternoon. It was the time that best summed up the House. Grace was logging memoranda. Brett was out of the office 'meeting with' the Chairman. He'd put an out-of-office message on his email explaining this, which seemed excessively conscientious to Grace.

'So how was it?' said Rosemary.

'Fine.' Grace continued staring at the Excel spreadsheet on her screen.

'Did you get on well?'

'Ish.'

'What?'

'We got on well-ish.'

'You should make more of an effort with him.'

'I did.'

'I think he's got a soft spot for you.'

Grace turned to Rosemary. 'Do you?'

Rosemary nodded.

'What gives you that impression?'

'He's been ever so friendly to you the last few days.'

'He's just being "professional"', said Grace, as if it were a swear word, and turned back to her screen. An email from Reuben had popped up:

—hello. how are you today? Since their initial spate of emails a few weeks back, he had not emailed her at all. Not since she'd asked him to send her a photo to jog her memory. She had been disappointed, obviously, but had kept a lid on it. After all, how disappointed could you be about someone you'd never met? There was no photo attached to this email. Perhaps he hadn't got her last message.

'He likes you.'

'He doesn't like me in that way, Rosemary. He's just being friendly because he's into "team bonding" and all that crap.' In a way it was quite sweet that he actually cared about team bonding. Even his birthday chart idea, although she had mocked it, was quite sweet. She wouldn't have thought Brett would bother about birthdays. 'I'm not his type. And he's totally not my type.'

—Yes, fine. Busy. She'd play it cool, pretend she hadn't even noticed the huge gap in their correspondence.

Rosemary flinched at the word 'crap' even though Grace, who didn't consider it a swear word, often used it in her company. 'Well, I think he's lovely. Anyway, beggars can't be choosers.'

'What!' Grace clicked Send and faced Rosemary. 'I'm not a beggar!'

Rosemary gave a mild smile, apparently unaware that she was walking beneath a deluge of outrage dammed only by the flimsy twigs of Grace's sensitivity. 'No, sorry, dear. That wasn't very nice of me. But you know what I mean.'

Grace knew what she meant but thought it extraordinary that Rosemary, who had been single for ever as far as she knew, should be mocking her own singledom. Rosemary was what she feared becoming. Not that Rosemary seemed unhappy. One of the striking things about Rosemary was her contentment. Some people were easily pleased, Grace supposed. Rosemary was fifty-four and had worked at the House since she was thirty.

Since the age that Grace was now. In the next year she would be presented with a framed certificate of long service by the Clerk of the House, some John Lewis vouchers and the opportunity to have a free three-course meal in the Churchill Rooms. The prospect of this pleased Rosemary. She talked about it with pride and anticipation. The prospect would have depressed Grace. Vicariously, it did depress her. One of her waking nightmares was that she would still be working at the House as a Band C committee assistant in twenty-five years' time. Unlike Rosemary, Grace had never deliberately applied to work in the House and had simply fallen into her job: it was a temping contract made permanent, which she had taken after graduating to allow her time and money to think about what she really wanted to do. She had been thrilled at first: living in London, working in an iconic location, treading the corridors of power, rubbing shoulders with people who were making history. The money was terrible – indeed, when she had asked if she could have a higher starting salary, the semi-aristocratic woman who oversaw her appointment implied that it was vulgar to mention money and that the prestige of the place made up for the low pay. Grace comforted herself that she wouldn't be at work for a third of the year – the recesses were amazing. The university timetable would continue for her. August would remain a happy month. She had to hide her complacency from friends who were immediately plunged into the harsh regime of twenty-eight days' annual leave.

—busy with what? replied Reuben.

—Work.

—what sort of stuff?

—Oh, you know, the usual boring stuff. I can't be bothered to go into it.

—i know how you feel. i had an appraisal this morning. my boss said I needed to learn how to play the game. hate that phrase. hes such a bell end. pardon my french.

—No problem. I thought you were in a temp job though? Surprised they're doing appraisals already.

—well it was more of a meeting to see whether he wants to keep me on permanently but seeing as i dont play the game he probably wont.

—Oh right. Bummer. Or maybe not bummer. Doesn't sound like you like the job much. I know what you mean about 'playing the game' though. Last time I went for a promotion (which I didn't get) the chair of the interview panel said exactly the same thing to me.

The chair had been a middle-aged clerk called David Rowlings. Throughout their one-to-one post-interview feedback session he had stared at her from beneath hooded eyelids and let an occasional ironic smirk play around the corners of his mouth.

'The thing is, Grace, as in many areas of life, you need to play the game.'

'What is the game? I didn't know there was a game.'

'If you didn't know there was a game, that's probably why you didn't do very well at the interview.' Though David was younger than Hugo and had been in the House for less time he was higher up the departmental ladder.

'If you're not going to tell me what this game is, I suppose I shall have to work it out for myself and then learn the rules,' said Grace. The meeting was freighted with a flirtatiousness she was sure she hadn't initiated but it was hard not to respond to David's arch pronouncements in kind.

'Have you ever thought that perhaps you ought to look elsewhere for a job, that perhaps the House isn't the place for you?' he asked, his froggy lips still in a half-smile.

'Are you telling me that I'm never going to get promoted here?' David's flirtatiousness was giving her licence to be blunt. 'Are you basically saying my face doesn't fit?'

'I'm not saying that.' David was unperturbed. 'I'm just saying that sometimes one comes to a crossroads in one's life and one needs to take a different turning rather than just plodding along the same old path ...' His voice lifted. 'Do you know what I think, Grace?'

'What?'

'Maybe the best solution would be to find yourself a nice rich husband ...'

Grace stared at him. She wasn't sure if he was joking or not. She backed out of his office, self-consciously aware of her body, even though she was wearing nothing particularly revealing. On the way back to her office she considered complaining to HR but Rowlings would deny all knowledge.

'I'm sure he was joking,' said Rosemary, when Grace ran through it with her. 'That's just David's way. Everyone knows that's what he's like. Anyway, he's probably right really. I wish I'd found myself a rich husband. Too late now. Not too late for you though ...'

Rosemary's words had been cold comfort. Though she knew it wasn't objectively too late – she was only thirty – everyone else was beginning to pair up, settle down, have babies. Her last long-term boyfriend had been at university. Since moving to London, she'd only had flings with men who had turned out to be unsuitable in one way or another: mad, married, alcoholic, cokehead, commitment-phobic, chronic stoner, or sometimes a horrifyingly toxic combination of these traits. For as far back as she could remember she had been convinced someone would fall in love with her at first sight. Not that she considered herself an amazing beauty – often she thought she was quite plain and she knew she ought to lose some weight – but she felt she was unusual and she was certain one day someone else would feel this too. Perhaps Reuben was the someone she had been waiting for. The other week in the *Guardian* magazine she'd read about a woman who'd got together with a man who had dialled her phone number by accident. This online correspondence with Reuben could be the tale they told their children of how they met. She applied herself to his latest email:

—what a coincidence. youre a girl after my own heart. i hate people that play the game

—So do I.

—this boss ive got at the moment is one of those people thats played the game all his life. basically a total yes man.

—I think that's what you have to be to get on. Conform.

—yeah conform but also embrace change. my boss is one of those people who embraces change. mind you hes one of those people that would embrace whatever the management told him to embrace. if he was in 1930s Germany hed have joined the nazis.

—He's that bad? That's quite a harsh thing to say about someone.

—i often divide people up into nazis and non nazis, the collaborators and the resistance. the germans werent inherently evil ... its just that most of them, like the majority of any population, did what they were told to save their own skins. they were weak. they were yes men. like my boss.

Grace's mental image of Reuben as a laid-back, vaguely hippyish musician shifted.

Hugo loomed up behind her monitor with the agitated expression that came over him whenever work needed to be done.

'We must send out a revised press notice immediately. The one we sent out yesterday had the wrong room number on it and Mervyn King's name was spelt wrong.'

'How was it spelt wrong? Surely there's only one way to spell King?'

'Not his surname, his Christian name: it's Mervyn with a "y" not an "i"—'

'First name,' Rosemary piped up from the other side of the room.

'What?' Hugo glared at her.

'First name, not Christian name. You can't say Christian name these days. We did it in Equality and Diversity training.'

'For God's sake ...' Hugo clapped both hands over his forehead. 'Or am I not allowed to say God any more?' Shuffling away with slightly more purpose than usual, he called over his shoulder, 'Print it out, Grace, and bring it in for me to look over before you send it out again.'

Ten minutes passed in this way and when Grace checked her inbox again, there was another message from Reuben:

—sorry, that last email probably came across a bit harsh. hope you dont think im some sort of nutter. just pissed off with my boss. i just always feel its a waste of my time being at work. i wish i could make a living out of my music.

—Don't worry. You're probably right. About the Nazis, I mean. Yeah, it's a bummer that art doesn't pay. Mind you, you're lucky to have a thing you really love doing.

—dont you have a thing you really love doing?

—Hmm. I can't think right now. She wondered if he was trying to get her to talk dirty again.

—oh go on

—Drinking gin. Eating cakes. Having a laugh. I can't imagine having a job I really loved doing unless it involved drinking gin.

There were a few other jobs that vaguely appealed – PR executive; curator; events organiser; journalist; fashion buyer; advertising copywriter – but when she looked in the paper or online for them, she felt exhausted by how much experience you needed and what a supercharged character you had to be:

'hard-working, driven and determined'; 'innovative and highly organised self-starter with superb eye for detail and great initiative'; 'able to prioritise workload, work well under pressure and cope with tight deadlines'. Some ads made no sense: what was a 'full 360 role' or a 'boutique consultancy'? How did you know if you were 'results-orientated'? One ad read: 'ambitious, competitive and money-minded graduate wanted'. Grace could not imagine a more unpleasant-sounding individual.

At university she had never met any motivated self-starters who enjoyed tackling new challenges with great initiative. Most of her friends had enjoyed sitting around getting stoned, eating cornflakes and talking about trivia. Anybody who fitted the description of a job ad would have been considered a complete wanker. When Grace envisaged jobs she wouldn't mind doing, she generally envisaged the bits in between the prioritised workload: cups of coffee in stylishly executive settings cropped up a lot. Coffee-drinking was the highlight of her current job. Ideally, as she had told Brett, she didn't really want a job. Sometimes she thought David Rowlings had been right: she should try to meet a rich man who would look after her. Obviously, she never voiced this as it sounded totally wet, not to mention completely unfeminist. But, really, trying to 'have it all' was knackering: what sane person wouldn't rather stay at home watching telly, doing a bit of cooking, maybe having a couple of kids and sitting in cafés with other mothers? Admittedly, housework was tedious, but only as tedious as logging memoranda. Even without kids, she was sure she could fill her time with creative pursuits – painting, learning to play the piano, perhaps even writing a novel.

When she told people where she worked they always said it must be interesting and, out of politeness to them and the faintest sense of self-aggrandisement, she always said it was. In actuality, her tasks were repetitive and the reports the Committee produced were stultifying in their dryness. The Members of the Economic Scrutiny Committee were obscure backbenchers – no one notorious or glamorous, no rising political stars. To them, she was simply there to service them administratively: an interchangeable back-office bod. She barely exchanged more than a few words with them, and those words were only ever about whether they had got their papers on time or what room the next meeting was in. The few times she'd had an opportunity to talk more she didn't know what to say: she had to be careful not to reveal any party bias and her knowledge of politics was broad-brush and hazy, more about personalities and gossip than hard facts. Although she sometimes watched *Newsnight* she could never remember the details of government policies, the same way she could never remember how to calculate percentages or how to defrag her laptop. Whenever she was around Members she felt mealy-mouthed and suppressed. In fact, whenever she was in the House in general, she had to pretend to be someone she wasn't: someone respectful of hierarchy and rules, who knew her place and wasn't resentful that it was at the bottom of the pecking order. The job wasn't so bad that she wanted to get out immediately and a lot of the time she felt relieved she wasn't overly stressed; Grace was not one to push herself. But, for a long time, she had wondered if this was all that work would ever amount to: eight hours a day sitting in a swivel chair wondering when real life was going to start.

Unfortunately, she had the distinct impression Reuben was not a rich man. After all, he was only doing a temp job. He sounded like a tortured artist, slightly bohemian. Trouble was, she knew she wasn't the kind of girl rich men went for, not enough of a trophy. Also, she never liked the rich men she encountered. They were like Brett, only worse.

As she was thinking about all this, Brett bounced in from his meeting, looking, as always, very pleased with himself. Grace considered him as he slid eagerly into his swivel chair, woke his computer from sleep mode and began attacking his emails. Brett was not a young fogey, unlike many of the men in the House, and, perhaps because he was Australian, he couldn't exactly be described as a stiff: he was one of the new breed appearing more and more in Parliament. Grace found them more dismaying than the fogeys because they were ruthless, had limitless energy and, unlike the fogeys, who at least appreciated old things and had yearnings towards culture, they had no soul. This had struck Grace yesterday during lunch with Brett. His admission that he rarely read novels, for instance. If Brett and people like him had their way, the whole of Parliament, in fact the whole of Britain, would be as shiny and smooth as a newly opened Starbucks.

The girl he had checked out in the Debate yesterday was his type. A smart young professional with salon hair and a sadhu-esque ability to withstand the hot-coal torture of four-inch heels. The kind of girl who bought ready meals from M&S on her way home from the gym, read novels with whimsical drawings of women like herself on the cover, and dreamt of skiing holidays and spa weekends. The kind of girl who'd be able to get one of those exhausting jobs advertised in the paper. The kind of girl who would easily ensnare a rich man. That girl had been the equivalent of Brett. His equivalent, and entirely different from her.

10

At lunchtime the next day, Brett decided to go for a run around Westminster. His neighbours had kept him awake until 4 a.m. with their music, so he had slept through his alarm and missed his usual 6.30 run around Highbury Fields. He changed into his running kit in the gents and reckoned, as he swaggered back into the office to dump his work clothes before he went, that Rosemary and Grace were checking him out. His running kit consisted of metallic silver shorts, toothpaste-white trainers and a T-shirt with the Australian flag on it.

Hugo was waiting at the lift as he bounced past with a bottle of Powerade in his hand.

'Ah. *Très sportif.*' The lift slid into view. 'Shall I hold the door?'

'No, thanks, I'll take the stairs.'

The Secretary of State for Education was padding nimbly up the stairs in teenagerish ballet pumps as he jogged down. He pressed himself into the wall to allow her past and swore she also checked him out.

'Very impressive,' she said, referring to his dedication to keeping fit rather than his legs, he supposed, although who knew for sure.

'Not as impressive as walking *up* the stairs,' he said, grinning at her through the banisters as she climbed on up. For an older chick, she had pretty good legs herself.

'Don't shoot me.' He held his hands up as he jogged past a cop with a machine gun at the gate of New Palace Yard. The cop failed to crack a smile.

He dodged through the tourists swarming dozily around Parliament Square. Sometimes he felt like waving his pass at them as if he was trying to get backstage at a rock concert. The tourists were taking pictures of the anti-war protest in the middle of the square. The tatty encampment and semi-literate, scrappily painted placards offended Brett's aesthetic sensibilities. Fair enough if they had nothing better to do than protest but why be so messy, so lacking in style? Actually, it wasn't even fair enough: how come these people weren't at work? His taxes were funding their dole so they had time to hang around making a big deal about some war in a country miles away. The two misplaced apostrophes in one of the placards – *Its the kid's* – set his teeth on edge every time he saw it. *The kid's* what? What kid? Never mind the grammar, the sentence didn't even make sense in the first place and the manipulative sentimentality was nauseating: why did do-gooders always invoke kids? Adults were just as important, if not more so. At least adults earned money and got things done.

In St James's Park, his irritation thawed. The park was quiet beneath the grey sky. The big old buildings at the back of Whitehall and Birdcage Walk were pleasingly grand, solid and clean: the polar opposite of the makeshift tents in Parliament Square. This was how London should be. This was what the centre of government should look like. His breath misted in the cold air and his blood somersaulted through his veins. He pounded around the edge of the frozen lake, enjoying the power in his leg muscles and the lightness of his feet. In the muted, still landscape he was the only flash of colour and movement; just as he was amid the torpor of the Economic Scrutiny Committee office. He was young, he was fit, he was good-looking, he was clever, he had a great job at the heart of one of the most important cities in the world, he was doing really well at his great job, he was going to get an even greater job, he was crashing right into the back of his ex-girlfriend …

'Fucking hell,' shouted Nadine. 'What the—?' She turned round. 'Brett! Oh my God!'

'Nadine …' Brett came to a panting halt. They bristled at each other, their breath making empty speech bubbles. Nadine had teetered from a restaurant overlooking the lake, right into his path. Her gap-thighed legs struck scissor angles in their sharp boots. They were sheathed in stockings so sheer you could rip them with your teeth. She was wearing black leather gloves and holding a cigarette. The effect was halfway between fascist and fetish. A tall blond guy in a sharp suit was loitering a few paces behind.

'You nearly knocked me down. What on earth are you doing here, Brett?'

'I work round here, remember? What are you doing?'

Nadine composed herself and drew the blond guy's hand into her own gloved one. 'I'm having lunch with Oliver.'

'Oliver' was holding a cigarette with the awkwardness of a person who didn't often smoke. They were Nadine's fags. She had obviously upped her intake of self-conscious Silk Cuts since they had split up. Her smoking had sparked regular arguments between them even though Brett had to admit it did make her lips look sexy.

Oliver smiled, stuck his cigarette in his mouth so he could offer his right hand, nearly coughed the cigarette out, dropped Nadine's hand, swiped the cigarette with his left hand and re-offered his right to Brett as he coughed again. 'Oliver Parsloe-Haverton,' he drawled in a voice so posh it sounded as if he had a foreign accent. 'Pleased to meet you.'

'Brett Beamish. Pleased to meet you, mate.' Brett wrangled more of an Aussie twang into his voice than usual to show up the ludicrous stiffness of Oliver's voice.

'Ollie works at the Foreign Office.'

'Right.' Brett's mouth continued to smile but his eyes hardened. 'I work at the House of Commons.' Too late, he realised the Foreign Office was more glamorous than the House of Commons. Even its name smacked of exoticism, of far-flung places, of foreignness. The House of Commons sounded parochial, stay-at-home ... common.

'Ollie's going to be posted to Washington next year,' said Nadine, her sly glance at Brett made even slyer by the quick drag on her cigarette.

'Good for you, Oliver.' Brett felt a pain, like stitch, just below his ribs – some might have described it as heartbreak, but not him: heartbreak was for losers.

'How are you enjoying it at the Commons?' asked Nadine.

'Loving it. How's it going at Bradshaws?'

'I'm not there any more. I'm at Freshfields now. I got headhunted.'

'Freshfields.'

'Yes. One of the Magic Circle.' Nadine's smile curled tighter and she sucked slowly on her cigarette.

'Yeah, I know.' Brett tried not to be mesmerised by her lips. Wouldn't it be great if Nadine had literally been headhunted? Her pretty head chopped right off. With an axe. Or maybe a machete. She was so irritating. So smug. This Oliver – what was his name? Parsley-Haversack? – anyway, whatever his stupid name was, this Oliver was just the kind of upper-class Oxbridge prick that Nadine had always been angling for. Clearly, her dalliance with him had been an aberration. He'd been an exotic *amuse-bouche* among the roast beef and Yorkshire pudding that was her standard romantic fare.

Oliver ... *Ollie* ... Brett surveyed Ollie's corn-blond hair, his ruddy complexion, his frank blue eyes. To his credit Oliver gave no impression of gloating about Nadine, the way Brett would have done in his position. In other circs, he would probably be a decent bloke. The kind of bloke you could have a beer or watch the footy with. Cheerful, uncomplicated, unoriginal. He didn't wear his suit as well as Brett. A rugby shirt was more his style. Brett wished he was wearing his Paul Smith. His legs were suddenly silly and thin, the Australian flag on his shirt an over-emphasised, hickish point.

'So, are you still in that little bedsit in Holloway?' Nadine dropped her cigarette from her black leather fingers and ground it out with a knife heel as if the butt were Brett's face.

'It's not a bedsit, Nadine, it's a studio. And it's in Islington, not Holloway. And, yes, I am still living in the same apartment.'

'I've got a place in Chelsea now. Ollie only lives round the corner.' Her smile curled tighter than an overwound watch as she linked her arm through Oliver's.

'Well, that's just great, Nadine,' said Brett. 'I'm so pleased that everything's turned out so well for you. Anyway, if you'll both excuse me, I've got a few more laps of the park to do before I get back to work … Nice to meet you, Oliver.'

It took Brett three laps of the perimeter of the park to pound away his anger. He avoided the lake and didn't see Nadine or Oliver again, although at one point he passed the Labour Party's chief spin doctor pounding in the opposite direction, looking even more angry than he felt. A grim frisson of accord passed between them like an invisible relay baton.

11

—been up to anything interesting outside work?

Grace knew Reuben was angling to find out if she had a boyfriend. She wanted to keep him guessing, partly to tantalise him, partly to protect herself. The only thing she had done outside work in the past few days, apart from sit on the sofa and watch telly, was go out for a meal at the local curry house with her flatmates. She, Gail and Julia occasionally attempted to bond with each other: the result was evenings of forced cheer in which everyone secretly wished they had just stayed on the sofa. Or at least Grace secretly wished this. It was hard to tell with Gail and Julia: maybe their standards of enjoyment were lower. She told Reuben all this in not so many words and sensed he was delighted by her less than impressive social life.

—what are your colleagues like? he asked.

—Oh OK. Nice enough. Well, one of them's a bit of a pain. She hesitated to write 'prick': although she didn't think Reuben would be offended, the word would instantly make him think of sex and, if he wasn't attractive, she didn't want him thinking of sex in connection with her. The fact he still hadn't sent her a photo was suspicious. Soon she would have to demand one. It was too weird otherwise, not knowing what he looked like. Despite trawling through pages and pages of Google results for his name she could find nothing that corresponded to this particular Reuben Swift.

—which ones a pain?

—Brett. Our new committee specialist.

—whats wrong with him?

—He's just ... Grace halted, her fingers hovering just above the keyboard, and surveyed the smooth back of Brett's head across the office. What *was* wrong with Brett? He was far more friendly than she had assumed from her first impressions of his slick smugness. He kept them all stuffed on chocolate and swilling in cardboard cups of coffee and his insistence on remembering their birthdays was nerdily sweet. At that moment, he was printing synonyms for the word 'said' in neat block capitals (he never used lower case, so his handwriting always looked like shouting) on small Post-It notes and sticking them in an exact yellow mosaic around the edges of his computer screen. This was to help provide elegant variation in briefs and reports: *the Committee stated / noted / asserted / commented / maintained / pronounced / explained / elucidated / delineated ...*

... very professional, Grace concluded.

—i know exactly what you mean.

For the rest of the afternoon, while a tiny part of her brain was occupied with performing administrative tasks, most of her concentration was focused on conversing with Reuben about the falseness of professionalism and the soullessness of corporatisation.

—work is all about pretending to be something youre not. professionalism is a mask to hide the real person, wrote Reuben.

—Exactly. Although maybe if we didn't pretend and we all expressed exactly who we were all the time, we'd never get anything done. Work isn't supposed to be a group therapy session.

—but the ideal worker is like a robot. never gets ill or upset, is completely efficient and thinks about his job all the time. its inhumane the way worklife is so much about pretence. its like the way politicians always have to be abnormally squeaky clean in every single area of their life but they also have to pretend theyre as normal as the lowest common denominator ordinary joe. no one who is really successful is that normal. theyve just got a lot of self control maintaining a public mask of normality.

—That's definitely true about politicians. Probably true about Brett too but the House used to have a lot of quirky people working here. It didn't used to be like the outside world but the outside world is gradually seeping in.

—thats poetic.

Grace sometimes imagined the House as a medieval fortress – which it was, sort of – constantly lapped by waves from the Thames, waves that carried laptops and smartphones, smoothies and high-tech trainers, takeaway sushi and celebrity magazines. Until recently, no modernity had been allowed to spoil the reigning Puginalia. The House had been a realm of regal colours and serifed fonts. Even the fire-exit signs and the ladies and gents symbols on the toilets looked as if they had been fashioned by a man in a leather apron who belonged to a guild of master craftsmen. Grace suspected there might even be some peculiar law pertaining only to the House, which banned Arial on the signage. In the good old days clerks had been aspiring academics and writers, who dashed off reports in between writing theses and novels and discussing opera with their feet on their desks. Why were they all supposed to work so hard now? Whose idea was it?

—People like Brett: it's their fault, she wrote.

—americans, wrote Reuben.

—Brett's Australian.

—same difference. australia takes its lead from america even more than we do. i expect brett would get on well with phil and jenny.

—Who are Phil and Jenny?

—phils my boss. the one i told you about. jennys his secretary.

He told her more about them. From his descriptions she could imagine them perfectly: Phil, aggressively ordinary and reeking of fashionably unpleasant perfumes, and Jenny, a high-street honey, nicer than Phil but his female equivalent. In his faintly ungrammatical way, Reuben was a natural with words.

—Suburban types, she wrote.

—thats a bit snobby, Reuben replied. im from the suburbs.

—Sorry. I didn't mean to insult you.

—no its alright. youre right. they are suburban. commuter belt conspicuous consumers. ad mens dreams. lifed probably be a lot simpler and nicer if i was like them.

—Lifed?

—life would.

—What are you like, Reuben? I know nothing about you. It's getting a bit weird. You know what I look like. Come on, why don't you send me a picture of yourself?

There was a long gap before he replied again – as she was closing Windows at the end of the day she noticed a new message from him with an attachment.

sometimes the analogue tick tocks
nail me into a coffin of heavy oak
padded with the red of liver dinners
but the river glittering past
breaks this solid stone castle
into a reflected confetti
and sweeps it east out to the heedless sea
where i am free.

The subject line was 'counting out my life in photocopies'. The attachment was a picture of an intense-looking young man with ruffled brown hair and haunted eyes. He was sitting on a plastic chair in the corner of a room with a cigarette dangling from his long, sensitive guitar-playing fingers. He looked as lovely as she had hoped.

—Hey Reuben, I love your poem. You've captured exactly how I feel. Thanks for the picture, Gx.

Already she was imagining them wafting around bookshops hand in hand, both trailing long scarves. Corduroy in autumnal colours would feature heavily in their relationship. They would hang out in his bare-board garret overlooking the sea, drink wine, listen to his obscure record collection – all vinyl, of course – and have tender yet creative sex.

12

Time is money and money is time. Time is money and money is time. Time is money and money is time. The old man in front of Brett at the Dcbate checkout fumbled through every pocket before finally finding his wallet in his briefcase. Time is money and money is time. Brett tapped his finger on his tray in rhythm to this thought. The old man counted out £2.95 in ten- and twenty-pence pieces in payment for his Waldorf-style salad with grilled halloumi, crushed walnuts and red pesto. He was kitted out in checked lime-green strides and a pink and orange jacket. Both items, though hideous, were, Brett could see, expensively tailored from quality fabric. What kind of gentlemen's outfitters would sell such deranged gear? Clearly the bloke had myopically selected the fabric himself and was wearing made-to-measure. Kudos to the oldster. Still, it would be good if someone put a rocket up his arse. Brett was starving. Forgetting his composure for a moment, he let out a long agonised sigh. Like that of a giant tortoise, the old man's head rotated towards Brett, and his pale, bulging eyes regarded him with the stare of someone so ancient they are on a different planet. Implacably, slowly, he placed his five-pence change in his wallet and tottered away with his tray.

'Jesus, by the time I get to eat my salad it'll be cold,' Brett remarked over his shoulder to the person behind in the queue.

The person behind laughed. 'You know that was Sir Norman Goldstein.'

Brett turned. 'Oh God, no, I didn't realise.' The person behind was the hottie he'd spotted while lunching with Grace the other week. Her pass told him she was called Rachael Saunders.

‘Don’t worry about it.’ She smiled. Brett smiled back and so did the woman behind the till, though her smile was tinged with the embarrassment of disloyalty towards a Member. They knew their place, these till girls.

‘I’ve heard of Norman Goldstein but I never knew what he looked like … *Sir* Norman …’ Brett corrected himself with a fake cough. The idea of knights and lords was kind of fairy-tale and unreal and also kind of bullshit but some people in the House got pissed off if you didn’t bother with Members’ titles. Hard to know why as it wasn’t like you were dissing them personally, but perhaps dissing the concept of the aristocracy was the equivalent of dissing religion (another quaint and bullshit concept). Hopefully Rachael Saunders wasn’t a royalist, religious type but even if she was he didn’t want to piss her off.

‘Sir Norman’s quite distinctive,’ she said. They had both now paid for their lunches and were standing like museum exhibits in front of the glass wall that separated the inner and outer dining areas.

‘Yeah, he’s certainly got a distinctive dress sense,’ said Brett. He looked Rachael up and down. Her dress sense was perfect: short skirt, high heels and a tight top, he suspected, although this was hidden behind various folders that she was clutching to her chest with one hand while holding her lunch tray precariously in the other. ‘Are you meeting someone right now?’

She shook her head and pouted her glossy lips into an exaggeratedly glum expression. ‘No, I’m lunching all alone. My boss is off lunching with more important people than me.’

‘Shouldn’t put yourself down.’

‘I was only joking. But he is lunching with various Cabinet members.’

‘You wanna join me? I’m lunching alone too.’

‘Sure. Yes. Why not?’

Before long Brett had learnt that Rachael came from Haslemere in Surrey. She was twenty-four and had worked in City Hall for the past three years. Her boss was Boris Johnson.

'Boris Johnson. Ha!' Brett grinned. 'Whaddya think of him?' Surely all right-minded people – hell, surely even wrong-minded people – thought Boris Johnson was a ridiculous buffoon?

Rachael regarded him levelly. 'Boris is wonderful.'

'Right.' Brett chewed on a rogue uncrushed walnut. When he had swallowed, he said, 'In what way is Boris wonderful?'

Rachael's gaze roamed over the glass ceiling like a dreamy blue searchlight as she explained the wonder of Boris. He was incredibly intelligent, he spoke fluent Latin and Greek – 'Useful,' Brett nodded – and he was so generous, so kind, such a fair and understanding employer. He'd taken her on straight from uni and allowed her to do so many things that were beyond the ordinary duties of a PA – 'Oh yeah?' Brett covertly eyed her breasts – and he gave her so many opportunities; he really wanted to help her grow and progress her career. Most of all he was just really, really good fun: 'The funniest man I've ever met'.

'Right.' Brett speared a cube of halloumi. 'In what way is he funny? Example?'

'Oh ... well ... the other week—' Rachael began giggling '—he was supposed to be going to this charity dinner in the City and he came in—' her giggles swelled '—and he was wearing his cycle helmet and these shorts and—' she pressed a dainty hand to her glossy mouth '—you had to be there really – sorry – it was just so funny—' She could barely get the words out between bouts of hysterics.

'Sounds like a blast,' said Brett. 'His hair's kind of a mess though, isn't it?'

'No!' Rachael coughed her laughter into submission and laid down her cutlery; she had barely touched her goat's cheese tart during her paean to Boris. 'No! His hair is absolutely wonderful. So thick and blonde. It's his trademark. I love it.'

'It's kind of like a haystack though, isn't it? I mean, it doesn't look very professional.'

'Boris's hair is completely Boris. He's a maverick. He's not your run-of-the-mill, grey politician in a grey suit. He's a character.'

Automatically, Brett smoothed his already sleek black hair and the perfectly flat lapels of his grey Paul Smith jacket. Had Rachael noticed the lining? To ensure she did he took the jacket off and slung it over the back of his chair so the lining spilled out extra trippily. This lunch was not going as planned. Rachael didn't yet know anything about his excellent résumé. It would have been more relaxing to eat alone – he'd even wondered if he ought to start bringing in sandwiches to save money. But, then again, Rachael *was* really hot, the kind of girl it was impressive to be seen with, and if he brought in sandwiches he'd have to eat them at his desk – it'd be too shameful to eat them in public–and then he wouldn't get to meet girls like Rachael. Making sandwiches was for losers anyway.

Since bumping into Nadine and Ollie Jolly-but-Dull, he'd been feeling a weird urgency, a weird sort of rushy feeling that sometimes made his heart pound. The other night he'd lain awake until 1 a.m. and woken at five. The neighbours hadn't even been playing their music. He needed to find a girlfriend pronto. His hands clenched into fists at the thought that Nadine had moved on quicker than him and he wanted to punch something: an effigy of Nadine preferably.

Rachael glanced up through the indoor trees to the annunciator in the dining area behind the glass. 'Oh my God – the time! Sorry, Brad—'

'Brett.'

'—Brett. Sorry. I have to dash. Boris is giving evidence to the

CLG Committee this afternoon and we've got to go through his briefing papers. It's been wonderful to talk to you—'

'No worries.' Remembering his manners, despite his irritation, Brett stood up as Rachael fussed with her various folders, which, impractically, did not fit in her minuscule handbag. His slighted mojo returned as he realised he towered above her. She really was a very petite girl, very *pliant*, probably. 'You know, it'd be really good to carry on this conversation, seeing as we only just got started. Fancy a drink sometime? Maybe in Strangers'? Are you around this evening?'

'Hold on' – Rachael looked at her mobile – 'message – Oh, it's Boris – Drinks? – Yes, why not?' She continued opening the message, her pink manicured nails elegantly scrolling down the screen. 'Ah, I can't do this evening. Boris is going to need me until late. How about I email you later when I've checked my diary?' A stupid little smile spread over her lips as she read Boris's message.

'Sure,' said Brett grimly. 'Mail me ... Actually, here's my card.' He extracted one from his snakeskin card holder and she examined it with amusement.

'Brett Beamish. How sweet! It almost sounds made-up. How funny!'

Brett watched her tittup away on her high heels. God, she was sexy. Shame she was also fairly irritating. When she had disappeared into a lift on the other side of the concourse he looked at the three-quarters of her goat's cheese quiche that remained. Though he was still hungry, decorum prevented him from shoving it in his mouth. Only complete derros ate other people's leftovers. The name Brett Beamish was not half as funny as the name Boris. In fact it wasn't funny at all. What the hell was she on about?

Back in the office he discovered from a click on Wikipedia that Boris's full name was Alexander Boris de Pfeffel Johnson, which had to be about the most ridiculous name he'd ever heard.

'What do you ladies think of Boris Johnson?' he asked Grace and Rosemary.

'I like him,' said Rosemary. 'He's a real character, isn't he? Not your run-of-the-mill politician, is he? Definitely a character.'

'Definitely,' said Grace. 'You can imagine he's a real laugh. I didn't vote for him as Mayor – I couldn't quite bring myself to vote Tory … Sorry, I know I've got to pretend to be neutral – but I've got to admit I was tempted to vote for him, just for the entertainment value. Wish there were a few more characters like him in politics.'

Brett's brow furrowed. What was this weird charm of Boris's that clearly only women could see? It was inexplicable. As far as he could tell the guy was a total clown who looked as if he had a mop on his head. Surely in the correct scheme of things, women should find him, Brett Beamish BA (Uni of Sydney), MBA (Melbourne), tall, handsome, fit, Paul Smith-suit-wearer, with great, smartly styled hair, far more attractive than bloody Alexander Boris de Pfeffel Johnson.

'Just because you *are* a character doesn't mean you *have* character,' said Brett. He reckoned he might have invented this, in which case he could add to his list of impressive traits: *super-quick coiner of aphorisms.*

13

After the picture, nothing. Grace waited for Reuben's reply to her last email, but for days her inbox remained resolutely filled with work. She examined her last email again many times, wondering if it had put him off. Perhaps the kiss beside the G was too much, her 'love' for his poem too strong. Perhaps he was suddenly disgusted by her negative attitude towards her job, the way she had identified with his plaintive little poem so readily. From several attempts at Internet dating she knew full well how a blossoming correspondence could be cut short without explanation – usually the other person got distracted by someone else, so the effort spent crafting a witty and alluring online persona was wasted. Reuben could have met someone the night before. She pictured him in the upstairs room of a dingy pub, watching an unknown band and hooking up with a tattooed muso girl who would understand all his musical references. The thought made her fingers tense over her keyboard with envy. After a week she lost patience:

—Is that it then?

Half a minute later a reply popped up:

—is that what?

—I just wondered where you were. One minute you're sending me poems and pictures of yourself, next minute silence.

A short gap. Grace wondered if she sounded a bit demanding, a bit neurotic. But then:

—did you miss me?

—I just wondered where you were.

—i was busy. sorry.

—Got any more poems?

Really she wanted more pictures, but she didn't want to seem shallow.

—have a listen to this.

An audio file with the title 'Lost in the Forest' was attached to the email. Surreptitiously, Grace plugged her iPod headphones into her computer, downloaded the file and clicked Play. The song was sparse and melancholy, nothing but an acoustic guitar and Reuben's low, sombre voice. The lyrics referred to snow and isolation. She was transfixed. For the duration of the song she was no longer in her warm, ordinary office with her two faintly irritating colleagues. She was lost in a forest in the middle of winter. Reuben had talent.

—Wow, that was fantastic. Can you send me more?

He did. Several more songs, all of which were mournfully beautiful. And photos too, in response to the extra photos she decided to send him. There he was on a hill in a lumberjack shirt. Against a brick wall in a leather jacket. Playing his guitar in what looked like a pub. With a beard. Without a beard. With a trilby. Without a trilby. Whatever he wore he looked cool. They swapped emails all afternoon. At one point she told him he was 'very photogenic'. Really she wanted to say 'absolutely fucking gorgeous'.

That evening she ended up telling Gail and Julia about him. For once, they were all in at the same time so it made sense to cook together. Over supper, the inevitable subject of their lamentable love lives came up and it was hard for Grace to resist revealing that maybe, just possibly, her love life was finally taking a turn for the better. She played them Reuben's songs on her computer, having sent them, along with his new pictures, to her private email address so she could commune with them at home.

'He's really good.'

'And really good-looking.'

The pair gathered around her computer, while Grace flicked through his pictures.

'Yeah, gorgeous.'

An absurd glow of pride warmed through Grace, as if she were responsible for Reuben's looks.

'You definitely don't remember seeing him at that evidence session?'

'No, it's really weird. But then I probably wasn't paying much attention. And there were probably a lot of people in the public seats.'

'Is he on Facebook?'

'No, I've looked. He's not on Twitter either.'

'Weird.' Julia frowned.

'Unless he uses a different name?' said Gail.

'That's true.' Julia nodded. 'He could use a different name. Some people do, if they don't want to be tracked down by their school friends or something. You've Googled him obviously?'

'Of course. I can't find anything that fits with him though.'

'Are you sure Reuben Swift is his real name?'

'I presume so. Why would he make it up?'

Gail and Julia stared at her as if she was completely naive.

'He might be married …'

'… Have a girlfriend …'

'Yeah, but why bother contacting me then?'

Julia pulled a mock dim-witted face. 'Because he wants to have an affair. *Duh*!'

'Yeah, but if he wants to have an affair he's going to have to reveal who he is at some point when we finally meet.'

'You're going to meet him?'

'I hope so. Bit pointless carrying on writing to each other if we don't meet up.'

'Yeah … be careful though. Make sure you let us know where you're going when you do meet him.'

The next day she couldn't wait to log into her Outlook, to tell him how much Gail and Julia had loved his songs.

—I played them to them last night. They think you're brilliant!

There was a slight delay.

—er … cheers … grace i know this might sound a bit uptight but id rather you didnt play those songs to anyone else. like i said yesterday im not really ready to share them with anyone else except you.

It did sound uptight but she supposed artistic types were well known to be a bit precious.

—Sorry. I didn't realise.

—no probs

—Btw are you on whatsapp? Might be easier to message each other on whatsapp.

—whats whatsapp?

—You know: an instant messaging app. I just find email a bit cumbersome.

—im a bit traditional when it comes to communications. i only do email.

—Is that why you're not on Twitter? I looked you up and couldn't find you. I couldn't find you on Facebook either. Unless you use a different name?

—no im not on twitter or facebook. i dont do social media.

—Why not?

—i dont want people keeping tabs on me

—What people?

—government, big business, the powers that be.

—Do you think they really bother?

—of course. its a way of keeping control of the population. i dont want to give away a load of info about myself. who knows what they might do with it.

—I just thought Twitter could be a good way of getting your music out there, getting known, but I guess if you don't want to be known ...

—not at the moment no

Now was the time to go for it. She took a deep breath and wrote:

—Look, do you fancy meeting up sometime? It'd be nice to meet in person.

There was a suspiciously long pause. His pauses were as eloquent as his messages. As she opened his reply she felt slightly sick.

—sorry im q busy at the moment. i would like to at some point soon but right now ive got q a lot on

What a cheek. He hadn't seemed busy yesterday when they'd bonded over his music, when he'd sent her all those photos. What a bloody cheek. For the rest of the morning, Grace performed her tasks with angry efficiency. Brett and Rosemary did not appear to notice her mood. In fact, they seemed equally preoccupied. The office was silent except for the tapping of keyboards and the occasional sniff from Rosemary, who had a cold. Just before going for lunch in the Terrace, Grace bashed out one more email to Reuben.

—Have you got a girlfriend or something? Are you married?

As she ate she staved off her nervousness about his potential reply by burying herself in her book: *Kitchen Venom* by Philip Hensher. Extraordinarily, it was set in the House of Commons, in her very department about twenty years ago, when Hensher himself had worked there. The Journal Office clerks that featured in the novel spent their afternoons playing delicate little parlour games with each other, such as making lists of all the titles of

Trollope's books. Grace suspected one of these clerks might be a thinly veiled portrait of Hugo but when asked if he had known Hensher, his expression had become uncharacteristically humourless. 'I knew him vaguely,' he had said. 'He really didn't take his job at all seriously and spent most of his time ringing up his agent or proofing his manuscripts. He was never going to be a high-flyer.'

At various points as she read and ate, Grace had the distinct feeling of being watched, but whenever she looked up the other diners were engrossed in their food. All the way back to the office the same feeling crept over her but every time she turned around there was no one, or at least no one looking at her. She bought a stamp for her mother's birthday card from the post office in Central Lobby and was relieved to reach the privacy of the lift, although, even there, she kept checking the ceiling for hidden cameras. Back in the office, there was no reply from Reuben. She couldn't believe she hadn't thought of it before Julia and Grace had suggested it. She must be stupid. His silence answered her question: of course someone who looked like he did would have a girlfriend.

14

'I used to come here quite often with Boris, of course.' Rachael slurped her vodka and tonic and squinted hazily around the Strangers' Bar. It was her third V&T, as she called them, in less than an hour.

'Of course,' said Brett, alarm frozen to his brow at the speed of her drinking. Maybe it had been a bad idea to buy her doubles. Because she was so pristine, he had assumed she wouldn't be a big drinker, that she would be into maintaining her perfect figure and he would need to buy doubles to loosen her up, but he had forgotten there was a whole tribe of metropolitan chicks who drank rather than ate. Nadine had been one of them – 'Clear drinks have less calories,' she used to say, which always sounded like total bullshit to him.

'Do you want another?' asked Rachael, rising unsteadily to her feet even without her high heels, which she had kicked off one drink back. Her red toenails glinted through her sheer black tights. They were kind of sexy but Brett felt it was also kind of disrespectful to be shoeless in front of Members.

'Do you think we should go eat?' Brett was beginning to feel a little wobbly himself. He wondered if her tights were in fact stockings, or maybe hold-ups. With lace at the top.

'Just one more and then we should.' She placed a red fingernail against her bottom lip and strained to see the bar. 'I think … I'm gonna have … a white wine spritzer …'

'Do you think you ought to be mixing drinks? Vodka, then *wine*? … Always best to go up in alcohol content, not down …'

'Hard to go much further up than vodka unless I start drinking meths … No, don't worry, clear drinks have less calories.'

'That wasn't what I was—'

'Just one more and then let's go and eat. Where we gonna eat?' With every drink, her posh accent crumbled a little more at the edges. Like Nadine, her classiness was only skin-deep. This was precisely why girls like them were so hot for stuck-up private-school dickheads.

'How about the Churchill Room?' He had checked out the menu on the Refreshment Department web page and it wasn't *too* expensive. Hopefully, she'd only want a main course, perhaps even just a salad.

'I have already been there a few times with Boris—'

'We can go somewhere el—'

'No, that's fine. I don't mind going again. What was it you wanted again?' She was already halfway to the bar, weaving her way through the forest of rumpled grey suits. Leering gazes followed her progress and Brett swelled with renewed pride in being seen with her.

'An OJ. Straight up, no rocks.'

'What?' Her pretty lips curled. 'What's that in English?'

She was a pain, this girl. Good-looking, for sure, but a pain. Only pride was preventing him from bailing out early. Plus, once started, he liked to finish a job.

'An orange juice on its own with no ice cubes,' Brett enunciated with surgical precision.

'You don't want a shot of something in it? A little V? Or a little G? Or maybe a bit of W?' She pronounced it 'wuh' like a child.

'What's "wuh"?'

'Whisky!' She laughed for way too long. 'Wuh for whisky.'

'No.' Brett smoothed his tie. 'I've gotta heavy day tomorrow, gotta pace myself.'

Her nod and smile had a patronising tilt. She turned on her

stockinged heel towards the bar. She thought he was lame. Brett tugged his top button open, loosened his tie and lounged against the seat, deliberately casual.

'Only Members allowed tonight,' said the waistcoated flunky on the door of the Churchill Dining Room. The room swam yellow and muted beyond him.

'But I'man Occifer …' Brett gathered himself and waved his pass. ''n Officer of the House.'

The flunky examined the pass. Like all the catering staff in the House he was probably an illegal immigrant. Shouldn't even be allowed a pass himself. The indignity of being questioned by this uniformed little prick was totally out of order.

'You are not an Officer.' The flunky let the pass drop back against Brett's stomach as if flicking a crumb from a starched tablecloth. 'You are only allowed in Thursday evenings. If you book.'

'But I work for Boris,' interrupted Rachael.

'Who is Boris?'

'Boris *Johnson* … the Mayor of London.'

The few diners looked up in alarmed distaste at Rachael and Brett. They were presumably Members, though Brett didn't recognise any of them. Since walking along the corridor from Strangers', the booze had hit him like a blow to the head. The yellow room was spinning.

'Did you put vodka in that OJ?' he demanded.

Rachael turned and smirked. 'Might have done. Thought you needed a bit of livening up. Never trust a man who doesn't drink: that's what Boris always says.'

'*Jesus Christ* …' Brett steadied himself against a lectern which held the reservations book. She must have put in more than a single, more than a double even.

'You leave now,' said the flunky, who looked shocked by his blasphemy. Obviously originally from some godforsaken poverty-stricken Catholic hellhole. 'You are disturbing the other diners.'

'Whaddya gonna do? Call the Serjeant at Arms? Have us arrested?' Rachael was now rickety on her heels, her poise entirely evaporated.

The flunky signalled across the room to another more burly man in a waistcoat.

'Come on, lesgo.' Brett grabbed Rachael's arm.

'Geddoff. I can walk on my own.' She wrenched herself away.

'*Really?*'

'What's that supposed to mean?' They were now in the passage outside the flower room. Dying flower arrangements lay against the walls, waiting to be cleared away by the cleaners. The passage smelt of sweet rot.

'You're totally drunk,' said Brett.

'I'm not. I've only had a few.'

'A few too many … Where are you going now?'

Rachael was tottering under the stone arches towards a dim courtyard on the left. 'Why don't we go to the Sports and Social?'

Brett checked his Storm Aquanaut but, though it could apparently show the time underwater, it was impossible to read the numbers in the dark and Rachael was too drunk even to notice it. Not that he was bothered about impressing her any more. For once he was not going to finish a job. She was a waste of time. He was sick of girls like Rachael. He wanted to go to bed so he could get up early and run five miles around Highbury Fields before work, although the way his head was spinning it would be a major achievement to get up in time for work, let alone early enough for a run beforehand.

'No, I'm going home.'

'Aw, Brett, don't be boring … It's only – what time is it?'

'Nearly nine.'

'Come on, the night is young. Come on, Bretty.' She linked her arm through his but he shook himself free. Up close her breath smelt of booze – sweet and rotten like the dying flowers – and her two front teeth were smudged with lipstick.

'Don't call me that. No, I'm off. Let's face it, you'd clearly rather be here with your boss.'

'What?' Her face crumpled. She was on a tightrope, wobbling between anger and upset.

'You've talked about him all evening, you talked about him all lunch. Bloody hell, anybody'd think you were in love with the guy.'

The result was like puncturing a balloon of water. Her body deflated and tears erupted from her eyes.

Brett groaned. 'For Christ's sake.' Tears. Tears were such an embarrassing drag. Girls like Rachael could always turn on the waterworks instantly. Same with Nadine. Nadine would be hard as nails one moment, a puddle of salt water the next. 'Don't cry. Chill out. Jeez, I was only pointing out the way it seemed to me. No need to get upset.' Rachael had sunk to the ground, her legs collapsing beneath her like a deckchair. 'Come on, get up.' Hard to know whether to put his arm around her or not. Not, he decided. Tears were now streaming down her cheeks, dripping off her nose and chin. Sympathy would only encourage more tears.

She wiped them away with her hand, spreading watery snot across her face. 'I am in love with him,' she whimpered. 'I'm in love with Boris.'

Brett hailed a black cab on the corner of Parliament Square. He had sobered up and the grand, clean buildings that surrounded him were almost as solid and static as usual. He bundled the soggy mess that was now Rachael into the back of the cab and told the driver to take her to the address in Clapham that he had managed to glean, between her sobs, was where she lived. He wondered if he ought to pay for the cab but decided not – it'd be chivalrous but he had to be real: he couldn't afford it and, in any case, seeing as he wasn't going to see her again there was no point splashing his dough around.

'She's not gonna puke, is she?' said the driver. ''Cos I'm not taking her if she is.'

'Are you gonna puke?' Brett demanded.

Rachael shook her head.

'She's not gonna puke.'

'She better not …'

'Are you sure you don't want to come with me?' Rachael's face through the open window was a gruesome parody of coquettishness. Her mascara was bleeding down her cheeks and her lipstick was smeared around her mouth. She looked like a clown. Like a Halloween kind of clown. A cross between Alice Cooper and Robert Smith from The Cure. Brett was sickened. 'Are you sure, Brett?' she persisted. 'I'm really sorry about this evening. I'll make it up to you later.'

Despite everything she was still prepared to sleep with him. During their stumbling walk from the House to Parliament Square she had sobbed on about how she had been in love with Boris ever since she had first started working for him – he was so kind, so funny, so clever, so handsome; she wanted him so much she would do anything for him.

'I'm sure if you let him know he'd jump at the offer,' Brett had said, yanking her back from the hurtling traffic.

'No … to him I'm just a silly little girl. I'm too shy, I'm too fearful of rejection to tell him how I feel; I'm so shy and insecure really; people never realise it but I really suffer with anxiety …'

'Right. Whatever you say.'

Her glossy veneer was now blurred by tears and booze. A lesser man than himself might have jumped in the cab – it had, though he didn't like to admit it to himself, been quite a long time since he had last had sex. He was not a lesser man though. He was a morer … no, he was a greater man. He had standards. High standards. For himself and for those around him.

'No, Rachael, I don't want to come with you.'

He turned to the cabby's window.

'Take her home.'

No sooner had he crashed onto his own neatly made single bed than the music next door started up. He banged on the wall.

'Shut up!' His voice trailed off wearily, but he half hoped they heard: '… You stupid arseholes … Just because you haven't got proper jobs and your lives don't require any brainpower doesn't mean to say you can keep me awake …'

The music stopped. Half an hour later it started again. The plan for an invigorating dawn run around Highbury Fields dissolved like a laptop screen running out of battery charge.

15

The room where Grace was sitting was on an upper corridor of the House, a dimmer, less well trodden corridor than the ones below. It was the first official day of spring according to her House of Commons diary but the room was freezing. Even in the height of summer this room was always cold, as if it swirled with the ghosts of long-dead Members. At one end was a fireplace but it obviously hadn't been used in decades, probably not since the time of the painting above the mantelpiece which depicted *The First Parliamentary Point-to-Point Steeplechase*. According to a brass plaque this had taken place at Bicester in 1889. The men in the painting had portly bodies and jowly faces. Though it was more than a century later and they were wearing grey suits rather than red jackets and cream breeches, the men around the horseshoe of tables that day had changed very little facially. These men were some of the members of the Economic Scrutiny Committee. They were waiting for the rest of the members to turn up so the meeting to agree the Committee's Fifth Report of the Session could begin. Grace had begun to think of these words with capitals. She had begun to think in House style.

'Brass monkeys in here,' said one of the Members, rubbing his hands together with an exaggerated shiver. 'Is this an austerity measure – first day of spring and they immediately switch the heating off?'

'Talking of austerity measures, do you know what?' another Member said. 'I've found a way of saving money that ought to please my constituents. In the Tea Room, if you ask for beans *and* toast rather than beans *on* toast, it costs 25p less ...'

There were mutterings of interest and surprise.

'… but you *have* to make sure the beans don't touch the toast at all.'

'If you get soup in one of those takeaway cups rather than having it in a bowl, you get much more for your money.'

'Not very ecological, is it, though? Really we should be encouraging the use of bowls rather than takeaway cups. Leading by example …'

'… I know, but I often find that the soup goes cold quicker if I have it in a bowl, whereas …'

'Should we start?' said the Chairman, putting down the iPad he had been puzzling over like a bear with a house brick. 'After all, we are quorate … Where's Andrew?'

'I believe Mr Sharpe has been detained by a DL Committee,' said Hugo, who was sitting to the left of the Chairman. 'He informed the committee assistant he might be a bit late.'

'And Sheila?'

'Mrs Brenton assured us she would be here. As you know she's taken a very keen interest in this report.' Hugo was scrupulous in referring to Members by their titles rather than first names, which made him sound subtly mocking, though the intention was, Grace presumed, to convey respect.

'I think we should start.' The Chairman coughed and seemed to tap an imaginary glass as if he were on the top table at a wedding. 'Gentlemen, I call this meeting to order … Right, first thing on the agenda is—'

The door swung open and the vast bosom of Mrs Sheila Brenton MP sailed in, followed by the rest of Mrs Sheila Brenton. She was wearing an electric-blue dress splashed with enormous scarlet flowers, which made her look like an overstuffed armchair. The dress was startling, even by Mrs Brenton's garish standards. There were rustlings of eye-rolling amusement, even from Brett, who usually maintained an inscrutable professional glaze throughout committee meetings. Grace caught his glance and, to her surprise, a smirk flitted between them.

'Sheila … you're here … we've just started …' said the Chairman.

'Am I late?' Mrs Brenton looked at the hands of the clock on the far wall. 'I'm going by the nineteenth-century clock. By that clock I'm on time and by that clock' – she pointed to the annunciator screen – 'I'm two minutes late.'

'I like to think the Economic Scrutiny Committee is in twenty-first-century digital time,' said the Chairman. 'Never mind. Very glad you've made it. Sit down. Right. Agenda item one …'

Mrs Brenton eased herself into her usual seat in the horseshoe and glanced with imperious expectancy at Grace, who hurried to insert a set of papers into Mrs Brenton's ring-fettered fingers. Grace was not sitting within the horseshoe. Her place was next to Rosemary, behind a separate, smaller table in the corner of the room, on which were laid spare papers, as the Members generally neglected to bring the ones Grace had sent to them. She and Rosemary lurked, in purdah, handmaidens to the Members' whims. Grace was a subsidiary handmaiden to Rosemary, who took chief responsibility for the Members' comfort at meetings. Grace dealt with the little details: the papers that needed photocopying; the messages that needed delivering and receiving; the extra water that needed providing – 'delightfully still' or 'gently sparkling' – from the bottles with the House of Commons labels. She played a private guessing game about which water the Members would prefer; in general, old money, such as the Chairman, liked still, while the nouveau riche, such as Sheila, wanted sparkling, as if they thought bubbles were more bling.

Because her duties were so trivial, because she had no real

responsibility and the buck did not stop with her, Grace tended to drift off in meetings. If she had been allowed to join in, to say her piece when Members were bickering, it would have been easier to stay alert, but she was meant to be a silent, geisha-like presence. The fact she had no strong party leanings, despite her *Guardian*-reading, made her ideal for the job in one way, but she often feared her intellect might be rotting away through lack of use. She certainly felt her confidence in her abilities had rotted away. Sometimes she was jolted out of her daydreams by sudden laughter and found she had missed the end of a joke. Sometimes the Members' chunterings caught her attention – mainly when they weren't talking about official business but, that day, even the snippet about baked beans in the Members' Tea Room didn't interest her, which was unusual, as she was generally avid to find out about areas of the House she was forbidden to enter. Until Mrs Brenton walked in and provided a glint of comic relief, Grace had been submerged in a swamp of gloom that didn't contain enough light or air for daydreaming. She had been in this swamp ever since Reuben's last email and her realisation that their correspondence was not the beginning of a significant relationship. It was just a brief, odd blip along the monotonous line of her life. She hadn't heard from him since he'd rejected her offer to meet. Everything felt as if it was going to carry on for ever in exactly the same way: her Tube journey back and forth each day; the raw light of the carriages rattling through the black tunnels into infinity; the episodes of *EastEnders* watched each evening; the trips to Tesco to buy the same small-scale single-girl provisions; the inexorable routine of the office week – sending out papers, proofreading transcripts, organising meetings, preparing reports, filing, minuting, processing, collating. Nothing she did produced anything she cared about, anything that was hers. All it produced was more and more reports filed along the shelves, like long green caterpillars, and more and more papers which eventually had to be placed in green folders, then brown boxes and 'sent to the Tower', as Rosemary gothically put it. This was Victoria Tower, on the far south-west corner of the House, where papers stretching back hundreds of years were sorted and stored by archivists according to arcane and precise rules. Her name appeared, along with Hugo's, Rosemary's and Brett's, among the papers sent there. In decades to come, historians might peruse these papers. They might even cursorily note her name, but who she actually was would not matter to them. In the record of parliamentary history she meant nothing. This bothered Grace. Why it didn't bother the others she didn't know but it didn't seem to. Even Brett, whose ego was obviously bigger than hers, was apparently untroubled by the fact that the reports he wrote were co-opted by the Chairman and that the Committee persisted in the fiction that the Chairman had written them. Although, even if Brett's name had been embossed on the cover in gold letters, it wouldn't be that much of a step towards immortality – sometimes the recommendations in the reports influenced government policy and thus indirectly contributed to laws, but mainly they didn't; mainly they just added to the mass of printed matter that burgeoned as rampantly as Pugin's patterns all over the surfaces of the House. Committees were just a small part of the democratic process, which was something Grace had come to regard as a woolly, messy thing, like a badly hand-knitted jumper.

'You can see why dictators don't like democracy. It's so time-consuming and inefficient,' she had commented the other day as she filed a stack of letters in date order.

It was the first thing she had said all morning.

Rosemary looked worried and puzzled, the way she always did when conversation took a turn towards the abstract, but Brett laughed and said, 'So you'd like to live under a dictatorship?'

'No, obviously not.'

'Well then.'

'It would be OK if I was the dictator.'

'Dictatorships are always OK if you're the dictator. What kind of dictator would you be?'

'A benevolent one, I expect.'

'One that insisted on north London liberal values on pain of death?'

She laughed. Sometimes Brett could be quite funny. For a brief moment she had been lifted out of her swamp, but she soon sank back into it when the office grew quiet again.

'So,' Mrs Brenton was saying, in her comfortable coffee-morning voice, 'after the comma in paragraph 25, line 33, I think we should cross out "*and* this policy" and put "*while* this policy" … I think that reads much better … don't you think?'

She smiled brightly at the assembled men. They peered at the photocopied pages in front of them and nodded. Grace was sure most had only given the report a perfunctory skim and she couldn't really blame them since its title was *Financial Services: Evaluating the NAO's Framework for Benchmarking*. That Brett could get his head around such stuff meant he really was of a different species from her. She feared she had a frivolous mind. Certainly, her own pleasure and comfort were more important to her than any cause, and she was suspicious of those who made a big deal of their social conscience. The things that made her happiest in life were small and fleeting: a bike ride on a sunny day; a gin and tonic; a first kiss. Politics was so vast and abstract, who really cared? The Government missed the point about life. MPs pontificated and made laws but, in her own experience, people's individual lives still went on in much the same way they would have done had this or that Act not been voted for. In unstable war-torn countries she supposed politics mattered more and her apathy was the result of privilege but, even so, the things she wanted most were personal and nothing to do with benefiting mankind: an intimate relationship with someone she loved, a home of her own and a fulfilling job. None of which she had right now.

She wondered if politics even mattered that much to MPs in the final analysis. Their personal lives probably caused more heartache than anything that went on in the House. Right now, inside the seriously nodding heads of the thirteen people around the horseshoe, the most strange and rococo imaginings, the most unlikely hopes and fears, could be taking place. In committee meetings she sometimes wondered if most people in the room were just pretending to be grown-up. She hoped so at least.

The Chairman squinted at the report through the glasses he adopted for such occasions and said, 'Paragraphs 1 to 25, everyone agreed?'

Vaguely positive grunts from the men were punctuated with an emphatic 'Agreed' from Mrs Brenton. While the Committee continued to agree paragraphs 26 to 48, Grace studied Mrs Brenton: her manicured nails, her powdery skin, her carefully drawn lipstick and her gravity-defying hair. How on earth did she whip her hair into that stiff blond meringue? How long did it take each morning? What did it involve? Curlers, super-strong hairspray, a will of iron? Why did so many female MPs have such hair?

It was extraordinary that Mrs Brenton managed to come back and forth to Westminster each week, deal with constituents' problems, make speeches in the House, keep up to date with Treasury policies, attend weekly, sometimes twice-weekly committee meetings, debate bills, open fetes, judge school art competitions, network at official functions, be a wife to Mr Brenton and mother to their three teenage children *and* maintain immaculate nails and hair. Grace found it exhausting just doing a simple job for which she was completely overqualified. She watched Mrs Brenton twinkling lipstickily at the grey men around her and realised that, despite her monstrous embonpoint, her plain, powdery face and her dreadful clothes, despite her mundane mind and her unoriginal opinions, Mrs Brenton had utter confidence in herself on every front. This was her secret weapon.

Grace undid her own messy ponytail, pulled a tress of hair in front of her face, found four split ends and plucked them off. Her nails were short and had a two-week-old coating of chipped black polish.

'Are you some sort of *goth*?' Brett had remarked, the day she turned up with it on.

'No, I'm just tapping subtly into the goth aesthetic.'

'The goth aesthetic, eh?'

'Yeah, I read in the *Guardian Weekend* that the goth aesthetic is a key trend this season.'

Brett cracked up. 'Grace, you're a classic.'

Grace's mouth twitched at the memory. Brett did have quite a good sense of irony.

'I just don't think this recommendation is strong enough,' Mrs Brenton was saying, tapping her copy of the draft report with a peach fingernail. 'I think, instead of saying "The Committee recommends ...", it should say "The Committee *strongly* recommends ..." What does everyone else think?'

Everyone else nodded, including the Chairman. Everyone else thought Mrs Brenton was right. Hugo made a note of Mrs Brenton's amendment with his fountain pen and smiled his sycophantic yet superior smile.

*

The Committee agreed paragraphs 49 to 60 and paragraphs 61 to 75, changed a few 'ands' and 'therefores' and discussed whether paragraph 76 was too lenient towards the Financial Services Authority and whether paragraph 87 ought to emphasise further the responsibilities of the Treasury. Hugo scratched notes and stroked his beard while Brett stared into the middle distance but nodded every so often, so Grace presumed he was still listening. Rosemary sat upright with her hands clasped in her lap, primed to jump to attention. Occasionally, she glanced disapprovingly at the epic doodle of a trellis of daisies that Grace found herself drawing around her to-do list. Rosemary thought doodling in meetings was disrespectful, that it was committing some sort of contempt of the proceedings, so Grace carried on drawing daisy after daisy even when she felt like putting her pen down.

'Well,' said Hugo, as the staff made their way back to the office after the meeting, 'that went rather more smoothly than I thought it might.'

'Yes, the Chairman seemed pleased with the draft,' said Brett.

'Pleased with all your hard work, you mean,' said Grace, and even as she said it she regretted the bitterness of her tone.

Brett turned to her, apparently genuine hurt rumpling his smooth features. 'Yes, I did work hard on it, Grace. Contrary to the way it might have sounded to you, I wasn't trying to big myself up.'

Back in the office Rosemary disappeared to make a cup of tea, leaving Grace and Brett alone. Tension crackled in the air, louder than silence. Grace touched the space bar on her keyboard and the screen leapt into life with a cartoon sound like a spell being cast.

'Sorry, Brett. I didn't mean to offend you.'

Brett was filling his purple transparent stapler with staples. 'No worries.' He didn't look up.

Just before six o'clock, Hugo shuffled in, twisting his hands. He paced around the office peering at pieces of paper on the general noticeboard and at Grace's art postcards, making snuffly noises that could have been either disapproval or admiration. He stopped in front of the whiteboard on which their birthdays were written in Brett's neat capitals and said: 'Ah! My birthday on Friday. What a terrifying thought. Must have blocked it from my mind … as one tends to when one is as aged as I am.'

'I'm sure you're not that old, Hugo,' Brett said. 'You don't look old.'

'Oh, I am, I am.' Hugo stroked his beard as he mused over the date on the board, as if trying to remember how old he was. 'I'm older than I look.'

Grace stared at the floor and tried not to laugh. Brett was ridiculously insincere: Hugo looked like a very old man even though he was probably only in his early fifties.

'We ought to do something,' said Brett. 'That's why I put everyone's birthdays up there. I thought it'd be good for the team if we did something on everyone's birthday.' His voice was strained, Grace noticed, as if the prospect of celebrating Hugo's birthday was as appealing to him as a ten-hour-long committee meeting.

'I think you're right. What are people doing on Friday? How about I take you all out to my club for lunch? Given it's a non-sitting Friday, we can make it a long lunch, perhaps a very long lunch … It might possibly be quite jolly and it would, as you say, Brett, be very good for "the team".'

16

It was weird seeing co-workers outside the office. Even leaving the office together and huddling into the lift was weird and kind of embarrassing. Brett could feel the warmth of their bodies. The fresh scent of his Armani cologne did not ward off the waft of the others' combined odours: hairspray (Rosemary); musty crotch (Hugo); some sort of cheap perfume that smelt like one of those hippy shops in Camden Market he'd wandered into accidentally on his first weekend in London (Grace). He was the best-smelling person in the lift. And the best-dressed. And the best-looking … Brett sighed, momentarily exhausted and embarrassed by his own competitiveness in the face of such lame opposition.

'Six?' demanded Hugo, glaring at the sign above the lift door, which said MAXIMUM LOAD: SIX PERSONS. 'What kind of persons are they talking about? Anorexics? Starving Ethiopians? Giacometti sculptures? It barely fits four of us.'

Rosemary coughed an apology and tried to squeeze into the corner. How humiliating to be so fat. But then she should never have let herself get into that state in the first place. As the lift sank to the ground floor Brett adjusted his tie and smoothed his jacket. His hand glanced against his stomach. Even beneath several layers of expensive fabric it still felt taut. For the first time in several weeks he was glad to be Brett Beamish. For several weeks, without realising it, he must have not been glad to be Brett Beamish. Jeez, he had to pull himself together.

Outside the House in the gusty rain, Brett watched Rosemary open an umbrella and Hugo hail a taxi. He'd never seen them negotiate any equipment other than the printer or the photocopier. Apart from that excruciating lunch with Grace in Portcullis House back when he had been a total newbie, he had only encountered his co-workers in work scenarios.

'You should mess up your hair more often, Brett,' said Grace, when they were all squashed in the back of a black cab, crawling up Whitehall.

'What?' Brett ran his hands through his hair. It felt gross – the wax he'd applied that morning had turned sticky with the rain and was threatening to dry in clumps.

Grace was in the middle of the back seat between Rosemary and Hugo. She was looking at him strangely, kind of *down* on him, but maybe it was just because he was on the flip-up seat opposite, which was lower than the back seat. 'Yeah, it looks better a bit messy and windswept. What do you reckon, Rosemary?'

Rosemary, who was drowning in her own boobs and taking up way more than her third of the back seat, nodded. 'Yes, definitely. More rugged.'

'I wouldn't go that far,' said Grace. 'But it's certainly an improvement on it looking so anally neat the whole time.'

'What are you on about? Just because I take pride in my appearance, just because I don't want to go round looking like a derro, doesn't mean to say I look "anally neat".'

'Don't get your knickers in a twist. I was only joking.' Grace grinned. 'What's a "derro", anyway? Do you mean a tramp? We call them tramps in England.'

'Children, children … calm down, stop bickering,' said Hugo. 'This is my birthday, you know, and I thought we were supposed to be engaging in "team bonding", not petty squabbles about sartorial matters …'

'Sorry, Hugo.'

'Sorry, Hugo. Happy birthday again.'

Brett frowned out of the window at Horse Guards Parade where two poor bastards in red coats and feathered helmets were standing bolt upright pretending the rain wasn't bothering them. He glanced back at Grace, who was now also frowning out of the window. Actually she wasn't looking that scruffy today. She was looking quite nice. Very nice, he might almost go as far as to say – very nice in a boho way that wasn't really his scene. She had on a fitted brown suede jacket with a long, wafty scarf, a tight denim skirt and, instead of her usual scuffed boots, a pair of high-heeled green shoes with a strap across the ankle, Minnie Mouse-style. For once, none of her clothes looked like they had come from an op shop. Her hair was brushed and washed and swirled over her shoulders like a second scarf. Her eyes were smudged with a lot of dark make-up and her mouth was slicked with red lipstick. She'd made quite a big deal about this lipstick – frantically searching through her desk drawer for it, going on about how it was her favourite colour, then, when she couldn't find it, rushing out to the Boots near the Tube to get another one.

'How does *my* hair look, by the way?' asked Hugo, tweaking the ginger wisps that dusted his bald head.

'Very nice, Hugo,' said Rosemary.

'Your beard looks nice,' said Grace.

'Thank you, my dear.'

Hugo's club was on Pall Mall in a building that looked like a government ministry: grey and imposing with huge columns either side of the massive front door.

After checking their coats and signing their names in a register the size of the Domesday Book, they filed through a load of dusty rooms full of worn leather armchairs containing old men nodding over *The Spectator*. It was hard to differentiate between the furniture and the club members.

'... Very pleasant place to have a postprandial nap,' Hugo was saying. 'I often come up here on a Friday after work – read the paper, snooze in front of the fire, have a bit of tea, maybe a small sherry. Mrs Llewellyn gets rather annoyed sometimes – she likes me home on time – but, you know, a chap has to have his own space, somewhere to recuperate from the stresses and strains of life, cogitate over matters of import ...' The old men turned their heads as Hugo's well-fed voice rang out through the sleepy air and his brogues struck the parquet floor with uncharacteristically decisive steps. Not only was he proud of his club, Brett realised, he was also proud of his guests.

As well as a new girlfriend, Brett had been thinking for a while that he needed a club, a private members' club, somewhere to hang out when in 'town', even though 'town' was only two miles from where he actually lived. When he'd paid off his debts, he'd look into it. Maybe he ought to look into it now. Bugger the debts – you had to spend money to earn money. It'd be good to have somewhere to schmooze clients. He wasn't sure which clients he would schmooze since his job didn't involve clients or, unfortunately, as Grace had predicted, much schmoozing, unless you counted buttering up the Members, but a club was the sort of thing that someone like him ought to have. Not Hugo's club though. No, it would have to be somewhere zappy and go-ahead, full of attractive, successful people, most of them young women, preferably.

'It's usually roast beef on a Friday,' said Hugo, as they followed a waft of cooked meat and cigar smoke that led into the dining room. The atmosphere was so similar to the Terrace Cafeteria they may as well have lunched there. The club was like an extension of the House. No doubt Hugo's own pad was also a bolthole of polished mahogany and stuffed leather. His wife probably waited on him like the swarm of tuxedoed flunkies in this place, who were carving beef, pouring claret and manipulating Yorkshire puddings onto plates with silver serving spoons.

'This is cosy,' said Rosemary, as they were ushered to a table in the centre of the room, amid covert glances from the other diners, who, Brett noticed, were mainly glancing at Grace. She was the only vaguely nubile person in the vicinity, apart from himself – if you could refer to a bloke as nubile, which he wasn't sure about. It was probably just a chick thing.

He was surprised Rosemary wasn't more annoyed at sacrificing her Friday off to attend Hugo's birthday lunch. Had it been one of Grace's scheduled non-sitting Fridays, she would definitely have bailed out, but then Rosemary probably didn't have anything better to do, plus she was too loyal to Hugo to have made an excuse. She was wearing a boxy red jacket, the colour of a London bus, with a jewelled brooch in the shape of a giraffe on her lapel: an outfit that an MP like Sheila Brenton might have worn. Jeez, that dress Mrs Brenton had worn at the last committee meeting – you'd needed sunnies to look at her. He smirked to himself. Mrs Brenton had been well and truly buttered up by the B-Man's charm. After the meeting she had cornered him with her vast boobs and told him how 'incisive', 'articulate' and 'persuasive' his draft report had been.

'Your amendments really made a difference to it, Mrs Brenton. Really honed the argument,' he had replied.

'Do you think so? That's so nice of you to say. I always hope that my little comments are helpful.'

'The report wouldn't be half as strong without them, Mrs Brenton.'

'Oh, Brett!'

'Mr Beamish? Are you with us?'

Brett jumped. Hugo gestured to the waiter.

'You seem somewhat *distrait* today, Brett,' said Hugo. 'I think the staff are waiting for us to order.'

'Sorry ...' Brett took the menu. He hoped Hugo was paying because the food was not cheap. 'So what's the choice: beef, beef or beef?'

'I very much hope not,' said Rosemary, 'because I've just decided to go vegetarian.' When nobody reacted, she added, 'Mainly because of issues of cruelty.'

Brett noticed a low rumble emanating from a cluster of waiters near the carvery. A rumble of discontent. It seemed to be directed towards their table. Brett surveyed his co-workers. Nothing amiss as far as he could tell. No more amiss than usual. A different waiter began striding towards their table with a look of implacable determination usually seen on parking attendants. He was bearing down on them before the others had noticed.

Brett folded his menu very deliberately and cocked his head. 'Is there a problem?'

'I'm afraid I am going to have to ask you all to leave.'

'Pardon?' Hugo peered over his half-moon spectacles.

'Sir, I'm afraid I am going to have to ask you all to leave.'

'I am a member, you know,' said Hugo.

'I'm sorry, sir, but one of your guests is inappropriately dressed and, as you should know, club rules dictate that ...'

Brett peered down at himself – OK, an off-the-peg Moss Bros suit perhaps wasn't up to his usual standard of sartorial excellence but surely it wasn't *inappropriate*. Rosemary and Grace were also surveying their outfits in puzzlement.

'The young lady is wearing denim,' said the waiter. 'No denim is allowed according to club rules ...'

'It's a denim skirt,' said Grace.

'Club rules ...'

'Nobody said anything at the door. And it's quite a smart skirt. It's not like I'm wearing a scruffy pair of jeans and even if I was ...'

'This is really not on,' said Hugo. 'I'm going to take this up with the board.'

'I'd be grateful if you exited quietly, sir. You're disturbing the other diners.' The waiter was now practically pulling out their chairs and hauling them up. A couple of minions hovered nearby.

'If you weren't trying to throw us out then we wouldn't be disturbing them,' said Grace.

'The fact you are inappropriately dressed has already caused some disturbance.'

Grace glared around at the old men slurping up roast beef. 'Among who? Has somebody complained? I can't believe it …'

'Grace, keep your voice down …' Rosemary clutched her handbag like a lifebuoy. 'People are looking at us.'

'I don't care.'

'I'm terribly sorry, Grace. I think perhaps we ought to do as we're told.' Hugo placed a hand on Grace's back. His watery eyes had frozen into small grey marbles and were fixed on the head waiter. 'This is extremely embarrassing and upsetting for my guests and I can assure you I shall be writing a very strongly worded letter to the board …'

'Come on, Grace. Let's get out of here. It's not worth it.' Brett scraped his chair back. Who the hell was this jumped-up dickhead wielding his pathetic bit of power? He was all for rules in the right place but to make a huge public drama with some paying guests over a skirt was ridiculous.

They slunk out. Or rather Rosemary slunk, her face the same colour as her jacket. Hugo shuffled, his pride in both his guests and his club now crushed. Brett and Grace stalked in different ways: Brett nonchalantly with his hands in his trouser pockets and Grace haughtily on her new high heels. The old men returned to their roast beef.

*

'What an absurd rigmarole this is turning into,' said Hugo, as they retraced their journey back down Pall Mall and Whitehall in another cab. It had been decided they might as well go back to the House and lunch in the Strangers' Dining Room. 'Still, at least we can all now say we've been chucked out of a club ... How marvellously louche ...'

'Something to tell your grandchildren,' said Rosemary, whose blushes had faded to pink glee. She patted one of Grace's knees, peeking from the hem of the offending skirt. '"The day I got thrown out of a gentlemen's club."'

Grace smiled wanly. Brett suspected she thought it lame that Hugo and Rosemary should be so excited by such a minor transgression. She had suggested they go home and arrange Hugo's birthday lunch for another time. After all, it was a non-sitting Friday. But Hugo and Rosemary refused, mistakenly imagining Grace was upset and needed cheering up by a lunch somewhere posh even if it was back in the House. Brett knew she wanted to slope off back to Finsbury Park, get on with whatever it was she did when she wasn't being a committee assistant. She was so slack: a total bludger. Her idea that Friday shouldn't be a working day was a joke. Brett came in every Friday without fail. Always stayed till six at least even though everyone else was gone by three. It was easier to concentrate with no one around. Sometimes, on the way back from a latte run, he took detours around obscure parts of the building. Generally, the place was empty although last week he'd passed a weird bloke on a staircase near the Lords library. The bloke looked half anxious, half irritated, as if he'd been caught doing something he shouldn't. His face was familiar but unplaceable. Brett was sure he knew him. He glanced back. The bloke was standing in the same place and staring daggers at him.

'Everything all right, mate?' he'd asked, but the bloke had

turned and carried on up the stairs without answering. Bizarre. These days Brett was finding a lot of things bizarre.

'Brett … Brett … wakey-wakey … Are you ready to order?'

Brett shook himself to attention. Grace was waving at him from the other side of a table in the Strangers' Dining Room. She, Hugo and Rosemary were staring at him like they expected him to say something. They were surrounded by oak-panelled walls and dark heavy furniture. For a moment it was as if they were still in Hugo's club and the taxi ride back to the House hadn't happened. A guy in a tux was standing behind Grace.

Brett squinted at the menu that had appeared in front of him. The words on it were small and impenetrable, like a Hansard transcript. He blinked up at the waiter and hazarded a guess: 'I'll have the steak.'

'Are you not going to have a starter, Brett?' said Rosemary. 'We're all having starters.'

'A starter …' The words on the menu were now swimming in front of his eyes. 'Uh, not sure I … OK … the soup?'

'The soup.' The waiter scribbled on his pad. 'And how would you like your steak, sir?'

'Medium rare.' Thank God: the menu hadn't betrayed him. 'Please.'

'I'm having the steak too,' said Grace. 'Very rare.' She smiled at Brett. Her teeth seemed whiter than usual and it looked as if she had just reapplied her lipstick.

17

Something wasn't right with Brett. Grace only noticed it when they were finally ordering lunch in the Strangers' Dining Room but, in retrospect, he had been acting oddly all day. Considering these team-bonding birthday events had been his idea, he had been surprisingly morose, insular and un-Brettish ever since that morning. Almost as if, like her, he didn't want to be there.

Thankfully, Hugo's birthday hadn't fallen on one of her Fridays off, otherwise she would have been furious. As it was she was merely irked that she wouldn't be able to get away by three. By the time they had returned to the House after the skirt debacle, it was nearly two o'clock. Lunch was threatening to be a drawn-out affair with much fussing from the waiters and long gaps between courses. Hugo and Rosemary insisted on ordering starters, which meant Grace and Brett had to follow suit even though Grace hadn't wanted one for reasons of poverty as she wasn't sure if Hugo was paying, although she pretended she was worried about her waistline, and Brett, well, who knew, but he hadn't seemed to want one either. He could have been worried about his waistline too. Except he was putting away a lot of alcohol. By the time they were on their steaks he'd already ordered a third bottle of wine, having drunk more than his fair share of the first two. Such was his aura of health and efficiency, Grace hadn't imagined him a drinker. The odd beer with his mates to look sociable. The occasional martini in a swish bar when trying to impress a girl. A glass or two of good wine with a meal, but not bottle after bottle of the house red. Hugo had suggested Brett choose the wine – 'I'm sure, being a metropolitan sophisticate, you're more *au fait* with wine than I am' – but Brett hadn't even bothered to scan the wine list, let alone pontificate about grape varieties and vintages as Grace had expected, and simply told the waiter to bring them the 'cab sav'.

The other unexpected thing was how unruffled he had been by getting chucked out of Hugo's club. He hadn't even taken the piss. Instead, he'd demonstrated unusual solidarity, and when Rosemary fretted they might not be allowed into the Strangers' Dining Room either as 'ladies' were supposed to be 'formally dressed', he'd said, 'We'll just sit down and demand to be fed. Hugo's a clerk – they'll do what he says.' Hugo had looked doubtful but murmured, 'Of course they will.'

Yes, it was a subtly different Brett sitting across the tight stretch of white linen from Grace, chewing his steak. Thinking back over the past few weeks, she realised Brett hadn't been his usual self for a while. Definitely not as chipper. The newspapers were no longer arrayed in a careful flourish on the table in the break-out area and, like everyone else, he never bothered to break out there any more. The times he offered to fetch chocolate for Rosemary were rarer. One morning not so long ago he had come in twenty minutes late – later than Grace even – emanating gloomy fury and looking haggard, a look far more appealing than his usual vacuum-packed freshness. He had barely spoken that day. And then on Tuesday, after the meeting, he had been so touchy over her sarcasm about his report, and earlier that day he had been strangely embarrassed when she had complimented his messy hair. It had been rather endearing. Almost sweet. She had been so swamped in her own gloom, so vigilant about Brettisms – the way he still arranged his M&Ms in colour order before eating them; the way he still insisted on weekly team meetings in which he talked about 'mission-critical business' and 'cascading best practice' – that she had not noticed the un-Brettisms.

'How's everyone's food?' asked Hugo.

'Absolutely delicious,' said Rosemary.

'Very nice,' said Grace.

Brett nodded, his mouth full of steak.

'Don't know how you can both stand to eat it so bloody,' said Rosemary.

'Full of iron,' said Grace.

Rosemary had chosen the risotto of baby fennel, baby artichoke and cherry tomatoes and this time they listened dutifully to her reasons for becoming vegetarian, which stemmed from the volunteer work she was doing at her local city farm and how attached she had become to the pigs and chickens.

'But what about the suffering of all those poor baby fennels and artichokes?' said Brett. 'Ripped from the ground before they had a chance to grow up.'

Grace laughed.

'More wine, Grace?' Brett held up the bottle, his face impressively deadpan.

'Why not?' said Grace and their eyes met as he filled her glass. She flicked her gaze away to the clock above the door. Twenty-five past three. Still pudding and coffee to go. Maybe even brandies. Hugo would probably insist on brandy. Another hour it could take. She gulped her wine. Brett did the same.

'Brett assumed I was a vegetarian when he first met me,' she said.

'Did you?' Hugo continued demolishing his seared pigeon breast without looking up.

'I did,' said Brett.

'And why was that?' Hugo's attention was still trained on the pigeon.

'Because I'm a trendy *Guardian*-reading bleeding-heart liberal.'

Rosemary prodded her risotto and her gaze switched from Grace to Brett and back again, fearful at this forbidden exposé of political beliefs even though there were no Members around. 'Are you?'

'Am I, Brett?' Grace raised an eyebrow.

'Well, your heart probably bleeds more than mine …' said Brett.

'Whose doesn't?'

They laughed. Hugo and Rosemary didn't. A pleasant wooziness seeped into Grace's head. It was a Friday afternoon. The weekend had started. Everything felt soft and easy. So what if she hadn't got away at three? So what if she was still technically at work, when, by rights, she needn't be? Nothing really mattered.

'This is odd,' said Grace, surveying their surroundings.

'What?' Brett followed her gaze.

Grace turned to face him. 'Being here.'

They were in the Sports and Social. Two full vodka and tonics were on the table between them, along with four empty glasses, two smudged with crescents of red lipstick. Lunch seemed hours ago to Grace. Almost a whole other day. Her limbs felt casual and floppy with alcohol. Hugo and Rosemary had been shaken off in between leaving the Strangers' Dining Room and arriving at the Sports and Social. Brett had suggested another drink but Rosemary had to get back to tend to the baby hedgehog she had rescued from the road last night and Hugo had to get back to be tended to by 'Mrs Llewellyn'. The two 'young things' were advised to 'run off and play'.

So they had. And now they were sitting in a corner in the dingiest bar in the Palace, which was, as Grace said, odd, except that actually it didn't feel that odd, and she'd only said it did because … because … well, she was too drunk to think quite why she'd said it.

'I just wouldn't have thought this would be your kind of place,' she said.

'Why? Because I'm so anally neat the whole time?'

Lounging with his tie off, Brett was, as it happened, not looking at all anally neat at that moment. He looked like a whole other Brett. A better Brett.

'That really got you, didn't it, that comment?' Grace rested her head against the greasy velour upholstery. The Sports and Social was untouched by modernisation. It had sickly lighting, a stained and florid carpet, and was steeped in a fug of stale beer and the sweaty waft of dubious pies in a heated cabinet on the bar. There was a dartboard and a pool table and a fruit machine that winked relentlessly in the corner. There was even a jar of pickled eggs. Grace had been aware of the Sports and Social's existence but had never known where it was and, being disdainful of socialising at work, had never bothered to find it. The place was awash with dark suits and slightly hysterical Friday night hilarity. No Members were in evidence, or at least none Grace recognised.

'Do you ever get Members in here?' she asked.

'I don't know. Never been in here before.'

'I thought you had.' Brett had steered them with decisive familiarity towards the obscure door off the courtyard where the garbage crushers were kept.

'I've passed it. I knew where it was. I've pretty much memorised the whole of the parliamentary estate.'

Grace laughed.

Brett knitted his brow. 'What's so funny?'

'I don't know … sometimes … the things you say …'

'You don't take me very seriously, do you, Grace?'

'No, of course not. Should I?'

Brett retracted his chin in affront. 'It might be nice occasionally.' 'You're always taking the piss out of me.'

'No, I'm not.'

'Yes, you are!'

'You should feel flattered.'

'Really? Why's that?'

'Because …' Brett stopped. Something had caught his eye on the other side of the bar. Alarm flashed across his face.

'Are you all right?'

Brett focused back on her, his composure regained. 'Yeah, fine. Sorry, what were you saying?'

Grace scanned the bar and saw nothing but the same drunken suits as before. 'You were saying … that I should feel flattered …'

'Oh, yeah …' Brett glanced across the bar again. He pulled at his collar. 'Look, do you want to get some air … It's kind of stuffy in here …'

'I haven't finished my drink …'

Neither had Brett but, before she could remonstrate, he was already halfway across the bar, wading through the sea of grey and navy pinstripe. Grace picked up both their glasses and followed him. A girl in a red dress emerged from the suits, a glossy-haired, sharp-heeled girl. She caught the tail end of something that passed between the girl and Brett: an exchange of words, looks, she wasn't sure what, but definitely something, if only an atmosphere, and whatever it was flustered the girl briefly but she rearranged her lips into an aloof pout and teetered on, bearing a glass of white wine and a pint of beer between manicured fingers.

Outside in the courtyard, Brett was leaning against the wall, elaborately casual, his hands in his pockets. On seeing Grace he inhaled an ostentatious noseful of garbage-scented air.

'You brought my drink. Cheers.'

'You OK?'

'Yeah, yeah, sure. Just needed some air.'

'It was a bit claustrophobic in there. Sometimes, this place can feel so sort of … enclosed.'

Brett shrugged, as if to disassociate himself from such neuroticism.

'Actually, the only place in this building I don't feel hemmed in …' Grace craned her neck back and gazed up at the square of night sky caught between the towers and the crenellations. 'Do you want me to show you? You can bring your drink …'

Grace pressed button four in the lift and they slid up in nervously smiling silence, clutching their drinks to their chests. Grace strained for something to say but, as always in lifts, conversation was impossible. Her head was swimming, her mind pleasantly unfocused. 'Here we are,' she said, as they reached the fourth floor.

'Great,' said Brett, 'the suspense is killing me.'

They were standing in a narrow, murkily lit stairwell with a small window either side. The purposeful bustle of the House seemed far away. Beneath the brass light switch was a sign that read, *Please Do Not Switch Off*. Grace pointed at it. 'Very unecological.'

Brett nodded and peered out of the windows. Only their reflections were visible, softened yet dramatic, and, Grace suspected, more attractive than in actuality. Beyond their reflections was darkness. She laid her hand on the door.

'"Authorised personnel only",' read Brett.

'We are authorised.' Grace pushed. The door fell open and the night breeze rushed towards them. It was like stepping onto the prow of a ship.

Brett stood in the centre of the roof and wheeled around 360 degrees.

'Awesome!'

Up close, the minarets and buttresses of the Palace were as unreal as a stage set. Being face to face with Big Ben was like viewing the surface of the moon. The real moon was an echo floating behind it. Above the jumble of spires, courtyards and crenellations the edges of the sky could no longer be seen. It stretched, ultramarine, shot with street-light orange, from east to west, north to south.

Brett clinked his glass against Grace's and they leaned side by side against a low parapet and surveyed the messy jewel box of the city lights. Grace could feel Brett's heat against her arm. She wondered if he could feel her heat, and if, like her, he was thinking about it. She sensed he wasn't thinking about the view any more. She was aware of the rise and fall of her chest, of her breath coming quicker and her heartbeat gathering pace. The silence between them had thickened. It wasn't awkward, not like in the lift, but it was expectant.

'Now the suspense is killing *me*,' said Grace.

Brett turned, pulled his head back to look at her, then leaned in and did exactly what she had been expecting him to do since the moment they first sat down alone in the Sports and Social. He smelt fresh and expensive despite their epic drinking session, and his mouth tasted chemically sweet, of tonic water. She supposed hers did too.

'I think this section of the team has bonded quite well today, don't you?' she said, when at last they pulled apart.

18

The Monday morning after the Friday night, Grace went into work with nerves as sharp as a new pencil, and dressed with so much care that as she was leaving the flat Gail said, 'Looking smart. Got an interview?'

'No, just the same old, same old.'

'Someone you're trying to impress at work then?'

'No, course not. They're all a bunch of stiffs.'

'You're not meeting that Internet guy, are you? What was his name? Rupert?'

'Reuben. No, nothing came of that.'

She felt a pang of regret. Reuben would probably have been much more her type, if he'd only allowed her to meet him, but, as Rosemary had pointed out, beggars couldn't be choosers. Gail and Julia would have been entertained to hear about Brett but, out of self-preservation, she would only tell them about him if things panned out in her favour, and she suspected they wouldn't. Her phone had remained implacably inert all weekend. Every time she looked to check she hadn't missed a call, she sensed two wills battling silently over the air waves like weather fronts. Who would give in first? She was damned if she would. There was no way she wanted to make Brett any more conceited than he already was. Also Brett was the kind of guy who would expect girls to follow 'The Rules' and would respect those that did. Grace hadn't actually read *The Rules* but she had a vague idea what they entailed: not calling first; not being available on a Saturday if called after Wednesday; retaining your mystery; generally establishing uptight boundaries; and behaving like a spoilt princess.

She was amazed by their brief liaison. Not just by the sitcom cliché of doing it in the stationery cupboard but because she had done it with Brett. Brett Beamish! The man she had least expected ever to liaise with. The word liaise amused her, always had. Even in the job application sense it sounded lascivious. The 'Essential Skills' for her own post included 'excellent oral communication and ability to liaise tactfully and confidently with a wide variety of people, including Members and senior colleagues'. Well, she'd certainly shown some excellent oral communication when liaising with a senior colleague.

As she had knelt to take his penis in her mouth, her gaze wandered over the box labels – *mailer gummed manilla recycled trapezium flapped* and *100 buff square-cut files*: phrases so strange she had been momentarily distracted from the extant strangeness of the situation.

'Whasso funny?' Brett had demanded.

She had lifted her head, let his penis spring away. 'This.'

'What?' Brett cupped his genitals in alarm.

'This.' She gestured around the small dark room with its office supplies laid out neatly by the unwitting Reg Doig. If only he knew. *Oh no …*

'What? Whassamadder?'

She collapsed in a fit of groaning laughter. 'I was just thinking about Reg Doig …'

Despite her suspicion that they were unlikely to liaise again, Grace had found herself on Upper Street on Sunday afternoon, ostensibly to check out boutiques she couldn't afford but, if she was honest, she'd hoped after a day and a half of electrical silence to bump into Brett. If his flat was near Highbury Tube, Upper Street would be his main stomping ground. It was a suitably upmarket area. Nothing less than the best for Brett. Her gaze slid into every plate-glass restaurant window but he was not in any of them. Islington suited Brett well. It was his milieu, his manor.

She reached the Angel with a see-saw sensation of disappointment and relief. It would have been hard to explain her presence had they bumped into each other. He would have only flattered himself that she was stalking him.

Her attempt to get to work before him so she could establish a subtle upper hand was foiled. She arrived at exactly the same time as Rosemary, and Brett was, of course, already at his desk looking as immaculate and inscrutable as ever.

'Hello Rosemary. Hello Grace. Good weekends?'

'Very nice thank you, Brett,' said Rosemary.

Grace nodded, set her bags down without eye contact and, with precise movements designed to deflect Brett's own impermeable poise, fired up her computer and began slitting open the post with the blade of her letter opener.

The morning ground on. Rosemary chattered about her hedgehog, who was going to have to be let out into the wild eventually and whom she would miss so much: 'I'm worried he might have lost all his natural survival instincts.' When she went out to make a cup of tea, Grace and Brett remained fixated on their separate screens, apparently immersed in work. Disappointment rumbled inside Grace. Obviously she knew Friday night had been an aberration but, in the cold light of Monday morning, she wished for once in her life, something – if she was honest, some *man* – would hang around a bit longer, make things change, make London a little cosier. Disappointment segued into irritation, which began to drip biliously into her gut. Irritation at herself and irritation at Brett. For God's sake, he had put his penis into her vagina! A major boundary had been crossed. Some appreciation was due. Was he embarrassed? Was she the kind of girl he wouldn't want to be seen with? But then was she kidding herself too? Brett was an alien species. A corporate automaton. Although she wasn't as left-wing as he thought, as far as she could glean he believed in ultra-free market capitalism. He was a neo-con. He didn't think recycling was important. And to top it all, lest she forget, he lined up his M&Ms in colour order before he ate them. No: she couldn't dismiss him that easily; there was still something about him that intrigued her. Perhaps it was simply his conventionality. She was used to outsiders. Outsiders always wanted to know her. She thought about Reuben, who had not contacted her for ages, not since her email demanding to know if he had a girlfriend. Reuben's correspondence reeked of outsider discontent. Brett was an insider. Also, face it: he was good-looking. The hot half-lidded way he had looked at her when they were lying in the stationery cupboard had triggered a delicious bitter tension in her stomach.

How dare he! How dare he be so conceited! What a completely up-his-own-arse conceited wanker he was. He'd probably been laughing about her with his friends over the weekend. Laughing at how easy she was. He probably thought she was a slut.

'Grace?' Rosemary's voice interrupted this inner monologue.

'What?'

'Oh.' Rosemary feigned an exaggerated double-take. 'No need to sound so grumpy. I was only wondering if you could do me a tiny little favour.'

'Go on.'

'Could you possibly go into the stationery cupboard and get me another printer cartridge. This one's getting very low on ink. You know how I can't get up on that ladder …'

Inadvertently, Grace caught Brett's eye. A soupçon of amusement flavoured his expression.

'Yeah, OK.' She slunk out of the office, her own face blaring red.

There was no evidence of their shenanigans. All the stationery in the cupboard was stacked in neat, blameless piles. The room still smelt of nothing but cardboard and ink. She climbed to the top of the movable ladder and reached for a printer cartridge. If Brett came in now he'd be able to see right up her skirt, right up to the lace at the top of her special hold-ups, which she wished she'd been wearing on Friday night instead of her woolly tights. Despite his drunkenness Brett had been unsurprisingly virile. He wouldn't have allowed himself to be anything else. He was as efficient at sex as he was at writing concise, factually accurate briefs. They had spread their coats on the cold hard floor and lain down. She had fumbled in her purse for the condom that had been nestling there for longer than she cared to admit, even to herself. She had not come. Brett had. Quite quickly. He put the used condom in an envelope and put the envelope in a wastepaper bin in the corridor on the way out. She worried about the cleaners emptying the bin, his sperm jiggling away among all the parliamentary waste. Paranoia washed over her: what if the condom was found and somehow – DNA testing? Sniffer dogs? – traced back to them?

He didn't invite her back to his. 'My flatmate's kinda funny about people staying over,' he said, as they kissed goodbye at Westminster Tube. 'He's very Christian. A real God-botherer.' This was the first she had heard of a flatmate, let alone a very Christian flatmate, but she let it go. She was feeling tired and wretched and in need of her own empty bed. Drinking all day had left her with an early-onset hangover.

Back in the office, she changed the cartridge, self-conscious about standing in the line of Brett's gaze, even though he was studiously not looking at her.

'Thank you very much,' said Rosemary.

'That's OK.'

She returned to her chair and touched her computer into life. A message from Brett lit up her inbox.

—Fancy meeting up this evening then?

Her first instinct was no: make him work, don't roll over at the first sign of encouragement.

—OK. Where shall we meet? She ignored her first instinct.

—How about Southwark Travelodge, 6.30?

—Why do we have to go to a hotel? You can come to my flat if you want. Or I could come to yours. Or we could have a drink beforehand. You know: talk.

For ten long minutes nothing, then:

—OK. How about you show me the delights of the F-Park.

19

As soon as they crashed onto Grace's unmade bed after drinks in some dive bar round the corner from Finsbury Park Station, Brett worried the mess might put him off his stroke. Fair enough, she'd had no chance to clean her room as they'd gone out straight from work, but, still, he couldn't believe she had let it get so scummy in the first place. Crusty knickers strewn about. Bedlinen that hadn't seen the inside of a washing machine in weeks. Old cups of tea with green fur growing in them. A rail with clothes flung haphazardly over it: no wardrobe colour coding *whatsoever*. Even her shoes weren't paired up, just chucked in a heap in the corner: high heels, walking boots, flip flops, trainers. The number of high heels was unexpected. Perhaps he could encourage her to wear them more often. He liked the green Minnie Mouse shoes she'd worn the day they got it on. Why she didn't wear high heels all the time, he had no idea.

'So, this is your room … the lair of Grace … Grace's place …' He removed a dirty plate from under his shoulder where he'd landed on it and placed it on the unvacuumed floor.

'Yeah.' She kicked some of the knickers under the bed. 'Haven't got round to tidying up in a while …'

'I like those.' He pointed to a pair of strappy stiletto sandals.

'Thanks.' Without prompting she put them on and as she was also wearing hold-ups – a major improvement on the tights from the other night – he was able to focus on these and the stilettos and they got down to business very successfully.

'Are you hungry?' she asked, afterwards.

'Kinda.'

'Shall I cook you something?'

'That's very kind but you don't need to bother …' If the state of her bedroom was anything to go by, her kitchen would be an environmental health hazard.

'It's no bother. I'm starving … I'm going to cook something for myself.'

'OK.' He was pretty weak with hunger, now he thought about it.

They surfaced from the stale, tangled sheets, put their clothes back on and shuffled into the kitchen. Her flatmates were in there: one plump, one skinny, both kind of plain and both wearing dressing gowns even though it was nowhere near any normal person's bedtime. They fluttered and blushed when Grace introduced him.

'Very nice to meet you, Brett.'

'We'll get out of your way in a minute …'

The way they melted into their bedrooms with their plates of toast made Brett wonder if Grace had warned them about his potential presence, told them not to cramp her style. The flat was so small and the walls so thin they must have overheard what had been going on in her room ten minutes before. The idea sort of pleased him.

'You actually do cook, don't you?' he said, watching her chop garlic like a pro. The kitchen, though not totally up to his exacting hygiene standards, wasn't as hellish as he'd feared. Presumably the flatmates had some influence over it and were cleaner than Grace.

'Yes, of course. What do you do?'

'Eat out, mainly. Or get takeouts. Or ready meals. I don't have time to cook.'

'What are you so busy doing?'

'Working. Living.'

'Cooking is living.'

Nadine, like him, had hated cooking. Hadn't known how to. Thought it was a waste of time and didn't eat much in any case. When they lived together they had mainly eaten out. For all that she wasn't into food, Nadine was a total restaurant whore – liked to tick the top places in *Time Out* off her list: St John, Ottolenghi, Nobu, et cetera et cetera. At home they ate M&S ready meals or things from tins. Brett had an abiding memory of Nadine perched on a tall kitchen stool, long legs dangling, daintily forking up tuna in spring water straight from the can, then lighting a menthol Silk Cut. Nadine was too highfalutin to cook, too pristine. Too feminine.

Yet the way Grace cooked was feminine too. A different type of femininity. Kind of earthy, Nigella-esque, except, unfortunately, Grace didn't resemble Nigella. You could tell she enjoyed her food but, unlike Nigella, she wasn't quite pretty enough to carry off a big arse and plump thighs with total success. She could've done with losing a few pounds. He'd asked about her exercise regime earlier that evening and she'd laughed, said the word 'regime' sounded really fascist and she didn't have one as such, but she occasionally went to a yoga class.

They ate in the depressing lounge, which was decked out like the rest of the apartment with wallpaper the colour and texture of porridge. An old-school gas fire, the type that'd probably end up suffocating Grace and her flatmates, hissed on one wall. In front of it stood a clothes rack, festooned with functional knickers. The window dripped with condensation. Hard to know whose knickers they were. Grace's possibly. Apart from the hold-ups her undies were disappointingly unsexy. But then her flatmates didn't look up to much in the underwear department either.

'Tasty.' He twirled a forkful of spaghetti carbonara into a spoon.

'Look at you!' Grace laughed, hand to her mouth.

'What?'

'The way you eat spaghetti … it's so …'

'What?'

'I don't know.' She laughed again. 'It's so you, I suppose.'

'You don't like my forking technique?' He twirled up another mouthful. It was good. Heavy-duty carbs, though. Even if Nadine had been able to cook, she'd never have cooked anything so fattening. Cream was *verboten*, pasta too. He'd have to run it off in the morning; that's if he could get away that evening: no doubt it'd seem ungentlemanly to just shoot, eat and leave. Sleeping with Grace, actually sleeping, would be weird. Sleeping was really intimate. More intimate than fucking. If he stayed over and they got the Tube to work together they'd end up spending a full twenty-four hours in each other's company. He'd have to wear the same shirt and undies two days running. Tomorrow there was a committee meeting. He didn't want to blast the chairman with BO. Grace probably didn't have a spare toothbrush. And those stale sheets …

'You're looking very spruce today, Brett,' said Grace, the morning after they had not spent the night together. 'Very fresh and well pressed.'

As per usual Grace was ripping the piss. Yesterday evening he'd told her he had to get home to get his washing out of the dryer and iron a shirt for work. This was more tactful than saying he wanted to go for a run, as he didn't want to make her feel bad about her weight.

'Brett always looks spruce,' said Rosemary, puzzled.

'I know but don't you think this morning he looks especially *soigné*?'

'If I knew what swanyey meant.'

'Cared for, groomed.'

'Brett always looks groomed.'

Brett caught Rosemary's eyes flicking between the two of them. She might not know what *soigné* meant – neither did he – but she wasn't stupid. If Rosemary discovered there was something going on it'd be around the department faster than a rat up a drainpipe.

—Don't you think you should quit with the flirty digs? he emailed.

—They're not flirty. Don't flatter yourself, came the reply thirty seconds later.

The following day they didn't meet up and did not exchange emails so it was easy to maintain their previous mode of amused contempt. This was the way things should be. They should call it quits now. The whole office-romance gig was just not his scene. Unprofessional. She was nice, Grace, more his type than he had initially thought but, basically, not really his type, not long-term. For a start she was older than him – only three years but, still, her body didn't have quite the fresh tautness he required in a woman. Maybe it never had. Also, she was probably looking to settle down, pop out a few sprogs. By the time they got to their thirties that's what women always wanted.

Nadine had been his type. She was in his ballpark. They had the same goals and ambitions, the same perspective on life. They looked right together: the kind of well-dressed, good-looking couple that other people envied and admired. A power couple. Now she and that Parsley-Haversack bloke were swaggering around being top dogs. A sharp pang prodded him just below the ribs whenever he thought about what he'd lost. No, Grace was just a blip in his otherwise smooth upward trajectory. A bit of fun that he was going to cut short. The only problem was Grace seemed to be cutting it short without his say-so. This was irritating. If anyone was going to cut it short it was him. It went without saying that he was in the driver's seat. Brett tried to settle down to work but it was hard. Grace's non-communicative presence was distracting. What was she thinking? What was she so busy doing? She never used to be busy. Now she was all brisk and bustling. For his benefit, he was sure, except she never looked his way. Her coolness was surprising and impressive. A girl like Grace – decent but not obviously hot – he would've expected to be more grateful. Especially as there didn't seem to be anyone else on the scene, not anyone definite, anyway.

'I do have one admirer,' she had told him the other night in her messy bed.

'Yeah? Who's that?' He pictured some wimpy geek into poetry and art-house movies.

'Oh, nobody.'

'What's his name?'

'I don't want to talk about him really.'

'Why'd you mention him then?'

She had flopped onto her back and stared up at the ceiling. 'Because you asked me if there was anyone else on the scene.'

He hadn't told her about Nadine. Or, at least, not the full unexpurgated works. Only an edited, slightly amended version, in which he had dumped Nadine because she was too – he couldn't think what lie to use – 'too in love with me,' he had said finally. 'And I didn't feel the same way about her.'

'Why, were you too in love with yourself?'

'Shut up! Of course not.'

Both Tuesday and Wednesday nights, he found himself sitting on his single bed, eating an M&S ready meal for one and wondering what Grace was up to. Probably something similar. Except her meal wouldn't be from M&S and it probably wouldn't be 'ready'. He thought about the way she had chopped up the garlic, the confidence in her hands. His mind roved to an image of her tipsily laughing as she fell back naked onto her chaotic bed. His hand hovered over his phone and he contemplated calling her, inviting her over. 'Get in a taxi. I'll pay,' he would say. She wouldn't care about his shitty studio, the grim bathroom shared with people of dubious personal hygiene. Unlike Nadine she didn't have high standards. With a girl like Grace, he wouldn't always have to be on guard, keeping up the B-Man façade. Except a taxi from the F-Park, how much would that be? Fifteen quid? Twenty? The sight of his bank balance, which he had checked earlier that day, had sent him into a panic. No, if he couldn't do things in style, he wouldn't do them at all. He dropped his phone, picked up his half-finished plate and sighed loudly.

Thursday was Grace's last day that week. It was her turn to take Friday off, slacker that she was. He'd overheard her and Rosemary discussing it, the fake surprise in Grace's voice: 'My turn again?' Late that afternoon he watched her thumping the Speaker's stamp down repeatedly onto a stack of envelopes. She knew he was watching her. She looked like she wished the stamp was a nail gun and the envelopes were his head. Fuck it, he was going to crack. He liked her. So what if she wasn't specifically what he was looking for? You couldn't always have Miss Right. Sometimes you had to settle for Miss Right Now. It would be a laugh to go out one more time. Plus he wanted to have sex.

—Are you mad at me? he emailed, when she had sat back down.

—No. Why?

—You haven't spoken to me in three days.

—I'm being discreet.

—So discreet I might as well not exist.

—What do you want, Brett?

—Fancy meeting up tonight? I'll take you somewhere nice.

A pause. Then, finally: OK, where? Southwark Travelodge?

—No, I thought we could grab a kebab first. (Joke.) How about the Oxo Tower?

He'd put it on his other credit card. The one that wasn't totally maxed out. Hell, if you couldn't live in style you might as well not live at all.

The thing about Grace was she was easy to please. Not grateful exactly, but she appreciated stuff that girls like Nadine or Rachael took for granted. He could have just bought her a kebab on the Holloway Road and she'd probably have appreciated it. After all, even the menu at the Oxo Tower entertained her: 'Buttermilk and maple syrup *emulsion* … what on earth is that? … Black pudding wontons … vichyssoise foam … chorizo *dust* … This place is insane …' Eventually she settled on lobster bisque with daikon and wasabi salad, followed by venison with spiced pumpkin purée, trompette mushrooms and cocoa-nib sauce (because she 'liked the idea of chocolate with meat'); both were the most expensive items on the menu. Determined not to seem stingy, Brett had urged her not to hold back. To offset the cost he went for the slightly cheaper duck salad with Jerusalem artichoke custard and hazelnut and raspberry vinegar dressing followed by pot-roast cod, white onion and bay leaf compote, sautéed chicken liver and bacon gnocchi.

'This soup is *amazing*.' Noisily, she slurped up the bisque. 'Like the essence of the sea. Want to try some?'

Before he could say no, she had pretty much forced her spoon into his mouth. Tasting each other's food was so uncivilised, looked like you didn't get out to high-quality joints very often, but still …

'Mmm, mmm. Very nice … argh, stop …' A drop of bisque

dripped on his tie, his fifty-quid Armani tie. Damn. Frantically, he dabbed it with a napkin dipped in fizzy water. 'Bloody hell.'

'It's only a little stain.'

'This is Armani.'

'I'm sure you can wash it.'

'You can't wash ties.'

'Dry-clean.'

'Christ, I'm gonna look like Hugo. Food all down me.'

'Everything good, sir?' A waiter glided over.

'Delicious,' said Grace. 'This soup is amazing. How do they make it?'

'The chef, he basically gather all the shells of the lobster and he boil them for very long time and then he grind all up very, very smooth with a special machine for grinding and there you have. Of course, he put in cream and several flavourings: garlic and wine and so forth … I'm so glad you like.' The waiter slid away.

'You can't ask them for recipes,' said Brett.

'Why not? He didn't mind. He was pleased I liked it.'

Brett shook his head, smiling in disbelief. You didn't talk to waiters. You were polite to them but you didn't engage them in conversation. Again, it made you look hicksville. Outside the sky was turning red over the jagged horizon.

'You can just about see the House.' Grace pointed to the eerie silhouette of their workplace in the distance, seagulls circling its spires like bats in a horror film. 'Is that Big Ben? Maybe it's the Victoria Tower. Amazing view. Like the spires are pricking the sky, making it bleed.'

He squinted at the horizon. 'You could say that. Or you could just say the sun was setting over Parliament.'

'Brett, where is the poetry in your soul?'

'I don't know.' He shrugged. 'I must have mislaid it.'

'Yeah.' She looked at him with an expression he couldn't read and turned back to the view. 'The House looks so pretty and peaceful from far away. Who would think what a viper's nest of intrigue and back-stabbing it is.'

'Yeah. I guess.' He took a large slurp of wine and tried not to worry about his bank balance.

'I love hotels.' Grace threw herself across the tightly made bed later that evening. 'They're so brilliantly bland.'

'I wouldn't usually stay in a Travelodge.' Brett couldn't decide whether it was sweet or pathetic that the Southwark Travelodge was so thrilling to Grace. 'I mean, if I was on holiday I'd stay somewhere better than this. At least four-star.'

'Brett, you're such a conspicuous consumer,' she called from the bathroom, where she was now having a pee with the door open.

'What's the point of consuming if it's not conspicuous?'

'What about being green?'

'Bugger that. We're in the age of consumer choice and I fully intend to make the most of it. To hell with all you greenie doom-mongers. Would you mind closing the door while you're in the dunny?'

Grace had no shame. Nadine would never have gone to the toilet with the door open. Nadine was obsessed with preserving her feminine mystery. To the extent that he was once horrified to find a tube of haemorrhoid cream in her medicine cabinet when he went to find a Band-Aid. Nadine had an arsehole? Nadine had an arsehole with piles? Needless to say Nadine had never let him go anywhere near her arsehole when they were in bed, had several times wordlessly slapped away his enquiring fingers when they ventured in that direction. The good thing about Grace's lack of shame was she was up for anything in the sack. Yeah, she might be a bit embarrassing and say bizarre things but she was a pretty reasonable sack artist. Maybe it was because she was a bit older. Nadine had prided herself on being good in bed and though she knew all the moves – apart from the no-fly arsehole zone – there was something, occasionally, *strained* in her performance. As if she had read up instructions in some self-help guide or a women's magazine. Which, knowing Nadine, she probably had. He heard the shower raining down.

'What are you up to?'

'Consuming all the facilities to the full, seeing as you're paying for them. Why have we come here anyway? Are you embarrassed by me?'

'What?' Brett flicked on the TV and lay back on the bed. He wondered if he ought to have a shower too. At this rate Grace would be cleaner than him. Surreptitiously, he sniffed his pits. Total freshness. The 24-hour deodorant he had applied that morning was doing exactly what it said on the tin. Even more surreptitiously he slid his hand down his undies and fossicked around. Just as he pulled his hand back up and was sniffing it, Grace sauntered in, hot and pink, wrapped in every towel the hotel had laid on and wearing the free plastic shower cap.

'Why are you sniffing your hand?'

'I'm not sniffing my hand.'

'Yes you were.'

'I was rubbing my nose.'

'You never answered me.'

'What?'

'Are you embarrassed by me? Is that why you've brought me here? Or is your flatmate actually your girlfriend?'

'No! I told you, my flatmate is very religious and would be really upset if I brought anyone home.' Brett laughed with relief. If only she knew. He thought of his studio, the fact you could open the fridge while lying in bed, and the shared bathroom with the unnerving stain behind the toilet and the shit splatters that the other tenants left in the bowl. Perhaps he could risk her seeing the truth behind his façade. See how non-judgemental she really was. He certainly couldn't keep on treating her to fancy meals and mediocre hotels. In fact, a low-rent girl like Grace could be ideal. Trying to impress Princess Nadine, keep her in the style to which she was determined to be accustomed, was what had got him into his crap accommodation/never-ending money-angst scenario in the first place.

'Why don't you find a more normal flatmate?'

'Because … I don't know. Why don't you find some more normal flatmates?'

'Julia and Gail are normal … Too normal.' As if she'd never seen such things, she examined the spare pillow in the wardrobe, the useless runner of fabric laid over the bottom of the bed and the half-size kettle beside the basket of teabags and coffee sachets. 'It's like a clean slate, a hotel, isn't it? Nothing to do, no distractions. Like being reborn.'

He pretended not to understand. It was her usual kind of oddball remark but he knew what she meant. In a hotel they were liberated from their real-life personas, their jobs, their crap flats, all the stuff they judged each other on.

'I remember reading this thing Slavoj Žižek said – have you heard of Slavoj Žižek?'

He arched an eyebrow. 'What do you think?'

'He's this Slovenian philosopher. Anyway, he said the only times he ever felt truly relaxed were when his flight got delayed and he had to spend the night in an airport hotel. He spends those nights watching the international weather channel.'

Brett snorted. 'Is he a Communist?'

'I think he might be a Marxist. He's some sort of cultural theorist.'

Brett snorted again.

'I know how he feels though,' Grace continued. 'Not that I've ever had a delayed flight but I get that feeling in all hotels.'

'My flight was once delayed at the layover in Singapore, flying back from Oz.'

'Did you get put up in a hotel?'

'Yeah.'

'Was it relaxing?'

'I'm always relaxed. I'm not some sort of neurotic Commie bullshit merchant.'

'You're never relaxed, Brett.'

What was she talking about? 'What are you talking about? I'm ice-cool.'

'I've never met anyone so controlled and uptight.'

'Shut up! I'll give you controlled and uptight.' He wrestled her, laughing, onto the taut pristine sheets. 'Is that shower cap supposed to turn me on or something?'

20

Suddenly life had sparkled into Technicolor and the House of Commons was Grace's favourite place. Instead of dragging herself to Finsbury Park Station and sitting slumped on the Victoria Line in an existential gloom, she looked forward to work. The office was now the dramatic centre of her life. Sometimes they caught each other's eye during meetings and the flicker of naughty complicity made Grace feel warmer inside than a steak and kidney pie from the Terrace Cafeteria. She started doing sit-ups every morning and always wore decent underwear, although part of her thought Brett should accept her as she was, greying knickers and all. They had clandestine lunches in the pizza place on Strutton Ground and, once, during working hours, took the lift together and snogged all the way from the ground to the third floor, on a knife-edge of excitement that any moment a Member or a colleague might stop the lift. She tried not to think about whoever might be watching them if there was a hidden camera in there.

Occasionally Grace worried she was letting the side down by going out with Brett, though she wasn't quite sure what side this was or why she should be on it. Life for Brett was black and white, which she found surprisingly comforting. He was not neurotic, at least not in the way she was used to from men. Reuben had seemed more like her usual type: angst-ridden and dissatisfied. Maybe this marked the beginning of a new chapter in her love life. Maybe she'd had a lucky escape.

Brett knew what he wanted and how he was going to get it and he didn't waste time moaning or feeling sorry for himself. She liked his irreverence. When he mocked her indecisive, wishy-washy liberalism, she wondered if he was right. She realised that corporate types like him saw themselves as decent and hard-working, that trying to climb a career ladder was sensible and self-reliant: the right thing to do.

'It's not a crime to want to better yourself,' said Brett. 'You don't have to have this negative attitude about money. Money makes life more comfortable. You can do more stuff, go more places. It's more fun to be rich, basically.'

'Yeah, but I hate the inequality in society: the rich get richer and the poor get poorer,' said Grace. 'It's not fair.'

'Grace, life is not fair. That's the way it is. It's a sad fact but there you go. You've gotta make the best of things, not be a whinger.'

'Am I a whinger?'

'A whinging Pom? Nah … maybe a bit.'

He mocked her arty pretensions, but she sensed he also liked them. 'I've never had an arty chick before,' he said, which made her feel wayward and bohemian, even though she knew she wasn't really. They were entirely different from each other but they had a good time together and that, for the moment, was enough.

Three times on a Thursday when the House had risen early and no one else was about, they had conspired to repeat the stationery-cupboard liaison. She was surprised Brett took such a risk since he was normally so law-abiding and respectful of their workplace, but she supposed, like her, it excited him to transgress the rules so much and, in any case, he was still reluctant for her to come back to his place.

The third time, emerging red-faced and ruffled from the stationery cupboard, they almost tripped over one of the cleaners vacuuming the corridor. The cleaner kept his eyes respectfully focused on the carpet but Grace couldn't help turning back once she had passed him and was disconcerted to find him staring straight at her with a look that could have contained anything from dislike to collusion to indifference, she wasn't sure.

'That guy *knows*,' she hissed to Brett as they descended to the ground floor in the lift.

'What guy?'

'That cleaner. Didn't you see him?'

'He doesn't know. So what if he does?'

'He might blackmail us.'

'He doesn't even know our names. He's a cleaner. He probably can't even speak English.'

'He could easily find out our names. He knows our desks.'

'You're being paranoid. If he does know, he probably thinks good luck to us. I'm sure those cleaners get up to all sorts.'

'Good luck to us? He probably hates us 'cos we earn so much more money than him – well, you do – and he's working for peanuts.'

'Enough already with all this middle-class guilt. Even if he does know and he does try to dob us in – which is highly unlikely – it'd just be his word against ours; he's got no proof, nothing's written down.'

Grace realised this was why Brett's emails to her had remained so bland. When she wrote, Guess what kind of underwear I'm wearing today? he had hissed, '*Don't* send me stuff like that,' as soon as Rosemary had left the room. 'You do realise the IT guys can read all our emails?'

'Of course they can't.'

'They can. They have access to our Outlook accounts.'

'They can't possibly read everyone's emails all the time.'

'Whatever, just don't send messages like that to my work account.'

He wouldn't even let her send such emails to his private account while at work, lest the IT guys could also read those.

—sorry for the long delay. ive had a lot going on at home, been having a bit of a bad time, but im back now. are you still up for meeting up?

Reuben was so far from her mind these days that his email, received out of the blue one sunny spring afternoon, was a depressing reminder of a former time, an unhappy time, when the only crumbs of enjoyment during her working day came from mutual online moaning with him about their colleagues. She had moved away from all that negativity. Brett was encouraging her to apply for better jobs in the department. He said he would help her with applications, coach her for interviews – 'I'm a master at interviews. Stick with me and I'll get you out of Band C and into Band B2 in no time. Hell, I can probably get you into B1, like me.'

This sudden email from Reuben was presumptuous. It didn't even address the contents of her last email to him: there was no reference to whether he had a girlfriend or not. He couldn't just suddenly barge into her life after ignoring her for weeks. Attached to the email was a poem, entitled 'vending machine sandwich':

vacuum-packed
sealed from the world
in a small airless chamber
rotating round and round
waiting to be chosen
while my edges dry and curl
quite soon I will be
out of date

She read it with a wry smile and wondered what Brett would make of it. Brett had probably never read a poem in his life. It would certainly never cross his mind to write one. For him, Reuben would definitely be a whinging Pom. She highlighted the email with a red Action flag – an Action to be completed once she'd finished collating the weekly circulation – but forgot all about it until after lunch, which she and Brett spent at the pizza place on Strutton Ground as usual.

'You don't think anyone's guessed, do you?' she asked Brett as they walked back through the inner courtyards to their office. 'About us.' A sudden sensation of being watched made her glance up at the windows above but there was no one.

'Nah, course not.'

'This place feels so un-private sometimes.'

—I'm kind of busy myself these days so I'm not sure I'm up for meeting any more, she replied when she saw the highlighted email again. Reuben did not reply. The next day she received no emails from him, nor the next. The next day was a Saturday and by that point she had forgotten all about him again.

'What's happened to that admirer of yours?' Brett asked one evening a few weeks later.

'Oh.' Grace started to attention, remembering Reuben hadn't replied to her last email. 'He's still around.'

'Who is he?'

She detected a bat's squeak of jealousy. 'Just some guy.' She smiled mysteriously. It was good to keep Brett on his toes.

'What does he do?'

'He's a musician.'

'That's not a proper job.'

'Yes, it is. It can be.'

'Does he actually make any money?'

'I'm not sure. A bit, maybe. But he has a day job as well.'

'An unsuccessful musician.' Brett adjusted his collar ostentatiously, as if to make sure he was the picture of success.

'You're so fucking conceited.'

'We are in the presence of Honourable Members. Perhaps you could adjust your language accordingly.'

They were sitting on the Terrace as the sun went down, drinking vodka and tonics from the Strangers' Bar – 'V&Ts', Brett called them, with a smirk, as if remembering a private joke. The Thames was lapping at the wall that ran from one end of the House to the other. Grace recalled Reuben's poem and wondered if she had been too quickly dismissive of him. She sat back and sipped her V&T, suffused with largesse. Perhaps she could just meet him for a drink. If he was having a bad time and needed someone to talk to, what was the harm? When you were happy it was easier to spread happiness. You had more patience with other people's misery when you had a boyfriend and more stoicism in the face of the less satisfactory parts of your life because at least one part of it was sorted. She wondered if Brett was actually her boyfriend, whether he would consider himself as such. She hadn't dared broach the subject. Perhaps this evening was the time.

One of the BBC's long-time political correspondents appeared on the Terrace, magnificent in his white linen suit, with his great domed head and manly moustache. He was as solid as the statues of Slim and Montgomery on Whitehall and seemed, like them, larger than life.

'Look,' said Grace. 'Thingy off the news.'

'I like him,' said Brett. 'I don't know why the BBC don't make him the main political guy rather than that dweeb with the glasses.'

'Which dweeb with the glasses?'

'You know: the one with the glasses that make his eyes look massive. Geeky black-framed glasses. Bald guy. Bald in a crapper way than that guy.'

'Oh him, yeah, I can't remember his name either. I like him though. He's sweet. I like his big eyes.'

'You would. You like the underdog, don't you?'

'How do you know?'

'I just do. You're that kind of person.'

'You're not the underdog ...'

The Secretary of State for Education emerged from the bar with a white jacket draped over her shoulders in a glamorous yet schoolmistressy style. Her arms were folded beneath this makeshift cape and a drink nestled in the crook of her elbow. She smiled across at them, approving, Grace imagined, of what she probably assumed was a nice clean-cut young couple in love. Members viewed people in simple terms: hard-working families, benefit cheats, asylum seekers, Middle England, the squeezed middle. In Members' eyes she and Brett were young professionals. Sometimes it was reassuring to be reduced to a cliché, to submit yourself to the easy mainstream and leave behind the misfits like Reuben.

'Good legs for an older chick,' said Brett, slurping his vodka in the direction of the Secretary of State.

'Who? Her?'

'Yeah.'

Grace glanced as inconspicuously as possible back at the Secretary of State but in the gathering darkness, silhouetted alongside a man she didn't recognise against the bright open door of the bar, it was difficult to make out much about her figure. Grace's feeling of well-being began to diminish, as if with the fading light, and she wondered, with a shiver, where she and Brett were going to spend the night and when the customary wrangle over why they couldn't go back to his would begin. Brett's secrecy about his home life was beginning to annoy her. It showed a lack of trust that was preventing their relationship – in her mind it had gone beyond a liaison – from moving on. She'd exposed her crappy lodgings to him. He should do the same. The inequality in what they knew about each other gave Brett the upper hand.

This was why he was doing it. There was something about where he lived that would demean him in her eyes. Something he didn't want her to know.

'Let's go back to yours tonight, Brett.'

'No, I'll come back to yours.'

'I want to come to yours.'

'I want to come to yours.'

'Why can't we go to yours? I don't believe all this stuff about your flatmate.' Even if the religious flatmate did exist, Grace couldn't believe Brett would care about upsetting him. But a glassy look had come over Brett's eyes, then over the rest of his features, and all at once he was as impermeably double-glazed as he had been when she first met him.

'OK, don't believe me.'

'I don't believe you.'

'Fine.' He downed his drink in one gulp and thumped the glass on the table.

'What's the secret? Why can't I come back to yours?'

'There's no secret. I just don't want you to.' He stared over her shoulder at the river beyond.

'It's very hard to have a relationship with someone who won't let you come back to theirs.'

Brett's jaw hardened. 'I don't consider that we're having a relationship, Grace.'

Grace stared at him. The sluice gate in her brain between sobriety and inebriation opened as quickly as his screen had come down. All the vodka flooded through. She could feel her cheeks filling with blood – a mix of shame and fury.

'I'm not in the market for a relationship.'

'Not in the "market"? What are you? A commodity?'

'It's been fun but—'

'But what?'

Brett shrugged and glanced over his shoulder to make sure nobody was listening.

'Are you ending it?'

'Grace, I don't think we have the same goals.'

'You're ending it just like that? Here?'

'Don't shout. There are Members around. And cops.'

'I don't give a shit. "Goals." Fucking hell.'

Nobody turned round but the atmosphere was ruffled. People were alert, eavesdropping. Grace felt uninhibited and reckless. Her chair scraped as she stood up.

'It's this kind of uncontrolled behaviour that makes me think we're not right for each other.' Brett sat back, glass-cold, as if daring Grace to punch him in the face. Instead she chucked the rest of her vodka in it.

'Steady on,' said the BBC reporter as she stalked past him and into the bustle of the bar, where she had to elbow her way through the mob that was squawking, cackling, arguing and opining like a Hogarth scene sprung to life. Her voice rose in increments.

'Excuse me . . . excuse me . . . let me out . . . can you please let me out . . .'

She emerged breathlessly from behind the heavy oak door of the bar into the carpeted calm of the corridor and burst into tears.

They didn't talk the next morning and both kept their eyes averted from each other, although Grace noticed Brett was wearing a different suit. The one he had been wearing yesterday would have been taken to the dry-cleaners' already on the way to work. She imagined his clenched fury, his *controlled* fury as he had taken the Tube home, damp and sticky from the vodka and tonic. Never before had she thrown a drink in someone's face. It was a soap-opera milestone in a girl's life. She could already imagine herself in a few months' time, laughingly relating the incident to other people. Not that she was laughing now. She was still furious. *It's this kind of uncontrolled behaviour.* She gritted her teeth at the memory of Brett's complacent expression. The cold splash of tonic had wiped that off him, replaced it with a look of fish-mouthed shock.

'Have you heard the news?' Hugo burst in on an unprecedented gust of energy, for once looking as if he was wearing something other than slippers.

'What?' Everyone looked up.

'The Election's been announced. Parliament is going to dissolve next Tuesday. Better do a dissolution recess note, Grace – we're only going to need a skeleton staff for the next six weeks, maybe even longer, what with Whitsun as well.'

The recess note was a chart detailing when each of them would be in the office and how they could be contacted at home. Once Parliament had been dissolved there would barely be any work to do.

'Just bits and bobs. Tying up loose ends,' said Hugo. He was finding it hard to keep the glee out of his voice.

Ordinarily, Grace would have been thrilled too. Six weeks of rising late and mooching about, only having to slope into the office for a few token nods towards 'keeping on top of things'. Hugo said he didn't expect her or Rosemary to come in at all during dissolution once they had tied up their loose ends. Grace foresaw that Brett would be able to avoid her for ages. By June their liaison would be old news. He'd never have to account for his sudden change of heart. She foresaw the emptiness of the weeks ahead. There would be too much time to brood. Depression loomed.

Brett announced that he would come into the office one day a week during dissolution but hoped to do some work shadowing in the City to 'keep his hand in'. An old mate from his MBA, who now worked at RBS, was probably going to be able to wangle him a placement there.

Hugo's eyes nearly popped out from under his shaggy eyebrows. 'Your work ethic is truly Stakhanovite, Brett.'

'I enjoy work, Hugo.'

Grace quickly Googled *Stakhanovite work ethic*. She knew Brett hadn't a clue what it meant either but was too proud to ask Hugo to explain. He wouldn't like the Commie aspect once he'd Googled it himself, which she knew he would do as soon as Hugo had gone.

'Well, in the words of Voltaire: "*Chacun doit cultiver son jardin*" …' said Hugo. 'In my case, literally. Our garden has been very neglected of late and I think Mrs Llewellyn is hoping I'm going to use the time to do a bit of weeding.'

'Each to his own,' said Brett.

'Yes: *chacun à son goût*.'

'Are those Voltaire's words too?'

'No. They're mine.'

Compiling the recess note would involve communicating with Brett to find out his movements over the next six weeks and all his contact details, including his home address. Grace's gut tightened at the prospect. She decided to send a group email to Hugo, Rosemary and Brett, placing his name last on the address list, in defiance of the unspoken convention that names should be listed in order of staff seniority. It was the kind of detail Brett noticed and he would pick up on her dismissive intent.

Hugo and Rosemary replied quickly, Hugo specifying his address was Highgate rather than what his postcode suggested, which was Holloway. A short while later Brett curtly offered his mobile number and personal email address.

—I need your home address too, Grace wrote back, her gut

tightening even more as she pinged the message into the ether. She'd lost all heart for a showdown and a low-level hangover was beginning to throb through her.

—I prefer not to give out my home address, for reasons of security and privacy. I trust you will understand, he replied, cc-ing Hugo, so no private retort or further demand for his address could be made without making her look like a stalker, as he would probably cc Hugo in on his reply.

For the rest of the week their eyes slid away from each other whenever they accidentally met.

'You're both being very quiet,' said Rosemary at one point.

They both shrugged and muttered noncommittally in reply.

21

For Grace, life in general dissolved along with Parliament. It became shapeless and fuzzy around the edges. Days merged into one another. Sundays felt like Mondays felt like Tuesdays felt like Wednesdays. Gail and Julia went to work before she got up. The daytime streets around Finsbury Park were filled with people she didn't usually see: the very old, the very young, the very infirm, the drunk and drugged – people who also led indistinct lives unstructured by the usual nine-to-five.

The run-up to the general election was a vague buzz in the background of Grace's consciousness, but she didn't follow the parties' campaigns closely. According to the opinion polls the current Prime Minister was bound to get in again and, even if the current Opposition finally won, Grace couldn't imagine much would change for her personally; mainly because there was only a cigarette paper between the two main parties in terms of policies and, in any case, she had learned from working at the House that Members were pretty similar – you got nice and nasty, polite and rude, easy and difficult from across the political spectrum. She couldn't vote herself as she wasn't on the electoral register; she'd forgotten to fill in the form when it had come round. So much for Brett thinking she was a raging leftie. She couldn't remember if, as an Australian national, he was allowed to vote. If he was, he obviously wouldn't vote Labour.

The weather was unseasonably hot, which made Grace feel even more disorientated and blank, as if the sun were cauterising her nerve endings. She spent a lot of time lying on her living-room floor with her laptop in a square of sunlight, lost down a rabbit hole of virtual information. Brett's old MBA mate had come up trumps and sorted him out a work placement at the Royal Bank of Scotland's headquarters on Bishopsgate. Grace Googled the place. It was a thin metallic wedge, the edge like a blade thrusting into the street. She searched for the staff that worked there, but could find no mention of Brett, unsurprisingly, and only pictures of the Board, who were mainly bald middle-aged white men with pinched mouths and heavy faces. The few women on the Board were similar but with hair, sensible unsexy hair. They were much older than Brett. Still, she imagined some young women worked there. The kind Brett would describe as 'hotties', striding about purposefully on uncomfortable heels, clutching folders of complicated documents to their chests.

Grace's eyes glazed over as she clicked from one part of the RBS website to another. The bank's brand colours were dark blue and grey. Nothing about the website was graphically stimulating. Phrases such as 'interim management', 'key performance indicators', 'corporate action' and 'economic insight' floated across her vision. She discovered some pictures of the Economic Advisors. They were younger than the Board. The only handsome one was a black guy with a first-class honours degree in Economics and Politics, who had won the 'prestigious Walter Bagehot Best UK Dissertation prize' for his doctoral thesis. Since then he had worked for two US investment banks. Arrogance burned from his eyes. His name was Terence Mbua. She clicked back through a blue and grey blur to the Google main page. Finance was so boring. How could Brett, Terence Mbua et al. stomach it? She supposed they focused on the main prize, dollar signs kerchinging in their eyes. That was the difference between those who got rich and those who didn't: they had the stamina to withstand the butt-grinding tedium of reaching the money. Once you had the money you had power and power wasn't boring at all. *They've got the real power*: Brett talking about bankers. The relish in his voice had been tangible.

She could see Brett would like it down there in the City, encased by glass and steel, the sharp architecture echoed by the sharp outfits of the workforce. The same way he preferred the modernity of the Debate in Portcullis House to the fustiness of the Terrace Cafeteria. He would be among his people. No doubt he'd meet the kind of girl who 'shared his goals'. The Economic Scrutiny Committee office wasn't his element. It was simply a stepping stone to better things. Grace closed down her laptop and for the rest of the afternoon she lay in the sun like a cat.

22

'Hi Grace!' Brett bared his teeth in what she supposed was a smile as soon as she walked in. They looked even whiter than usual against the tan he had picked up over dissolution. 'Good break?'

Grace grunted and logged on to her computer. It was as if they barely knew each other. He was being odiously professional.

'How was your break?' she asked evenly, once Windows had loaded up.

'It was very nice, thank you, Grace. I mainly spent it at RBS, shadowing one of the investment teams.'

'Right.'

'I learned a lot. It was an interesting challenge.'

She stared at him a split second longer than necessary, flinging invisible darts of hatred. Crisply, he turned back to his screen, and so did she.

Her inbox contained densely packed strata of bold type: 129 unread messages. Most could be chipped away immediately: newsletters and invitations to conferences from think tanks that had mysteriously acquired her email address: delete, delete, delete; departmental circulars; internal job adverts for posts way above or below her qualifications; pointlessly cc-ed messages: delete, delete, delete.

Subject: what are you up to?

She blinked, paused, rewound and delved into the Deleted Items. Reuben Swift. 03.23. A week ago. No message in the body of the email. Back to the inbox with a prickle of adrenalin. Boring, boring, boring. Delete, delete, delete. Then:

Subject: are you ignoring me??

'What kind of things did you do at RBS, Brett?' asked Rosemary.

'Oh, you know: analysed markets, crunched numbers, schmoozed clients, contributed to reports ... that sort of thing.'

'Sounds very high-powered, doesn't it, Grace?'

'Mmm.' Grace glowered into her screen and wrote No, I'm not ignoring you. I just haven't been at work.

'Expect it's a lot more exciting than this old place.' Rosemary hoisted her bosom over her keyboard and settled into her chair, with her usual placid smile.

'What could possibly be more exciting than the Economic Scrutiny Committee?' Brett grinned and Rosemary tittered.

'Jocularity on the first day back: how cheering,' said Hugo, shuffling in with the air of someone who had misplaced something but couldn't remember quite what. 'Just been on the phone to the Chairman. He wants to take the whole Committee for drinks on the Terrace tomorrow evening. A sort of welcome back to the new session and thanks for all our hard work last session. I think it will be rather fun. Another chance for team bonding.' His beatific beam encompassed them all. Grace smiled back weakly. Sometimes it must be very nice, very nice and simple to be Hugo.

—i know i forgot when i sent that email, Reuben replied. i got your out-of-office thing. are you still very busy then?

—Not particularly.

—pleased to be back?

—What do you think?

—what did you do while you were away?

—Not much.

—are you cross with me or something?

—No. Why do you ask?

—all these short answers. you sound grumpy.

—Sorry. I'm just not in a great mood.

—i know how you feel. although im feeling better since you got back in touch.

—That's nice. Her mood softened. Hope sprang eternal. Look, are we actually going to meet? Stop all this beating about the bush.

—OK.

—When?

—how about tmr eve? but theres something I need to tell you first.

23

'Shame you're not coming this evening,' said Rosemary, as she watched Grace gather up her bag and prepare to leave.

'You're not coming to the Chairman's drinks?' Brett looked gobsmacked. In his eyes, she was obviously putting her career in severe jeopardy.

'I've got a prior engagement.' Grace noted him surveying once more her pink dress and high-heeled sandals. They were the shoes she'd put on the first time he'd come round to her place. He'd tipped his head in surprise when she'd arrived that morning, had clearly assumed she was dolled up for the Chairman, or, more precisely, for him.

'You look very nice, dear,' said Rosemary. 'Going somewhere special?'

'Just meeting a friend … in town.'

But, after leaving the office, she did not head out of the House. Instead, she went down the stairs, turned left through the double doors into the shadowy quietude of the main committee corridor, past the paintings of former prime ministers: dreamy-eyed Ramsey Macdonald, lounge lizard Neville Chamberlain, a young Winston Churchill beginning to revert to the characteristics of a plump, querulous baby.

So, all this time Reuben had been working in exactly the same place as her.

—Why didn't you tell me before? she had asked, when he dropped the bombshell.

—my jobs very secret. im not allowed to talk about it.

—Why don't you have a parliamentary email address? She

had, of course, instantly looked him up on the global address book but there was no record of him; he didn't appear to exist.

—because im not directly employed by parliament.

Her first thoughts were: Secret Service, MI5, MI6 – she couldn't remember which was which or which one was more James Bond. He could be a policeman, which might also explain the secrecy and lack of parliamentary email address, although the artfully dishevelled, haunted-looking person in the picture didn't look much like a policeman. He didn't look much like a spy either, and she couldn't imagine either a policeman or a spy writing such plaintive soul-searching songs. Her interest was piqued anew. More than piqued, in fact. She couldn't wait to meet him. Brett had been a wrong turning. Finally, perhaps, she was on the right track. Still, she ought to be sensible: for safety, she had suggested they meet in the House, somewhere far from the Terrace so they would be unlikely to bump into Brett, although, actually, it might do Brett good to know she had another suitor.

—how about the roof? the roofs my favourite place here, Reuben had replied.

—It's my favourite place too.

In the distance all was dark, womb-like red. The corridor ran the length of the House from the Commons to the Other Place, as the Members portentously called it. Grace liked the childish differentiation in colour between the two Houses, as if the Lords and Members had been so quarrelsome that the Queen had declared: 'Now, now, children, look here: *you* are going to be red and *you* are going to be green and that's all there is to it.' Everything kept to this colour scheme, from the ribbons tied around Bills to the portcullises on the napkins in the cafeterias.

There were two lifts: one which said Members Only and one which didn't. Grace called both and the Members Only pinged into view first. Whenever Grace took this lift she always half hoped a Member would tell her off so she could use one of her carefully rehearsed rejoinders, such as, 'I thought I was living in a democracy.'

On the ground floor, she walked along several corridors to another lift, which she took to the fourth floor. Perhaps Reuben was one of the builders. One of the hunky ones. The builders were all contractors, not directly employed by Parliament. But being a builder wouldn't be very secret. Unless he was involved in building some sort of anti-terrorist system for the House, whatever that might be. Somehow, he didn't sound like a builder though. How many sensitive singer-songwriter builders were there? And he'd given the impression he had an office job. She stood in the narrow stairwell which looked out onto an inexplicable section of roof. The last time she had been there was with Brett. The memory of that night was curiously unmoving, which proved to her that, despite her bruised pride, she had moved on. The stairwell was flooded with low-angled sunshine, which concentrated the tranquillity. Pure silence was rare at work. The office was often quiet but there was usually some sound: the agitated ant steps of typing, the suck and whirr of the printer, Rosemary's sniffs and coughs. Work was not conducive to contemplation. Work was the opposite of contemplation. Activity versus thought. She gathered her nerves. Just being in this strange, separate, elevated place Grace always felt as if she was breaking a House rule, and yet, according to the sign on the door, she was definitely authorised personnel. She tried to check her lipstick in the light switch but the brass wasn't shiny enough to give a clear reflection and all she could see of her face was a ghostly blurred shape with a smudge of red where her mouth was.

Taking a deep breath, she pushed through the door and was up against the sky. Perched on the parapet that bordered the roof was a man in his early forties: bespectacled, besuited, brown thinning hair cut close to his skull, a plumpish face, the nose a little too long, the mouth a little too close to the nose. A nondescript office worker whom she might have passed on a corridor a dozen times before without noticing. He looked nothing like the man in the pictures sent by Reuben. She glanced around but there was no one else on the roof.

'Sorry, I'm looking for—' Unsteadily, the man stood up and lurched towards her. His glasses magnified his eyes so they looked startled. 'You're not … Are you Reuben?'

She took the man's proffered hand. It felt clammy and she caught a vinegary whiff of alcohol on his breath.

'Grace.'

'Yes.' She disentangled her hand and stepped back, conscious of how tall she was in her heels compared to this man, who was nowhere near six foot three, nowhere near deliciously overpowering. A knot of unease began to tighten in her stomach. 'Look, what's going on? Are you really Reuben Swift?'

'Yes.' He sounded uncertain but defiant.

'You're not the man in those pictures.'

Reuben smiled nervously. 'They were from a long time ago.'

Grace didn't smile back. 'They weren't pictures of you.'

The defiance evaporated. 'I … I can explain … Do you want to … Why don't you come over here and sit down? … Look, I've brought a picnic …'

Several House of Commons napkins had been unfolded and laid in a neat patchwork on the asphalt. They were weighted down by a number of sandwiches in plastic containers, two small yoghurts, two plastic cartons of fruit salad, a bag of Maltesers and a Bounty: all items from the chiller cabinet in the Terrace Cafeteria. An enormous bunch of lilies and white roses in a cut-glass vase towered over the picnic offerings. It looked like it belonged on the reception desk of the kind of hotel Brett claimed he usually stayed at.

'Do you like the flowers?' Reuben smiled hopefully.

Grace stared at him. 'They're … very nice.' Whoever this person was, he seemed unpredictable and needed to be pacified. She wondered if and how she was going to get through this evening. By rights she could just leave now. She had been encouraged here on false pretences. When he revealed he worked in the House, she should have known something was amiss. He'd lied to her from the beginning. He was definitely not the man in the pictures, and his speaking voice sounded nothing like the singing voice of whoever had sung the songs he had sent. She doubted he was even a musician, struggling or otherwise. She couldn't imagine him with a guitar. She couldn't imagine him ever doing anything bohemian or artistic. He looked like a thwarted office drone and she suspected that was exactly what he was. Only horrified curiosity and fear of what he might do next were keeping her rooted to the spot.

'I'm glad you like them,' Reuben was saying, 'I got the flower woman to do them for me. I've got to take the vase back but you can take the flowers home. They're for you.' He spoke quickly, agitatedly, as if trying to pin her there with conversation.

'Thank you … You shouldn't have … You mean the flower woman downstairs?'

'Yes. I asked her what sort of flowers you might like. I don't really know much about flowers, but I thought, well, I wanted to get some for you and this was what she decided. I thought they were nice. I hoped you would too.'

An image of this small strange man earnestly discussing bouquets with the glum-looking woman who created all the House flower arrangements flitted through Grace's mind. She'd often peered into the flower room as she passed and envied the woman's romantic job, although the woman herself always looked thoroughly no-nonsense in her sleeveless padded jacket and tweed skirt. If she wasn't grappling with flowers and chicken wire she was stolidly reading the paper or eating her lunch, oblivious to the heady gorgeousness surrounding her.

'What did you say about me?'

'I just said I wanted some flowers for a friend … something really pretty …' His smile was now more confident. Grace was appalled by the description of herself as his 'friend'.

'She didn't think it was a bit weird? I mean, you could've gone to Strutton Ground or somewhere … There's a flower stall …'

Reuben gawped. 'No, I … The thing is I thought … Actually, I didn't know about that stall. Anyway, she was very happy to do it. I paid her.'

'OK … sorry … I didn't mean to sound ungrateful … They're very nice.' To avoid his eyes Grace bent towards the flowers and sucked up a transporting waft of sweetness. 'You needn't have though. I wasn't expecting all this sort of … fuss.'

'I wanted to.'

In the pause that followed, he darted around and held up a bottle, still dripping from a silver ice bucket that looked as if it had been swiped from the Refreshment Department. 'I've even bought some House champagne. Do you want some?' Before she had a chance to answer, he was ripping off the metal seal and the bottle was clamped between his legs, his face screwed up as he eased out the cork. Suddenly it popped over the parapet. Champagne spurted onto the asphalt and, with clumsy haste, he slopped it into two plastic glasses.

'Please don't go. I know this probably all seems a bit weird, but I'm really happy that we've finally met and … you know … you've only just got here and the night's still young and all that.'

He pushed an overflowing glass into her hand. His magnified eyes had a skittish look.

Grace placed the glass on the ground, swiped her phone and pretended to open a message. 'Hold on, I just need to answer this text.'

—Brett, am on roof of House. URGENT. NEED YR HELP. Please rescue me from mad date.

'Sit down, sit down ...'

She flinched as Reuben's damp hand pulled her by the wrist onto the floor. His lack of boundaries suggested he was drunker than she had originally thought. Drunk people scared Grace. You never knew which way they were going to turn. Especially when you didn't know who they were in the first place.

They sat facing each other in the shade of the parapet. Small gold weathervanes, shaped like flags, glinted in the lowering sun. The view stretched eastwards beyond the curve of the river to the fat phallus of the Swiss Re building and further east still, to the tip of Canary Wharf winking on and off like a colossal lighthouse. Grace felt hobbled in her dress and heels, horribly aware of her breasts straining against the tight bodice, and of Reuben's eyes frisking over them. If she suddenly needed to run it would be hard. She considered taking her shoes off: in bare feet she would be more mobile, but Reuben might interpret this as a louche gesture. She did not want him to interpret anything she did as louche. Instead, she sat with her legs folded beneath her and her skirt smoothed down, until this began to give her pins and needles. Reuben, with his collar cutting into his neck and his paunch pushing against his belt, also arranged himself like a person unused to sitting on the ground. In hot countries people lolled with ease on the floor. What a bunch of stiffs they were in England. And they didn't get much stiffer than in this place. Although here on the roof, unwatched by colleagues and policemen, it felt as if they were in a place beyond the ordinary rules of House conduct. Which was why Grace had previously always enjoyed coming up here. Anything could happen and no one would know. No one would know. She glanced around. Surely there must be CCTV cameras? Not that CCTV cameras were any use really. They would merely record whatever was about to happen. She glanced at her phone and willed Brett to reply. The roof no longer felt like a safe place to meet.

Reuben was opening the plastic containers, offering her first a prawn mayonnaise sandwich, then a roast beef and horseradish. '... I didn't know what you'd like, whether you were a prawn person, never quite know with seafood, some people don't like it, do they? Anyway, I got a selection ...' The wind scraped an empty container across the asphalt. Grace leaned over to rescue it and pulled away a strand of hair stuck to her mouth. If only she could discreetly rub off her red lipstick, which, like her breasts, Reuben's eyes kept hovering over. '... It's nice up here, isn't it ... Quite a good place to get away from it all, you know? I thought it would be a good place for our first meeting.'

The way he said 'our first meeting' had a loaded heaviness. The knot in Grace's stomach was now so tight that she knew she wouldn't be able to eat anything. Even the champagne was hard to swallow. Reuben was planning a second and third and fourth meeting in his head ... meetings spinning off into infinity. He'd built this first meeting up in his mind even more than she had. From the champagne, the location, the flowers – above all, the flowers – it was obvious this meeting was a pinnacle for him, or perhaps a lower summit from which the ultimate pinnacle of his ambitions for their relationship would be reached. Everything about the situation, everything about him, from his big, eager eyes to the stumbling way he spoke in his old-fashioned Cockney accent, made her cringe. She knew she had not disappointed him, whereas she was now going through the motions, humouring his delusion. The fear of what he might do next had paralysed her. Her legs felt weak, as if they might not hold her up if she tried to escape.

'Why did you send me photos of someone else?'

Reuben looked at his soft white office hands, so entirely different from the long, artistic fingers of the man in the photographs. 'Why do you think?'

'But how was it ever going to work? I mean, as soon as we met, I was going to know … I suppose that's why you put off meeting me …'

'I hoped you might … I don't know …' He buried his chin in his neck. 'I thought we got on well via email. I felt like you understood me.'

His beseeching gaze made her feel claustrophobic, and her skin crawled at what he might be thinking: *you have amazing beauty*. That she had been pathetic enough, desperate enough, egotistical enough to believe him; that at one time she had even fantasised about having sex with him. Reuben was the least likely person she would ever have sex with.

'Who was that man anyway? The one in the photos.'

'Why?'

'I'm curious.'

Reuben grinned, as if curiosity equalled romantic interest. 'Just some guy, someone I found on the Internet. I knew you'd like him.'

'How did you know?'

'I know what kind of girl you are.'

'No you don't.'

'But you did like him. That's why you wanted to meet up.'

Grace ignored this. 'You're not a musician, are you? None of those songs was yours.'

He stared at the asphalt. 'No.'

'You stole someone else's music and photos.'

'He doesn't need them any more.'

'What do you mean?'

'Look, believe me, I didn't harm anyone by taking them.'

'You stole someone's identity. I'm sure that's against the law.'

'I do write poetry. All those poems I sent you, they were written by me. I've written loads of poems. I'm trying to get them published.'

'I don't care if you wrote those poems. You stole someone else's identity.'

'You said you loved them. You said that poem about the outside seeping in, that it captured exactly how you felt.'

'Why didn't you tell me before that you worked here?'

Reuben shrugged and wouldn't meet her eye.

'I should have realised, the one about the House, only someone who worked here could have written it. I don't understand. What do you do exactly?'

'Oh, just boring stuff … very similar to you … I work in the Lords though …'

'Why didn't you tell me? It doesn't make any sense.' There was no way this man worked for MI6; idiotic to have even considered it. He wasn't well-dressed enough for a start, nor self-contained enough to be privy to state secrets, and, from his tentative demeanour, she knew he had no power in his job.

'I wanted to create an air of mystery or something … I suppose.'

Grace snorted. There was something childlike in this man's artlessness.

Reuben smiled, uncertain whether she was laughing with or at him. 'Did you tell your colleagues you were coming here?' he asked.

'No, I haven't told them anything about you.'

This produced a conspiratorial grin, as though he liked the idea of being an illicit secret. 'I haven't told my colleagues either … You didn't tell that Brett Beamish then?'

'You remember his name.'

'You told me all about him.'

'I don't think I told you *all* about him.'

'You said you didn't like him.'

'I didn't say that. I think I just said I found him a bit annoying at first. He's not that bad.'

A constipated grimace rumpled Reuben's face. Grace dropped her airy tone. 'Don't worry, I haven't told him about you.'

'Good. It doesn't matter about him anyway … I don't give a toss about him …'

'No, that's fine … no reason you should …' She recoiled at his aggression and glanced at her phone. Nothing. She studied Reuben again, racking her memory for whether she had ever seen him before. His face was so nondescript it was impossible to tell. He looked like many people she had passed on the corridors over the years. 'Look, tell me one thing: you didn't come to one of our evidence sessions, did you? That's not when you first saw me.'

'It is. That inquiry was relevant to something our Committee was doing. My clerk wanted me to come along. You obviously didn't notice me.' His voice was now flat and accusatory.

'No. I didn't.' She didn't bother to hide her frostiness. She now felt irritated with him for being so unattractive and irritated with herself for being flattered into such a mad situation. She checked her phone again. Why hadn't Brett replied? Probably too busy schmoozing the Chairman. She started to attention. Reuben's hand was on her knee.

'Why do you keep looking at your phone, Grace? It's a bit sort of … I don't know … It's making me feel like you don't want to be here.'

'Stop it. Get off.' She jumped up, batting his hand away.

Immediately, he was on his feet and blocking the door. 'You're not going, are you?'

'Yes, I am. This is too weird.'

'Don't go. You haven't had anything to eat yet.'

'I'm not hungry … Look, who are you? This is so weird. I can't believe I've even come up here. Who are you? I don't understand what you were thinking, contacting me, pretending to be someone else, it's completely bizarre …'

Reuben was eyeballing her like a cornered animal.

'I don't even believe your name's Reuben Swift.' His pass was stuck into his breast pocket. If she hadn't been loath to get near him she would have leaned over and pulled it out. At that moment Brett burst through the door.

'What's going on?' He stood, fists semi-clenched and swinging at his sides.

'What are you doing here?' Reuben's gaze swerved from Brett to Grace and back again. 'What's he doing here?'

'She told me to come.'

'You can't just barge in. This is my private place. I invited Grace up here. We're having a private picnic.' Reuben took a step forward.

'Let's just go, Brett,' said Grace.

'No.' With surprising force, Reuben shouldered her out of the way and pushed her behind him with a sweep of his arm.

'Hey, don't touch her.' Brett grabbed Reuben's upper arm.

Reuben shrugged him off. 'What you gonna do about it?' Fury surged into his face with the same curdled expression of someone about to vomit. In a split second Grace saw how Brett appeared to him. His neat hair. His smooth face. His expensive suit. His arrogant stance.

Brett took a step back and surveyed Reuben as if from a great height. 'Sorry, but who the hell are you?' He addressed Grace. 'Who the hell is this?'

'Brett, leave it.' Grace edged away from Reuben.

Brett turned to Reuben. Just as he was about to open his mouth and issue an insult, Reuben's fist shot forward and Brett reeled backwards, clutching his jaw. Reuben chucked his glasses aside and Brett dived towards him. 'Fucking little prick.' Brett's fist met Reuben's mouth. Something cracked. Grace tried to pull them apart but was knocked sideways. She watched from a couple of feet away, clutching her mouth with both hands, as the pair grappled, raining punches and kicks at each other. She could almost feel each blow.

Reuben kneed Brett in the balls. Brett doubled over, wincing, then suddenly rose up and wrestled Reuben to the ground. The vase of flowers crashed over. Water spilled on the napkins and over the picnic. Reuben blindly thrashed about, crushing lilies and roses beneath him. He landed another punch on Brett's jaw. Brett punched Reuben in the eye then got him in a headlock. Both men were grunting and puffing, their breath ragged. Picnic items were scattered around and, for an absurd moment, Grace regretted the money that Reuben had wasted on them.

From one angle the two wrestling bodies looked disconcertingly tender, as if they were cuddling. Brett let out a yowl as Reuben jabbed him in the stomach and threw him off. Reuben fell onto the champagne bottle with a smash. Glass exploded over the asphalt. Blood sprayed across the sandwiches and blossomed on the napkins.

Reuben staggered to his feet. Brett was now close to the edge of the parapet. Stone walls sheered beneath them. Brett had his back to the drop. Reuben lunged towards him and, as Brett dodged sideways, Reuben kept lunging into empty space. His scream cut through the chaos. One moment he was there, the next he had gone over the edge.

In the moments after his scream died, Big Ben began to strike seven, drowning out whatever sound he made as he hit the ground. When the strikes had finished the silence was so intense it was almost loud. Brett and Grace froze. The lush scent of crushed lilies floated into Grace's nostrils. She stared at Brett. Despite the heat, she was suddenly cold. So cold her teeth began to chatter. Before she had a chance to speak, Brett grabbed her arm.

'Let's go.'

Part Two

24

She's beautiful. Not obviously, not the kind of girl that ordinary blokes would slaver over, but I can see her beauty. Her name is Grace Ambrose. It is a beautiful name. A pale, floaty name. It suits her. Very carefully I wrap the lanyard around the pass and put it in my pocket. I keep my hand around her lovely face all the way through the revolving doors at the entrance to the building. Really I should hand the pass over to the policeman on the security desk but I don't. Instead, I swipe my own pass over the reader and hurry along the colonnade, past the stone lion with its tongue out and the unicorn with its bared teeth and the workers and Members who are mainly going in the opposite direction: towards the exit. I take the back way to my office. You hardly ever see anyone in these corridors. Only a few cleaners are around – they lurk in the shadows after hours along with the ghosts of this place. All the cleaners are black and all of them keep their eyes on the floor as I pass, as if they're not supposed to be there. I feel bad: them being black, me being white, them cleaning up after me and all the other overwhelmingly white people who work here during the day. But, really, I wonder if I should feel that bad. After all, I bet when they're out of this place they stand up tall and look people straight in the eye. I bet they have a good time when they're not here. I bet they have a better time than me.

Alone, safe in my office, I study her more closely. The photograph has been blurred by being swiped across card readers so many times but her beauty shines through. Her eyes are huge and blue. Blue as a rare jewel. What jewels are blue? Sapphires? Her eyes are like sapphires. No, that sounds too …

femme fatale. She's not a femme fatale. Her beauty is sort of … quiet. Like a Brontë heroine or something. The Kate Bush type. Her eyes are like blue skies and her hair is like a sunset. Blimey, that's poetic. I'm going to write that down. Actually her hair's not like a really flaming sunset; she's not a ginger: it's more like the end of a sunset, darkish red, maybe auburn. I expect auburn is the word she'd use. You can imagine her on a moor with her long auburn hair flying about in the wind. She's got pure, pale skin. Pale and interesting. She is smiling at the camera, smiling at me. There is something shy in her smile, something a little bit knowing too. As if she has a secret. A secret life. I suppose we all do but hers looks more interesting than most.

Her photograph is framed by the usual grey square and at the top edge of the square there is a green stripe rather than a red one like on mine: she works in the Commons, not the Lords. It's good to see that, like me, she is not an Officer. But I reckon even though she is younger than me she is higher up: her face looks educated and clever. Clever *and* beautiful.

Her pass was on the floor in the Tube just outside the secret entrance to the building. Nobody else had noticed it so I picked it up. I had gone out to the Tesco Metro above the station to get a ready meal for tea; I couldn't face another sandwich from the vending machine. She must have dropped it on her way home. I wonder where she lives. I wonder what she is doing right now. I wonder if she's with her boyfriend. I bet she has one. Lucky bastard. Does he know how lucky he is?

I look her up on Outlook. *ambroseg@parliament.uk. Extension 6105.* She works for the Economic Scrutiny Committee. Her office is in the Palace, same as mine. I print out the floor plan of each of the different floors of the House. The Economic Scrutiny Committee is in Room COH-14 on the third floor in the top left corner of the Palace if you face towards the river. It is on the other side of the inner courtyards from my office, diagonally opposite me, nowhere near any of my usual routes. I would never have any legitimate reason to go there. However, I could easily bump into her in one of the cafeterias. I may well have passed her in a corridor already. If I have, it's surprising I wasn't struck by her beauty then.

Apart from Economic Scrutiny reports, the only other things I can find from Googling are her Facebook and Twitter. Her Facebook has all the privacy settings screwed up tight, so I can't get any further than her profile picture, in which she is smiling and wearing a skimpy vest top. She looks really sexy. Her Twitter has the same picture. I log on as myself (well, @hallogallo, my photo-less Twitter handle) and discover she's an even less active Twitterer than me: only ten followers and only following twenty people, most of whom appear to be friends. Since joining last October, she has tweeted twice: hello – anybody out there? and I feel a bit stupid doing this.

I go back to the intranet and bring up the New Starters list, just on the off-chance. There are New Starters up there that started two years ago. Two years in the House is two minutes compared to the length of time a lot of people work here. It's not unusual to have forty years of 'service' or more. I've been here fifteen years. Fifteen years and what do I have to show for it?

The New Starters pop up: fresh-faced and perky and yet to be ground down by the weight of this place. She's not there but I scan the others out of interest. Emma Hargreaves. Luke Evans. Jane Askew. Kalpana Gnanasegaram. That's a name and a half. Paul French. Giles Every. Godwin Ncube. Lot of silent letters going on with these new starters. And a few non-white people being employed as something other than cleaners. Finally the House is moving with the times. Jeanette Cozens. Craig Weber. Brett Beamish. What a stupid name. Looks like an idiot too: obviously really pleased with himself. One of those faces you want to kick.

Emma Hargreaves isn't bad, but she doesn't have the delicacy of Grace, doesn't have the wistfulness. Emma Hargreaves is obvious. Emma Hargreaves would never like someone like me. But maybe Grace Ambrose would.

25

I think about her all weekend. I manage to cut and paste her Facebook photo into my screensaver so I can look at her beautiful enlarged face every time my computer goes to sleep. Then I worry that some nosy parker – Jenny, perhaps, or Phil – might notice and ask awkward questions. I can't say she's my girlfriend: they wouldn't believe me. So I change my screensaver back to a picture of Kirsten Dunst in *The Virgin Suicides* and save Grace's picture into my personal files along with my Personal Development Plans and my poetry.

My Personal Development Plans aren't actually personal: they're just these forms we have to fill in every year and discuss with our line managers about how we are going to 'progress' our careers. Seeing as I've been in the same job ever since I started, have never been promoted, and have only moved up the ladder because my role has been upgraded over time, my PDPs are pointless. But you have to tick the boxes, jump through the hoops; you have to 'play the game', as Phil always says when we go through the annual audit of my 'progress' and I agree to do another course in Excel spreadsheets or Records Management so he can sign the box to say we have satisfactorily assessed and discussed my 'development needs'. This place is getting more and more corporate. In fifteen years I've noticed the changes: they're slow but every year there are more of them.

What would my real Personal Development Plan be? To get out of this place, to get a more exciting job, to get my poems published, to get a girlfriend. I always read the obituaries in the papers, even people I've never heard of, and the amount they've crammed into their lives amazes me: running away to sea at the age of fifteen; five kids and three marriages by the age of thirty; rising to the top of four different careers by forty; making a million, losing it all, making another million. These people are fearless. They have inhuman levels of energy, nerves of steel. I look for clues that explain their success: rich families, good connections, talent, beauty. The clues are usually there: successful people have usually been dealt a lucky hand. This makes me feel better.

I type her name so many times into the To box of a new email that it now comes up automatically … AMBROSE, Grace … but I can't think what to write. AMBROSE, Grace ... AMBROSIAL, Grace … her name reminds me of rice pudding and heaven … How do you approach a woman you don't know? Although, actually, I do know her, on a deep level. Instinctively, I know what she is like. You don't need to know someone to *know* them.

It's Sunday evening, just after nine. I've had my usual sandwich from the vending machine, practised my guitar (I'm teaching myself to play) and watched *Antiques Roadshow* and *Countryfile* on the annunciator. Surely now is a safe time. With butterflies in my stomach I pick up my phone and dial her extension, which I've memorised. Her phone rings. I hold my breath. What if for some bizarre reason one of her colleagues has come in to work on a Sunday and picks it up? What if she picks it up? The ringing stops. So does my heart. Almost.

'This is the voicemail of Grace Ambrose. I'm sorry I'm not at my desk right now. Please leave a message after the beep and I will get back to you as soon as possible. Alternatively, please send me an email. My address is ambrose g at parliament dot uk.'

Her voice sounds like crème fraîche. Exactly how I hoped it would sound, how I imagined it. Not surprisingly she's posher than me. Most people are. She's not too posh though. Not in-your-face-fuck-off-you-pleb posh. I like the way she says 'beep' rather than 'tone'. It's sweet. I like 'alternatively' too. 'Right now' is a bit American though. Disappointing.

I ring back and listen to her again. I imagine her saying my name. I imagine her saying other things.

That evening, I ring her ten times until every aspect of her message is burned into my brain: the slight lisp on the 's' when she says her email address; the emphasis on the 'sorry'; the emphases on the two 'pleases', which show she knows she is repeating herself. Then I have a bit of a panic that my number will come up on her phone so I sneak downstairs and into the Principal Corridor and ring her from one of the phones by the leather seats there so it will override my number. I mouth her words to myself as she says them and slide back on the leather. Oh Grace, if only you knew how many emails I have almost sent to ambrose g at parliament dot uk.

The thought occurs that I should send her pass back through the internal post. Anonymously, of course. But then I worry she might get suspicious and tell security. There might be some way they can trace where it has been sent from. What if they fingerprint it? Bring out the sniffer dogs?

I try to finish the poem I've started:

eyes like blue skies
hair like ~~a sunset~~ a dying sunset
skin like ~~a~~ the moon
your face is the promise of a wide open space
and yet for me you are ~~contained constrained confined~~ contained
within ~~four two by four~~ five ~~square~~ inches of plastic
that is the key to this House

~~your my~~ our nine to five prison

if only I had the key to your real house ...

The idea is good – open spaces versus confined spaces and all that – but I can't get it to come together. I wonder whether the moon sounds too like she's mooning me and whether 'five inches of plastic' sounds a bit sort of *rude*. Also my hours are actually ten till six – expect hers are too – but nine to five is more iconic. But that means the word 'five' appears twice. I get out the ruler from my desk and discover that her pass measures exactly 3.4 by 2.3 inches or 8.5 by 5.4 centimetres.

That night, I examine her photo again as I lie in my sleeping bag. I wonder what it would be like to kiss her lips, to stroke her skin, to have her in my bed. I wonder what her skin feels like – soft, obviously, but soft and cool, soft and warm? Same with her lips – soft and cool, soft and warm? It's frustrating not to know for sure. Back when I lived in my flat, I used to imagine, as the Tube trundled along the District Line, that there was a girl waiting for me, looking forward to me coming home so we could talk about our day and huddle together at night. This fantasy was so real I would be painfully disappointed when I got back and found my flat as dark and cold as usual and completely devoid of my dream girl. The world inside my head has always been more interesting than the world outside. I spend hours daydreaming, imagining potential situations from every angle. This is what I do with Grace. I place her in my flat, watch her make a cup of tea with my kettle, rifle through my records, sit on my sofa, lie in my bed. If Grace was in my bed I'd feel 100 per cent better about my flat. I'd definitely be able to live in it again.

After two hours lying awake, I get out of my sleeping bag. I know I have to do it. For once I have to grab the bull by the horns, seize the day, live in the moment. Obviously, I take precautions: I Google *sexy mens names*. Reuben is top of the list on Yahoo Answers. 'Swift' comes to me out of nowhere. It sounds cool. Cooler than Smith in any case. Once I've created a new Gmail account I quickly type a message and press Send before I have second thoughts. My heart is thumping like mad but when you do things at night, hidden from the cold light of day, it can feel like you haven't done them at all. Afterwards I snuggle back in my sleeping bag and drop off immediately, sleeping more easily than I have in months. The pressure to contact her has been weighing on me ever since I found her pass and with one line it has gone.

The next day, Monday, I carry out the other idea I had over the weekend. Seeing as I've got her pass, she'll have to get a temporary one from the pass office, which means she'll almost definitely have to come into the Palace through Black Rod's Garden Entrance and walk through the inner courtyards. If I position myself under the arch where the builders and kitchen workers smoke, she'll almost definitely walk past. To look authentic I've got a pack of Marlboro Lights and I'm smoking one. My mind went blank when I was faced with the wall of fags behind the Tesco Metro counter. I only go there very occasionally to get vital provisions like cheap booze. As the Marlboro Lights were directly in my eyeline that's what I asked for. The guy on the checkout gave me a pack of twenty and I felt too conspicuous to say I only wanted ten. Of course, I forgot to buy any matches so I have to ask one of the other smokers for a light.

Big Ben strikes ten and there's no sign of her. Five minutes go by, and another five. The quarter-hour strikes. I'm going to have to pretend to Phil that I was busy delivering something somewhere. People pass, some of them women, none of them Grace. Some of the women wear high heels that echo from yards away. The more attractive ones strut past with their noses in the air, ignoring the builders' stares.

My fellow smokers leave and are replaced by new ones. I get out another fag and ask one of the builders for a light.

'Monday morning,' he says.

'Yes.' What else is there to say? It is Monday morning.

'Another day, another dollar.'

'Yes.'

He sizes me up. Even though my suit is crumpled and looks shit, I know he thinks the fact I'm wearing one means I earn more than a dollar.

She walks past. The stupid bloke has made me miss her approach. I could have been feasting on the sight of her for much longer. We both turn to look. Her nose is red with cold but she still looks beautiful, even better than her photo. I like the sulkiness of her lips. My fingers feel sweaty and numb as I lift the cigarette to my mouth. I take a puff that makes me cough. Her eyes flick over the builder and she disappears into the shadows of the next courtyard, her low-heeled boots making hardly any sound. I'm glad she's not into heels otherwise she might be a bit taller than me.

The builder and I exchange a glance, a sort of silent mutual understanding that, in the words of The Band of Holy Joy, 'a real beauty's just passed through'.

'Back to the grindstone,' he says, flicking his butt into a drain, before disappearing into a dark passage marked *No Unauthorised Access*, through which I glimpse big pipes and a concrete floor: a brutal, macho place that's completely different from the atmosphere of my office.

I follow her but I don't manage to catch another sighting. She is walking too fast. I have to take a long-winded route back to my office, sneaking in through my own personal door rather than the quick way through Phil and Jenny's office. As I sit at my desk and log in to my computer I can hear them going on about their weekends.

'… and then I said to him, "But you're not even wearing a hat, Craig!"'

'… Oh my God, you didn't!'

'I did!'

Gales of laughter and desk-slapping. They are both so easily amused. It usually irritates me but at least it means today that they're too wrapped up in their own crap jokes to notice how late I am. One thing I'm good at is not being noticed.

26

—Who is this??

I can't believe it. She has replied immediately. Within ten minutes of getting into work.

—im reuben swift

Unsurprisingly, she wants to know who I am and how I got her email address. She sounds quite cross:

—You can't send random emails out of the blue and then not explain yourself.

—it wasnt random. i think you have amazing beauty, very unusual beauty and i just wanted to tell you that. dont be cross with me. Women love to be complimented. Best way to soften them up.

—How do you know what I look like? Already I'm drawing her in. I make out that I've seen her around and give her a load of flannel about how romantic and Brontë-ish she looks, although actually it's not flannel because it's true. She does look romantic and old-fashioned, in a good way. Things even get a bit saucy: some back and forth about me being 'a bit of rough'. I wonder if I've gone a bit far, been too suggestive too quickly. But a few minutes later she comes back, all pretend hoity-toity, so I know she's not that offended. We even have a bit of banter about the two dots above the e in Brontë and I'm chuffed when I prove that I'm quite clever by finding out that the two dots are a diaeresis and not an umlaut, like she thinks. She's pleased when I compliment her name and tells me she likes mine. I knew she would. I'm good at reading people, knowing what makes them tick. And then she asks me this:

—Anyway, tell me properly, how do you know what I look like? I've never heard of you. You can't have seen me around. This is really weird.

I need to think of something convincing. How would Reuben Swift have seen her around? What does Reuben Swift do? What sort of man would Grace like to meet? While I'm trying to conjure up her ideal man, I send her one of the poems I wrote over the weekend. Reuben is a poet, I decide. That can be one of the traits he and I have in common.

—i've written a poem for you:

eyes like blue skies
hair a dying sunset
skin like the moon
your face is the promise
of a wide open space
where the wind blows free
let's roll and fall in green

She likes it, she thinks it's sweet. I tell her I'm thirty-two, an aspiring musician, that I live in Essex (which is semi-true, even if I don't live there at the moment), near the sea (not true, but the sea sounds romantic and I want to throw her off the scent so she doesn't find out where I really live), and I'm doing a boring temp job (which means it won't seem weird if she can't find me listed as working anywhere in London, since I'm not a permanent staff member). The only thing I tell her that's fully true is my list of favourite bands. She responds with a list of her own, which is disappointingly mainstream but I guess I am a bit of an obscurist, then she asks why I won't tell her where I work. I make up some guff about not wanting to be defined by my day job. In my head this fits with my rebellious, slightly bohemian image of Reuben.

—you don't like to be defined by yr job do you? I reply, which is a flattering way of aligning her with Reuben.

—No. BTW, you still haven't told me how you know what I look like.

Oh God, I should've thought all this through before I started emailing her. Off the top of my head I make up a load of nonsense about how I had once seen her in one of her committee's oral evidence sessions, that I'd been temping at the CBI, working for the director-general's team and I'd had to come along and take notes. This is all cobbled together from frantic searches through her committee's web pages to find out what inquiry they were doing when I supposedly saw her. I reckon I sound just about plausible. She wants to know why I didn't come over and talk to her there and then. I tell her I was too shy, which would have been the truth had I really been there. Then comes the killer question:

—I wish I could remember you. I honestly can't remember. What do you look like?

Argh! How am I going to get myself out of this one?

It's nearly six o'clock. Our correspondence has gone on intermittently all day. If her hours are anything like Phil and Jenny's she'll be leaving soon, so I can legitimately hold off replying until tomorrow, and spend this evening finessing Reuben Swift's persona, including his appearance.

I need a good-looking bloke in his early thirties, someone who looks like a musician, someone who Grace would be likely to fancy. Soulful-looking, sensitive, an arty type. Someone she can't track down and someone that can't track *me* down. That evening I'm sitting on the chaise longue picking vaguely at my guitar while watching *Channel 4 News* when the answer comes to me. There's an item about Mark Kennedy, the undercover copper who infiltrated various eco protest groups during the mid-noughties. To create a fake identity he used the name and birth certificate of a dead boy, who had been born around the same time as him. I sit up. Yes! 'Reuben Swift' needs to be a dead person.

For hours I trawl the Internet for someone suitable. One of my eyes starts getting that flickery strain thing that feels massive until you look in the mirror and find out it's hardly visible. My shoulders feel so achy that I have to keep stopping and wheeling my arms around to stretch them. My right hand seizes up like a claw over the mouse. I am a brain connected to a computer. Everything but the virtual world disappears. I look through all the notable deaths from the past three years on Wikipedia. Any male musician within the right ballpark age-wise, I research further. I keep myself awake with endless cups of coffee until I feel so jittery that I have to calm myself down with a large whisky from the emergency bottle in my desk drawer.

By 1 a.m. I have found 'Reuben Swift'. He is, or rather, he was a twenty-nine-year-old from Southampton called Dan Sheridan who had a small amount of success with a band called Dead Gull, a name that seems unfortunate in the light of what happened to him. When I say small success, I mean gigs in local pubs and clubs, a few reviews in obscure online music mags. Small enough that I am pretty sure Grace will never have heard of them. Two years ago Dan killed himself. I can't find out how. People obviously think it's in bad taste to talk about the method. Dead Gull's Facebook page has loads of commiserating comments underneath, mainly from people in the Southampton area. Dan also recorded a number of solo songs under the name Lonely Gull. I find a load of them on his Bandcamp page. On YouTube I find a few videos of him singing along to an acoustic guitar about lost love, unrequited love and love gone wrong. His voice is pleasant, mid-range and he sings with an English accent, which I like. Best of all, he is good-looking but within the realms of reality; i.e. he doesn't look like a Hollywood star. He's pale, green-eyed, slim, with messy brown hair. He wears scarves, lumberjack shirts, boots, jeans, sometimes a hat. In some pictures he has the sort of beard that girls seem to like these days. He appears to be quite tall, judging from band line-up photos. Basically, I can't understand what he had to be so depressed about.

—im 6ft 3, slim, ive got brown hair, wavyish, and green eyes, I type, finally, in response to Grace's last message. And then, somehow, I can't bring myself to attach a picture of Dan. I'm not sure it's a good idea after all and I'm too tired to think it through properly and make a decision. I press Send and curl up, exhausted, into my sleeping bag.

27

She smiles at me! She sees me and she smiles. The next day, after only four hours' light sleep, I am standing bleary-eyed with the smokers again. I couldn't resist another sighting of her in the flesh. She walks past with another temporary pass slung around her neck, she looks right at me and she smiles. The cigarette nearly drops out of my mouth, I am so shocked. Definitely she was smiling at me. She smiled and then she was gone.

I've been feasting on that smile in my mind ever since. When I get back to the office, Phil says, 'Probs with the Tube yet again, mate?' so I know I can't wait for her another morning without him noticing my supposed lateness. I expect she'll be issued with a new pass tomorrow anyway, so she'll probably start coming in through the Tube entrance again. You can't loiter inconspicuously round there.

When I log back into Gmail, there are no new messages. I stare at the screen, willing her to reply. After five minutes I minimise the screen and try to concentrate on work, on logging memoranda although, obviously, I continually click back and forth between the memoranda spreadsheet and my Gmail. Suddenly a message pops up:

—Maybe you could send me a photo of yourself, to jog my memory.

All morning I worry about whether to send a picture of Dan or not. It seems wrong, but I can't exactly send a picture of myself now I've made out I'm some sort of tall, tousle-haired dreamboat. Oh, bloody hell. Perhaps after lunch I'll have more energy and be better able to make a decision.

*

Of course, after lunch I don't have the energy to make a decision. Well, I have nervous energy from all my worrying about what to do but it stops me from sleeping properly that night or the next night or the next night or the next. Each day I am so knackered that I worry I am not in the right frame of mind to decide whether or not to send Grace a picture of Dan. This is the sort of decision that needs to be made with a calm, clear head. I wonder if going for a run would help. I've never been a big exerciser, I'm more of an intellectual type, but people always say exercise clears your mind, burns off anxiety and releases endorphins. The nearest I can get to a run is jogging round and round the horseshoe table in one of the committee rooms at night, barefoot and in my pyjamas because I've got no running gear here. The committee rooms are big enough to get a bit of pace up, although there are a lot of chairs to negotiate. Ideally, I'd run up and down Committee Corridor, from the Lords to the Commons and back – it's got to be at least half a mile and it's a clear path; you could almost imagine you were in a forest at night, what with all the mad leaf patterns on the wallpaper and the wooden panels like a solid wall of tree trunks – but, even though there aren't any CCTV cameras inside the House as the Members won't allow them, there are regular security patrols, so it's safer to run around a committee room.

Once, I almost get caught. I hear a noise as I'm running so I duck behind the lectern that contains all the sound-recording equipment. The door opens and a guard swishes a flashlight around but he's too lazy to come in and do a proper check. After less than half a minute, he's gone. Thank God most of the security guards here are so weighed down with subsidised canteen dinners that they can't move or think very fast. I emerge slowly from behind the lectern, sweating like a bastard, and creep back to my office for a shot or three of emergency whisky. I don't go running again after that but I do spend about two weeks faffing around in this vein, not making any decision. Why is my life so hard? Why is everything a problem? Why?

Since finding Grace, instead of checking the Refreshment Department web page to see which eatery in the Palace has the best meal for under £4, like I used to, I have my lunch in the Terrace Cafeteria every day because it's the closest to her office, therefore the place she's most likely to go. So far she hasn't gone there but I don't want to go anywhere else, as, by the law of averages, if I stick to the same place, I'm more likely to spot her eventually.

A couple of weeks after my last communication with Grace, however, my resolve breaks and I decide to have lunch in the Debate in Portcullis House. I decide to carry on going there for the next week, just in case this is her regular eating venue. It'll be tough for me because I hate the Debate. It's shiny and modern and serves brightly coloured food from trendy countries like Mexico or Vietnam. The place gives me a headache. Light and noise bounce off all the hard surfaces. There's too much glass and glitter. Unlike in the Terrace or the Lords cafeteria, there are no safe dark corners: everyone is on show. It is the opposite of womb-like. If Grace is a fan of the Debate, I will be very disappointed.

I cross the courtyard of Portcullis House, blinded by the light flooding in through the glass roof and embarrassed by the clicking sound that one of my shoes is making on the marble floor. There's a drawing pin stuck to the sole. I sit under a fake-looking tree on the edge of one of the 'water features' and pull it out.

The tables outside the Debate are filled with good-looking young researchers, chattering like maniacs and laughing as if everyone is watching. I pick my way between them feeling self-conscious and check around for Grace with what I hope is a look of aloofness. She's nowhere to be seen.

The server makes a big song and dance about wiping away the splashes of sauce from the edge of the oversized plate containing my Szechuan pepper-coated Norfolk turkey escalope on garlic ciabatta with selected leaves. The Member in front has the same thing on her tray. She pays with a twenty-pound note and is ostentatiously friendly towards the African woman on the till, whose name, according to her badge, is Prudence.

There are no empty tables so I sit opposite a girl who's forking up some selected leaves with one hand and checking her phone with the other. Without looking up, she shifts her yoghurt to one side to give me more room for my plate. She's what a lot of blokes would describe as pretty but, to me, she's not as pretty as Grace.

And then I see her. Grace. Scanning the tables, with a tray in her hands. She's wearing this really sexy short flowery dress which shows off her legs and her curves. For one heart-attack moment I think she might take the spare seat between me and phone girl but some researchers get up from another table and she jumps into their place. Followed by a tall, dark bloke. Who seems to know her. She is having lunch with him.

My escalope goes cold as I watch them. The bloke is in his twenties; definitely younger than me, in any case. He's wearing a new-looking suit. Everything about him looks new actually: his shoes, his shirt, his pink and purple tie (which I have a feeling he probably describes as 'funky'). Even his haircut looks new. He runs his fingers through the sides of it before picking up his knife and fork and slicing his escalope into precise mouthfuls. He looks sporty, this bloke, sporty and fit: something about the squareness of his shoulders gives this impression, although it could be the sharpness of his suit that makes his shoulders look so square. He is, I suppose, what a lot of women would probably describe as handsome. He's handsome in the same way that the girl opposite me is pretty. Already I hate him.

I study Grace's face and try to work out who this bloke is to her and vice versa. Their table is too far away for me to eavesdrop but even if it had been right next to me, the racket in the Debate is such that I probably wouldn't have been able to hear them. I try to read Grace's lovely lips but I can't. For a start, the bloke is doing most of the talking. She is listening, occasionally nodding her head, sometimes smiling. Once she laughs. I bet he's not that funny. He looks too professional to be funny. They don't touch at all, which makes me think he's not her boyfriend. I bloody hope he's not. The way she's holding herself so carefully and listening to him so politely makes me think she doesn't know him that well. When she strode past me that Monday morning, the first time I saw her in the flesh, she didn't look polite: her hands were shoved into her pockets, defiant and casual, like she didn't really care about this place and its petty rules. I wonder if this guy is just a colleague. I bloody hope so. It pisses me off that he gets to eat his lunch with her. Why can't *I* eat my lunch with her? Something lights up in my memory and my mind scrolls back to the New Starters on the intranet. I'm pretty sure he's one of them.

They finish their lunches and he gets them both a coffee, looking really pleased with himself. She checks her phone while he's gone. Who's she expecting to ring? She looks up, straight at me, and my heart, which is already pounding like mad, goes even faster, until I realise she is staring through me. The bloke comes back with two cardboard cups and, now the Debate is emptier and the noise has faded, I hear him say, 'Here you are: latte to go.' His voice is really deep and up himself and, I'm pretty sure, American. *To go*. What a knob. I hate the word 'latte' too and I especially hate the poncy way he says it.

They leave with their 'lattes' and I follow them at a safe distance until they disappear into a lift near the Strangers' Bar. I need to make a decision about sending Dan's photo but I feel far too rattled now. Perhaps if I go to bed early and really try to get a proper night's sleep I might finally know what to do in the morning.

28

The next day I am as shattered as ever. The only strikes of Big Ben I didn't hear during the night were between four and five in the morning so I must have slept just two hours at the most. Phil surfs in on a tsunami of fresh ponce juice, with his hair gelled into a short, jagged fin. He looks around my office and frowns. I wonder if he suspects something. My sleeping bag is stowed, as always, in the bottom of my desk drawers but perhaps the room smells fusty. Mind you, how he can smell anything beyond his own aftershave, I don't know.

'Just realised we need to do a half-year appraisal for your PDP.' He taps the blue folder in his hand. 'That OK with you, mate?'

I nod. He pinches up the knees of his trousers before lowering himself onto the chaise longue. 'Everything OK, Gavin?'

I nod again. 'Yeah, fine.'

He considers me critically. I know I am being 'managed' right now. He's probably using some technique he learned on a management-training course: *for best performance results pretend to take an interest in the subordinate*.

'Gavin, if you don't mind me saying, you don't look fine.'

'Really?' I lower my head to avoid his gaze.

'You look completely knackered. And I can't help but notice you haven't been performing as well as you used to ...'

'Performing?'

'Your tasks.'

I stare at a ball of rubber bands on my desk. I've been making that ball for the past year and it's now bigger than my fist.

'Yesterday, you sent the wrong letters to the Speaker and the

Leader. The Speaker's office rang me just now.'

So this is why he's decided to do my half-year appraisal now.

'Very careless, Gavin.'

'I didn't realise. It was a mistake.'

'It's the kind of mistake we can't afford to make. Makes us look unprofessional.'

'I'm sorry. Sometimes I make mistakes.'

'The thing is, Gavin, attention to detail is very important.' Phil leans back, his voice growing leisurely, getting into his stride as a manager in a management situation. 'The House prides itself on attention to detail. It's in your core job description: excellent attention to detail.'

'All right, Phil, I understand. My attention to detail slipped a bit. I'm sorry. I've said I'm sorry. What do you want me to do?'

'Gavin, there's no need to get defensive.'

'I'm not defensive.'

'You are, Gavin. You're being defensive.'

'No, I'm not.'

'Even saying that is defensive.'

'You're having a go at me.'

'Gavin, I'm not "having a go". I'm trying to find out if there's any reason you keep having these little … lapses … in your attention to detail. Last week all the briefs were missing page 4, the Chairman didn't even get his papers this week and I know you haven't booked the room for tomorrow's meeting because it's not on the Wallsheet.'

'Oh.' I'm holding the rubber band ball, throwing it from hand to hand. I don't want to look at Phil. If I look at him I might tell him to fuck off. I shake my head. 'No, no reason. I'm sorry. I'll try to pay more attention in future.'

'Good man, good man. That's what I want to hear. Right, let's have a look at this PDP. Now, I can see here you haven't put anything down in Development Needs.'

'I haven't got any Development Needs.'

Phil pulls in his chin, puffs out his lips and raises his eyebrows. '*Ri-i-ight*.'

'I've been here fifteen years. I've been on just about every course they run. I honestly don't think there's much point …'

Phil consults his notebook, which presumably contains notes on how to conduct this conversation. 'How about Effective Time Management? That's a new one. Might help you get a bit more organised.'

I sigh so hard my shoulders droop.

'Gavin, you know how it is in this place: you just have to play the game …'

'Yes, I know.'

After we've signed off my PDP, Phil springs up and claps me on the shoulder. 'Remember, if you've got any problems, if you've got any issues, any issues at all, I'm always here. It's important you feel you can talk to me. You know: as your manager.'

He gives me the Chairman's draft report to photocopy. As the photocopier shunts and whirrs, I stand in a daze. I could measure my life in photocopying. Big Ben strikes one o'clock as I enter Phil's office, bearing the warm reports.

'Hot off the press.'

'Nice one.' He doesn't bother to look up.

'I'm going to get some lunch now.'

'Right you are, mate. I'm going to grab a sandwich in a bit. Just one thing, if you could …'

Grab a sandwich. I hate that phrase. Grab. Trying to inject dynamism into a boring activity. All part of the changes that are coming to this place, the gradual corporatisation. Eventually we'll all have to 'grab' sandwiches and eat them at our desks like Americans. Phil's got time to eat a three-course meal if he wants but he likes to big himself up and subtly put me down by pretending he's only got time to 'grab' a sandwich.

Phil's one of those people who embrace the changes. That's why he's got on. Mind you, Phil's one of those people who would embrace whatever the management told him to embrace. If Phil had been in 1930s Germany, he'd have joined the Nazis. I often divide people up into Nazis and non-Nazis, the collaborators and the resistance. The Germans weren't inherently evil. It's just that most of them, like the majority of any population, did what they were told to save their own skins. They were weak. They were yes men. Like Phil.

'... so is that all right then? You'll have it done by close of play today?'

Phil's been talking all the while I've been turning this Nazi stuff over in my mind. I stare at him blankly and he stares at me with irritation.

'Close of play, yeah?' He loves this phrase; makes him feel like a clerk: A-grade rather than B.

'Yes, boss.'

'Nice one, Gav.' He nods and smiles, doesn't pick up on my ironic tone in the slightest.

I have no idea what it is I am supposed to do by close of play today.

That afternoon, I email Grace again. I know I'm going to seem a bit random and I know I am going to have to deal with the photo issue eventually but, right now, I just want contact.

—hello. how are you today?

—Yes, fine. Busy. Weird: she sounds unsurprised to hear from me. It's as if there's been no gap in our conversation. It must mean something that we can communicate so easily.

—busy with what?

—Work.

—what sort of stuff?

—Oh, you know, the usual boring stuff. I can't be bothered to go into it.

She sounds grumpy. I wonder if it's because I haven't emailed for so long. I try to lighten the mood by telling her about my meeting with Phil. Immediately she jumps on the fact I'm supposedly a temp; why am I having appraisals? Christ, there's no flies on her. I make up some bullshit about how he was giving me an appraisal to decide whether to keep me on permanently. I give her my theory on why he would have been a Nazi. She sounds slightly shocked, tells me I'm being a bit harsh, so I have to backtrack, make out I'm just frustrated with my day job:

—i just always feel its a waste of my time being at work. i wish i could make a living out of my music.

Definitely the kind of thing Dan Sheridan would have said.

29

It is nearly midnight. I am sitting at her desk in the darkness. It took a lot to gear myself up to this. A lot of emergency Dutch courage. I had to sneak here carefully, along the edges of the corridors, ducking into a committee room at one point when I thought I heard a guard coming. Thankfully, it was nothing. Lately, I keep hearing things that aren't there, sensing people's eyes on me when I'm walking around the Palace but turning and finding nothing. Sometimes I feel I'm being watched even when I'm alone in my office. My only safe place is becoming unsafe. Now, I'm in her office. My hands are touching things that her hands have touched. I am sitting where she has sat. I am trembling.

It is obvious this is her desk. There are three desks in the room and hers is the only messy one. I knew, like the way I knew she wouldn't wear high heels, that she would have a messy desk. I can sense what she is like. As I've said before, I know her already.

There are postcards pinned to her noticeboard: art postcards. I unpin each card and risk switching on her green desk lamp so I can read the titles on the back. *Mariana in the South*, John William Waterhouse, *Starry Night*, Edvard Munch, *A Lady with a Squirrel and a Starling*, Hans Holbein the Younger, *Between Dog and Wolf*, Chrystel Lebas, *Fernsehturm*, Tacita Dean … the Royal Academy, the British Museum, Tate Britain, the V&A. In my head she wanders around these places alone on Sunday afternoons looking and feeling wistful. I'm not sure what she's feeling wistful about – being alone, hopefully. Only one card, as far as I can tell, has been bought by someone else – a picture of a girl in a bonnet by Vittorio Matteo Corcos called *Contemplation (en prière)* – with a message on the back in red pen: *This girl reminds me of you. Love Rx.* I peer at the front again. Though it is a nice picture and it does look like her I want to rip it up, as R is obviously a man.

I pin each card back, pressing the pins back into the old pinholes, and then go through her drawers. Among the unsurprising collection of paperclips and pens, I find headache pills, a hairbrush full of her hair, tampons, various sauce sachets from the canteens, mascara, lipstick and a Virgin Atlantic travel toothbrush and toothpaste set. She must have been to America. Bit jet-set. Only place I've ever been abroad is France – a day trip to Dieppe with school years ago. The lipstick is a lush pinky red. I imagine it on her lips. It would make them look good enough to eat. *Cherries in the Snow*, says the tiny label on the bottom. It smells of fake sweetness. I run it across my own lips, using the blank computer monitor as a mirror, and lick it off. It tastes of grease. I slip it into my pocket. I want to smell it when I'm alone.

The words from 'Suedehead' careen through my mind: 'You had to sneak into my room just to read my diary'. Unfortunately, there's no diary here, although in the bottom drawer I find printouts of her annual reports.

> Grace has performed well this year, effectively juggling administrative demands and always ensuring reports and committee papers are produced on time … Occasionally Grace needs to pay more careful attention to detail … Grace has grown in confidence in her dealings with Members … I have no doubt that with further experience of committee work, Grace could be successfully promoted …

At the end of each report, below her boss's spidery inkblot

signature, is her name in round bubble letters. She has surprisingly bad handwriting.

I close the drawers and investigate the desktop, making sure everything is replaced exactly as it was. There is a ring-bound notepad, which I sit back to devour. Her handwriting reminds me of girls at school. I almost expect hearts on top of the 'i's. It looks a bit thick, to be honest, though what was I expecting? Calligraphy? It's full of to-do lists, work stuff. As far as I can make out, her job is the Commons equivalent to mine. I rifle through the pages for more personal stuff. There are doodles of hearts and flowers, stars and butterflies. Rainbows arching from one side of the pad to the other. Stylised clouds and suns with long rays of light. Women with floor-length hair and flowing dresses. Like sixties posters for 'happenings'. Really big, intricate doodles that cover whole pages where she's pressed so hard the paper's curled up. She must've been at some meeting, mega-bored. Doodles reveal the subconscious, right? Her subconscious seems somewhat psychedelic. I wonder if she's into drugs. I hope not. I'm scared of drugs. Not that I've ever taken any. She is a bit alternative-looking but she doesn't look druggy. Perhaps she smokes pot. Is that what it's called these days?

I flick through the rest of the notebook with one eye on the door. How I'd explain myself if I got caught, I really don't know. There's a list of screening times for *Blue Valentine* at the Curzon Soho, a note that says *French House – 7.30*, a phone number for someone called Jules. I wonder where the French House is and who she went there with. Hopefully not Jules. The wanker. Probably got hair like Hugh Grant. Probably works in the City, earns loads of money. But maybe Jules is a girl. Julie, Julia. Posh girls often have boys' names. Like my clerk, Roberta. Other clerks call her Bobby.

Big Ben strikes midnight. The bongs seem excessive: like,

OK, we get the point, it's twelve o'clock, you can stop now. The building seems to shake with each chime. In ten hours Grace's bum will be back on this seat. Her full, round, perfectly shaped arse. The thought gives me an erection.

The desk to the right of Grace's is covered in animal memorabilia – soft toys, ornaments and postcards of giraffes, elephants, orangutans and so on. I've worked out, from studying the Economic Scrutiny Committee's web pages, that this desk must belong to Miss Rosemary Ballard, Senior Committee Assistant.

The person at the desk opposite Grace has to be Brett Beamish, Committee Specialist. He is, as I suspected, the prat I saw her with in the Debate. I looked him up again on the New Starters web page.

His stupid smug face grinning – *beaming* – out at me from the computer was despicable. An *Australian*. My only experience of Australians is of them being loud and full of themselves in various London pubs, back when I occasionally went to pubs. They're even more full of themselves than Americans. Plus they expect everyone to like them, whereas at least Americans have the good grace to know everyone hates them.

I wonder what Brett earns. Obviously more than me. The Treasury, an MBA … no wonder he looks so bloody pleased with himself. *When not poring over the finer points of economic policy, Brett enjoys travelling and tennis.* What toss. I bet he wrote that himself. Travelling and tennis: how bland can you get?

His desk is immaculate. There is nothing on the worktop and inside the drawers pens are lined up in size and colour order, paperclips and pins are stored in little compartments on a pull-out tray, and envelopes and compliments slips are placed in careful piles. *With compliments*. Fuck off with your compliments, Brett Beamish.

I've got an urge to defile his desk in some way. Scatter the paperclips, pull the tops off the pens, shit in the drawer. As soon as I think this last thought I slam the drawer shut. Sometimes my thoughts worry me.

30

Next day, I get her to open up a bit about her life outside work. She tells me about her flatmates. They are both women, which I'm pleased about. Although she doesn't state it outright I get the impression she's single, which is brilliant. In fact, I get the impression she's lonely, which is also brilliant. I manage to manoeuvre Brett Beamish into the conversation, wheedle out what she thinks of him. I nearly punch the air when she tells me he's a 'bit of a pain'. She definitely doesn't like him, in any case; basically thinks he's a corporate wanker in not so many words. We have a good bonding conversation about the fakeness of corporate life. And then, just as I'm thinking maybe we've built up enough of a rapport that I could send a real picture of myself, that she might have forgotten I'm supposed to be a six-foot tousle-haired hunk, she sends me this:

—What are you like, Reuben? I know nothing about you. It's getting a bit weird. You know what I look like. Come on, why don't you send me a picture of yourself?

I go to the loo, I come back, I make a cup of coffee. I click through the pictures I've saved of Dan Sheridan. I look at the two pictures I've got of myself. I look at the pictures of Sheridan. I look at my pictures. I look at his. I look at mine. It's no use. I send a picture of him, sitting in a corner, looking angst-ridden but handsome. I attach a poem entitled 'counting out my life in photocopies', which I wrote yesterday evening before I went snooping round her office. She replies within a couple of minutes:

—Hey Reuben, I love your poem. You've captured exactly how I feel. Thanks for the picture, Gx.

*

After everyone goes home, I lock my door on the inside so the cleaner can't get in. I lie on the chaise longue and fall asleep before Big Ben even strikes seven. Sleep comes like a bookcase of committee reports falling on my head. It doesn't feel like healthy sleep. More like a sort of death.

When I wake it's pitch dark. It seems like four in the morning but the annunciator, glowing alien green, says it's just after ten at night. Something has woken me, some sort of noise. Something falling for real. I lie very still. It's a noise from next door, from Phil and Jenny's office. I hear bumps and muffled giggles. I lie even stiller, terrified that the door is going to open. Then I remember that the door is locked from the inside and, in any case, Phil and Jenny, because I can recognise from the giggles that it is them, are not going to realise I am in here because they are too busy with their own naughty little activity.

I tiptoe over and lower my eye to the keyhole. A lamp is on in their office. I can't see anything except a strip of carpet and the corner of Phil's desk but it's obvious from the giggles and the grunts and the sighs what they are up to.

There's nothing that makes you feel lonelier than the sound of other people shagging. Though I shouldn't, I can't help but imagine what Phil is doing to Jenny. She's not so neat now with her head thrown back across the desk between her well-ordered file trays, not so efficient with her skirt shoved up to the top of her chubby thighs and, between them, Phil's spotty white bum pumping in and out. Phil's bum: what a horrible image. I try to push it out of my mind. I try to push the whole image of him and Jenny out of my mind but it's difficult because I can hear them panting and snuffling and a rhythmic squeaking of furniture and Phil's bottom keeps turning into mine and Jenny's thighs keep turning into Grace's. We are thrashing about on Grace's desk among her piles of unfiled paper. She's still got her boots on and her cherry-red lipstick. Her hair is all over the place. She wants me hard in her. Really hard. In her passion she kicks a half-finished cup of coffee off the desk … The image pops like a bubble because suddenly the message on the annunciator has flicked to THE THREAT LEVEL REMAINS SEVERE. The glowing screen is an all-seeing eye. I pull my hand out of my trousers.

There is a definite silence in the office next door. The solid silence of the House at this time of night. As if time has stopped. I know all the different silences of the House and all the small sounds that break the silences: the nearby hum of computers and faraway tides of traffic. I know what the House sounds like when everyone has gone home. I put my eye to the keyhole again but all is dark. They've gone. That was quick. I wonder how long they've been carrying on together. If this is going to be their regular trysting place – is that the right word? 'Trysting' sounds a bit too sweet for what they were doing – if this is going to be their regular shag pad I'm done for. My last safe haven gone. I might have guessed from their constant flirting that something was going on. But, because they've both got *partners* – how I hate that smug word – I assumed that's all it was: flirting; office silliness; ordinary banter between ordinary men and women.

Sadness floods over me, floods over my exhaustion. Other people are tough: they grab what they want. If they want two women, if they want two men, if they want a man and a woman, they have them. They don't care about other people's feelings. I should be the same.

I flop my head back and stare into the darkness. I've set myself on a particular track, of pretending to be someone else, and now I don't know how to turn back. If I tell her the truth perhaps she'll understand. Hard to tell how nice she really is, how forgiving of other people's insecurities. Maybe it will be OK if I meet up with her. Maybe I can pretend I've gone to seed since that picture was taken.

It's so unfair. I deserve Grace. I appreciate her far more than Phil appreciates Jenny. Despite all his smarm, Phil doesn't really appreciate women. He's proved that by cheating on his girlfriend. He's too in love with himself to be capable of truly loving someone else.

31

—Is that it then?

—is that what?

—I just wondered where you were. One minute you're sending me poems and pictures of yourself, next minute silence.

I can't remember when I last wrote to her. I've been having so many conversations with her in my head, I keep forgetting I haven't actually replied to her. Well, not forgetting exactly, but I keep losing track of time. It might be the whisky. And my insomnia is getting worse. I thought once I'd made the decision to send Dan Sheridan's picture I'd feel calmer, but no. Also, in real life, I couldn't decide how to respond to her last message thanking me for his picture so, as always, when in a state of indecision, I did nothing. Now she sounds pissed off.

—did you miss me? I ask.

—I just wondered where you were.

—i was busy. sorry.

—Got any more poems?

She wants more pictures really, I expect, but she doesn't want to sound shallow. Funny how her interest was piqued massively when I sent that picture of Dan Sheridan. The speed of her reply said it all: 'Hey Reuben, I love your poem'. I could feel the way she sat up straight at her desk, the energy as she typed. And that 'Gx'. First time she's signed off with a kiss.

—have a listen to this. I attach an audio file of Dan Sheridan playing 'Lost in the Forest', a sparse, acoustic number which has a sound that I can only describe as 'icy'. Icily sad.

Of course, she loves it.

She also loves 'Liminal Space', 'Black and White Film', 'Iodine' and 'Under the Lime Trees'. We discuss my influences: Nick Drake, Nick Cave, Leonard Cohen, Morrissey ... the miserable Nicks and the miserable non-Nicks. We discuss the meaning behind my lyrics – sex, death and madness, in not so many words – and what inspired my songs: the films of Fritz Lang, Berlin, Dungeness Power Station and the sound of foxes shagging at night (except I say 'mating' to protect Grace's delicate sensibilities, and even then I wonder if this is a bit strong – the fox idea came to me from a poem I read a long time ago). We discuss how these songs make her feel: sad, mainly, but 'in a good way'. She tells me all her favourite songs are 'bittersweet, halfway between sad and happy'.

At one point she asks me if I've ever performed these songs live.

—not these ones. im not ready to share them yet. except with you.

—Have you tried to get a record deal?

—no. i want to get together enough songs for an album first.

Without prompting she sends me some more pictures of herself: the one off her Facebook profile and another, in which her lips are the colour of the lipstick I stole from her desk and she's wearing a red dress which makes her breasts look fantastic. I send her a load of pictures of Dan Sheridan. She tells me I am very photogenic. I know she wants to say more. By home time I can tell we're both completely hot and bothered.

To my horror, she then tells me her flatmates really loved my songs.

—I played them to them last night. They think you're brilliant!

My stomach clenches. I feel cold. Her flatmates could easily play Dan's songs to someone who recognises him.

—er ... cheers ... grace i know this might sound a bit uptight but id rather you didnt play those songs to anyone else. like i said yesterday im not really ready to share them with anyone else except you.

There's a slight delay in her reply.

—Sorry. I didn't realise.

—no probs

She asks if I'm on WhatsApp and when I pretend I can't be bothered with that sort of palaver, she asks if that's why I'm not on Facebook or Twitter either, so I make out I'm one of those anti-Establishment types that doesn't want Big Brother keeping tabs on me. I reckon this fits in with Reuben Swift's persona.

—I just thought Twitter could be a good way of getting your music out there, getting known, but I guess if you don't want to be known ...

—not at the moment no

There is another delay, longer than before. I worry I've sounded too suspicious and weird, but then:

—Look, do you fancy meeting up sometime? It'd be nice to meet in person.

Oh God. I'm not ready for this now. I don't know if I'm ever going to be ready for it. Oh bloody hell. What have I got myself into? I've done this all wrong. I'm an idiot. It's never going to work. Oh fucking hell ...

—sorry im q busy at the moment. i would like to at some point soon but right now ive got q a lot on

She doesn't reply.

That lunchtime I go down to the Terrace. I need comfort food. I need to feel warm and cosy. Or as warm and cosy as I can ever feel, which is not very, these days. I choose the shepherd's pie and chips for £3.50. Shovelling forkfuls of food into my mouth, I glance around the other tables. They contain the usual assortment of pudgy, suited blokes and court-shoed women. No Grace. By the time I've finished, there is still half an hour left of my lunch break. I don't want to go back to the office and I definitely don't want to leave the Palace, so I decide to push the boat out and have pudding, even though it will tip my lunch 55 pence over my £4 limit. As I head towards the counter where the jam roly-poly and custard is drying out under a heat lamp, she passes me with a tray. I hold my breath. I turn back. She is wearing the red dress from the photo she sent me last night. I haven't seen her wear it before. It feels like some sort of sign. Like she was thinking of me when she put it on this morning. Like subconsciously she thought we might meet. She is surveying the tables. What if she sits opposite me? She'll guess who I am. I'm sure she will. What am I going to do? I'll have to say something. But what?

She takes a seat next to a security guard, two tables from mine. He moves his coat off the chair so she can sit and carries on talking to his mate. Amazingly, they barely notice her. I carry my pudding back to the seat opposite the one I had been sitting at, so I can see her face. My hands are sweating as I pass but she doesn't even look up. Her right hand is forking up her food, her left is holding open a book. She is eating the same lunch as me, except she's got broccoli instead of chips and she hasn't squirted ketchup all over her shepherd's pie: she's definitely posh. The room is emptying so I have a clear view of her across the tables. I spoon up my pudding and pretend to stare into the middle distance – that old Tube trick. Not that I've been on the Tube in a while.

She eats nicely, like the well-brought-up girl that she obviously is. Smallish bites, chewing with her mouth closed, occasionally dabbing her mouth with a serviette, and spreading it back across her lap. Lucky serviette. Her dress stretches gorgeously across her breasts. They are small but definitely in existence. Her hair is pinned up in some sort of bun-type thing. Very Brontë-esque. If anything, it makes her look even prettier than when it's down loose. Just her cool, un-officey clothes make her stand out, let alone her beauty. I can't believe the security guards aren't transfixed by her. I'm dying to see what she's reading. Eventually she lifts it up when one of the assistants comes to clear her plate. *Kitchen Venom* by Philip Hensher. I've never heard of it.

All too soon she stands up, checks the time on the annunciator – 13.48 – shoves her book in her bag – some sort of hippyish leather job – and leaves without a backward glance. I follow her at a careful distance. Along the function-room corridor with its potted palms and waiters in waistcoats stalking up and down with trolleys of white linen. It always makes me feel like I've wandered into a hotel. Two of the waiters eye her up. Up the stairs, past the medieval pictures of kings and queens, into Lower Waiting with the pointless stone fireplace and fake fire. Along the tiled floor to Central Lobby where a cluster – a catastrophe? – of people in wheelchairs are waiting to meet a Member. I sit on a leather seat and watch her buy a stamp for a letter – to who? – at the post-office counter. She then strides through the milling people and disappears, with a nod of her head to the doorkeepers, up to Members' Lobby. She has not looked at me once. Like I say, my ability to fade into the background can be useful. When I get back to my desk this message is waiting for me:

—Have you got a girlfriend or something? Are you married?

32

Now I know Phil and Jenny's dirty little secret, I can't believe I didn't twig before. The looks that flick between them during committee meetings, the giggling, the way they're always disappearing off together: it's all so obvious. The morning after I'd first caught them at it through the keyhole, I felt nervous about seeing them again. I didn't know if I'd be able to behave normally and I was sure they'd know I knew. Ridiculous, 'cos they were the ones who should have felt nervous, not me. Phil and Jenny are brazen though. They've got no shame. I'm more sensitive than them. I think it's because I'm more intelligent. I look at Phil and Jenny and I know there's nothing going on behind their stupid grins and their empty eyes.

It's the same with people on the Tube. Back when I used to commute to work, I used to watch people poring over celebrity magazines or nodding their heads to their iPods or talking absolute bollocks to each other, and I knew their minds were as shallow and brash as Saturday-night TV. And it's not just normal people, even the upper classes are the same: I listen to the Lords in meetings, boring on and on, and I know from the ordinary things they say that their thoughts are ordinary too. No wonder most people don't feel things like I do: they don't think as much.

I have to do a ring round, find out if the Lords on the Procedure Committee are coming to the weekly meeting. I get through to a couple of secretaries – brusque, brittle-voiced women, who insist on referring to their bosses as *Sir* So-and-so. I leave some messages on voicemails: 'I'm calling from the Procedure Committee … just trying to find out if Sir Anthony …' 'Sir' sounds so bloody arse-licking I'm glad no one is listening to me: I'm ashamed of myself. I get through to Lord Kilpatrick directly.

'Yers?'

'Hi, I'm just calling from the Procedure Committee.'

'What?' No doubt Lord Kilpatrick is holding the phone like an ear trumpet.

'I'm calling from the Procedure Committee … you know: the committee you're on …'

'Oh yers …' Lord Kilpatrick always sounds as if he is reclining on a chaise longue, letting a large lunch go down.

'Just wondering if you'll be attending the meeting tomorrow.'

'What meeting? Speak up. I'm very deaf, you know.'

I know. Deaf and mad and senile and with both feet in the grave. Quite often in this job I feel like a care assistant in an old people's home. Lord Kilpatrick and I go through the same rigmarole on the phone every week because he refuses to answer emails. He probably doesn't even know how to turn his computer on and would prefer it if I delivered messages to him by hand on a silver platter.

'The Procedure Committee meeting!' I shout.

'*What?* Speak up, man.'

'The Procedure Committee meeting.'

'*The Seizure Commies are meeting?*'

'The Procedure Committee meeting! You're on the Procedure Committee!'

'Who on earth are the *Seizure Commies*? I've absolutely no idea what you're talking about. Speak to my secretary.' He slams the phone down.

Lord Kilpatrick doesn't have a secretary, so I will have to type him a letter and send it through the internal post. Actually, I might as well hand-deliver it. I type up the letter, print it off and seal it in an envelope. Christ, my brain is meant for better things than this.

Trouble is, nobody realises I'm clever. I've got A levels – a B and two Cs in English, History and Art; quite an achievement for an Eastbrook Comp boy – but compared to most people these days, compared to someone like Grace, it's nothing. I bet she's got a degree. Mind you, even Jenny and Phil have got degrees. Jenny's is in International Hospitality Management and Phil's is in Business Studies – Mickey Mouse degrees, obviously, but still, degrees. There was no talk of getting a degree when I left school. Nobody in my family has any further education. In my family, you just leave school, get a job and earn your keep.

For the first few months I was pleased about getting this job. People were always interested to hear where I worked and I basked in the glory of it. I liked swanning around the echoey halls and padding along the long, warm corridors. I sometimes got a feeling that I can only describe as soaring, as if a part of me had flown out of my body and was hovering like a painted angel in the great arched ceilings. I suppose it was a feeling of possibility: that anything might happen. Months passed and then years and I never got promoted. I went for promotion interviews but I never got anywhere. I thought I said the right thing during these interviews but obviously I didn't. Or at least I wasn't convincing in the way I said I wanted to 'identify business needs' and 'cascade responsibility forward appropriately'. Basically they knew I was subversive. The Establishment is a monolith and it crushes anyone who doesn't fit in. Even though managerial types pretend they want people to 'think outside the box', they don't really. Free-thinkers are a threat. Mad really, as you'd think an insubordinate irritant like me could be easily brushed off by a huge institution like the House, but they don't like anyone sowing seeds of discontent.

Once, some pompous git at a feedback interview after another failed promotion attempt said, 'I don't want to speak out of turn but have you ever considered you might be happier in another organisation?'

I didn't know what to say. He was basically saying my face didn't fit. It made me want to dig my heels in, so even though I knew I had no hope I kept on applying for jobs just to prove to that git that he hadn't won. People who had arrived after me – stupid, ordinary people with the gift of the gab, like Phil – began to streak ahead. Soon they had more power than me, these stupid people, and they liked to throw their weight around. They were a new breed. The old lot, the lot that worked in the House when I first started, were slow and soft and polite. They held doors open for ladies and said things like, 'How do you do?' and, 'Indeed'. But they began to be crowded out by a fast, hard, new lot, who talked nonsensical management jargon and had fake smiles.

The change was gradual and it took me a while to notice it – like when you've been sitting in one position for a long time and you suddenly realise you're cold. I didn't notice when those soaring feelings stopped, but they did. One day I walked through Westminster Hall and felt nothing. Usually Westminster Hall was guaranteed to make me soar – it's so ancient and solid and huge and the musty air seems to have blown in on a draught from the Middle Ages. But that day it did nothing for me.

'Earth to Gavin … Earth to Gavin. Anyone there?'

I jump. Phil. Sliding into my office as if the soles of his pointy loafers are smeared with his hair gel. Even though I'm not sorry I make an apologetic noise.

'Do you want something, Phil?'

'Yes, actually, I do. Can you make up a set of nameplates for the witnesses for this afternoon.'

'Isn't that usually one of Jenny's jobs?'

'Jen's very busy CRCing a report right now so if you wouldn't mind …'

Judging from the laughter I'd overheard only five minutes ago, it was hard to believe 'Jen' was that busy.

'I'm quite busy myself.'

'Really? You didn't look very busy when I came in. You looked like you were in a world of your own.' Phil smiles but his eyes are cold. I hate him and he hates me. We both know we hate each other but we have to be civil or else … Or else what? I'll get a bad annual report. The office will descend into anarchy. The very fabric of day-to-day working life will unravel and reveal itself to be a threadbare rag.

'When do you need them by, the nameplates?'

'Asap.' He pronounces it like a word instead of letters.

'OK.'

'Good man.' He slides back out.

Good man? Christ. It's hardly like I'm about to defuse a bomb or perform open-heart surgery or weld a car panel. Phil's so pompous about our jobs – our *roles* – yet basically we do low-level admin; we're just paper-pushers.

As I make the nameplates I think about Elaine. The only other woman I've truly loved apart from Grace. There's a clue in her name. It sounds like an older woman's name. She was an older woman. Same age as my mum, to be precise. She was really nice, Elaine. I was a right bastard to her. And I don't say that in a proud way. I still feel bad about it.

We met at the Poetry Café in Covent Garden. I went there one Tuesday night after reading about it in *Poetry Review*, this magazine I used to subscribe to. Tuesday nights were open-mic nights where anybody could get up and read a poem. There were all sorts there: young, old, black, white, pretty, ugly, sane, mad (a lot of mad). You wouldn't believe so many people write poetry. It was quite encouraging because I'd always thought my writing poetry was a bit odd. No one I knew wrote poetry.

I didn't get up and read mine. But this middle-aged woman who had been sitting next to me on one of the rows of folding chairs was one of the people that did. Her poem was about foxes, the sound of them shagging at night, how she lay in bed alone and listened to them and wished she was a fox. It was pretty full-on, pretty sexy, especially for an older woman. I liked it, and when she sat down I told her so. I turned to her and said, 'I liked that.'

She smiled at me and said, 'Thank you very much.'

During the interval, she asked if I was going to read any of my poems.

'No, definitely not.'

She asked me why and I said I was far too shy.

'That's a shame … I'd be intrigued to know what kind of poems you write.' That was the word she used – *intrigued*. Nobody had ever used that word in connection with me before. It was far more suggestive than plain 'interested'. We got to talking about poetry. She was really easy to talk to. Probably because I wasn't trying to impress her. And she seemed genuinely interested in me – genuinely *intrigued*. When the interval ended I was disappointed because I wanted to talk to her more.

After the second round of poems, we did talk some more. In fact, we talked until the Poetry Café shut and then we talked all the way to Leicester Square Tube.

'It's been so nice talking to you,' she said. 'It'd be really nice to talk again.'

So we swapped numbers and she hugged and kissed me full on the lips. The following Saturday we met up again at the Poetry Library on the South Bank. She read me some of her favourite poems – all sexy, modern stuff written by women: I was sure she was trying to tell me something – and then we had dinner at Wagamama. She showed me how to use chopsticks and I ate a tiger prawn for the first time.

'Where have you been all your life?' she asked.

'Hornchurch,' I said. 'They don't have big prawns and chopsticks in Hornchurch.'

She laughed. 'You're funny.'

Nobody had ever told me that before either.

After dinner we walked across Hungerford Bridge towards Gordon's Wine Bar on the Embankment.

'There's where I work.' I pointed across the river to the House. From that far away it looked like it was made from dripping wax.

'It looks beautiful from this angle,' she said. 'Shame about all the ugly people inside.'

I looked at her, shocked. I didn't know what to say.

'No, not you.' She was all flustered and embarrassed. 'I meant the politicians.' She looked at me really sincerely. 'You're not ugly.'

In the middle of Hungerford Bridge we kissed properly. We never got to Gordon's. She took me back to her place in Crystal Palace there and then. Her house was very arty: full of books and proper paintings and antique rugs. Everything was cluttered and dusty. Unlike my mum, she wasn't into housework. Her mind was on higher matters. The way she acted wasn't like an older woman and even though her hair was grey and her skin crinkled around her eyes, she was still pretty. From some old photos in her hallway I saw she had been an absolute stunner in her youth.

To begin with I was going to pretend I was experienced but two minutes into getting down to it, she said, 'Is this your first time, Gavin?'

It seemed stupid to lie.

'A lot of firsts for you today,' she said. 'First chopsticks, first prawn …'

I was mortified but she made me feel at ease, showed me what to do. If there was an ideal woman to lose your virginity to it was Elaine.

We went out for three months. Happiest three months of my life. I felt more comfortable with her than anyone I'd ever known before. She was an education to me, in more ways than one: introducing me to high-quality literature, art and food. She gave me a crash course in being middle-class, I suppose. When I say 'went out' I really mean 'stayed in' because, during those three months, we didn't go out that often and when we did I'm ashamed to admit I felt embarrassed. I was worried people would think she was my mother. We did get funny looks but Elaine seemed oblivious to them. Even if she had noticed she wouldn't have cared because, in a low-key, un-show-offy way, she was very unconventional.

After three months I ended it. Pretended I didn't have 'feelings' for her any more but that was a lie and she knew the real reason was my stupid, conventional, small-minded embarrassment. She took it well, in the same calm, kind way she took everything. Without me spelling it out, she understood.

I was heartbroken. Stupid really, seeing as it was my choice. Weekends were long and blank again and I couldn't work out how on earth I had put up with the boredom of life before I'd met her. A month after our split I tried to contact her again, to tell her I'd changed my mind but she wouldn't have me back. In the kindest possible way she told me I was immature, that I'd hurt her and she'd been wrong about me. She'd thought I was the kind of person who didn't care about society's conventions. She'd thought I was bigger than I am.

I often think about Elaine, imagine what could have been if I'd been braver. We could still be lounging on her holey rugs, drinking lapsang souchong and reading the Sunday papers. Sometimes I Google her but she doesn't have much of a 'web presence'. The only thing I once came up with was a poetry competition she'd won with the poem about the foxes. I keep

the website in my Favourites. It's still there. I used t
connection to her when I looked at it. Like I was to
through the ether.

'Nameplates.' I place the plastic Toblerone-shaped
Phil's desk. He immediately reduces whatever he wa
on the Internet.

'Nice one, mate.' He scrutinises them. 'Hang abou
supposed to put Mr or Mrs in front of everyone's nam
titles … Jen?'

Jenny turns round from her prissy long-nailed t
We are.' Her pert little mouth, smothered in pink gr
at me. 'Sor*ree*.'

'I suppose you want me to do them again?'

'If you wouldn't mind, mate.'

I do mind, you bastard. I bloody do mind. Who
whether some tedious captain of industry gets calle
Why all this pandering to archaic conventions? W
matter?

'OK, Phil. Will do.'

I take the new nameplates in to Phil, who noc
satisfaction as if I'm a naughty schoolboy who has fi
the error of his ways. Jenny is sitting straight-backed,
still tapping away as if butter wouldn't melt in her m
your secret, you dirty cow. I know what you get u
right here, on that very desk.

Back at my desk I finish a poem I've been workin
days. In a sudden fit of impatience with myself, I ser
along with this message:

—sorry for the long delay. ive had a lot going
been having a bit of a bad time but im back now. a
for meeting up?

abstract level, and we would agree with Kate Soper's insistence on the social mediation of these natural phenomena. 'Even death', she writes, 'that notorious leveller, will not lay down in the flatness of its essence.'[29] Certainly maternal and infant mortality is not a stark and simple fact of nature, but is susceptible to social control and historical variation. Famine may be a natural given of the pre-social world but we know nonetheless that a more just distribution of the world's food resources could eradicate it. The diseases of the undernourished are every bit as social as the nervous breakdowns and heart diseases of the affluent.

It is not simply that the facts of nature are amenable to at least a substantial degree of social control. Appeals to nature, and particularly to natural inequality, have a hallowed tradition in the justification and legitimation of social inequality and social division. This has been widely recognized in the history of ideologies of class, estate, race and nationality. The irreducible differences between the sexes provide a fertile basis for such legitimating processes: 'The pattern of gender relations in our society is overwhelmingly a social rather than a natural one, but it is a social construction that caricatures biological difference in the most grotesque way and then appeals to this misrepresented natural world for its own justification.'[30]

Nowhere can this process of caricature and misrepresentation be seen more clearly than in the recently fashionable science of socio-biology. In categorizing the family as 'anti-social', and in accusing it (somewhat anthropomorphically no doubt) of being a 'selfish' institution, we invite the socio-biological retort that selfish mechanisms are inevitably the means by which 'selfish genes' seek to reproduce themselves. Socio-biology seeks to demonstrate that all human behaviour is explicable in terms of the tendency of genes – DNA – to

[29] 'Marxism, Materialism and Biology', in John Mepham and David Hillel Ruben, eds., *Issues in Marxist Philosophy*, vol. 2, Brighton 1979, p. 95

[30] Michèle Barrett, *Women's Oppression Today*, London 1980, p. 76.

maximize the conditions of survival and reproduction.[31] Sex difference is written into socio-biology at a fundamental level. Males, who are capable of fathering countless children, will naturally be sexually promiscuous in order to populate the world with their genetic successors; at the same time they will guard against the social obligations of fatherhood unless they can be sure the child is theirs. Females, whose reproductive capacities are finite, will seek to maximize them by selecting a reliable and well-providing mate and will not threaten the genetic succession by sexual deviation. To this elemental model we find accommodated explanations of the minute details of contemporary sexual and familial behaviour. As Lucy Bland points out, the theory enables socio-biologists to justify as natural the various trappings of present definitions of femininity and masculinity. Female coyness, male philandering, criteria of female attractiveness and so on – down to the finest details of male fantasy – are scientifically explained in articles in *Playboy* as well as in more scholarly publications.[32] Socio-biology is shot through with a political conservatism that waxes lyrical on the stupidity and ignorance of feminism, which it sees as attempting to halt (like Canute the tides) the necessary passage of genetic evolution. As is the case with a considerable body of work in palaeontology, primatology, evolutionary anthropology and so on, the 'findings' of socio-biology bear a suspiciously close resemblance to the sexist principles and assumptions of its practitioners.

Feminists have paid considerable attention to the sexist bias of natural, particularly biological, science in both its erudite and popular forms and it is not necessary for us to take up these arguments one by one. It must be repeated, however, that the argument from biology can be countered on a different level – that of social and political choice. It is a mark of progress that issues such as eugenics, abortion, euthanasia, the artificial preservation of life and the treatment of severely disabled

[31] Richard Dawkins, *The Selfish Gene*, London 1976; E.O. Wilson, *On Human Nature*, New York, 1978.

[32] '"It's Only Human Nature"? Socio-biology and Sex Differences', *Schooling and Culture*, no.10, summer 1981.

We went out for three months. Happiest three months of my life. I felt more comfortable with her than anyone I'd ever known before. She was an education to me, in more ways than one: introducing me to high-quality literature, art and food. She gave me a crash course in being middle-class, I suppose. When I say 'went out' I really mean 'stayed in' because, during those three months, we didn't go out that often and when we did I'm ashamed to admit I felt embarrassed. I was worried people would think she was my mother. We did get funny looks but Elaine seemed oblivious to them. Even if she had noticed she wouldn't have cared because, in a low-key, un-show-offy way, she was very unconventional.

After three months I ended it. Pretended I didn't have 'feelings' for her any more but that was a lie and she knew the real reason was my stupid, conventional, small-minded embarrassment. She took it well, in the same calm, kind way she took everything. Without me spelling it out, she understood.

I was heartbroken. Stupid really, seeing as it was my choice. Weekends were long and blank again and I couldn't work out how on earth I had put up with the boredom of life before I'd met her. A month after our split I tried to contact her again, to tell her I'd changed my mind but she wouldn't have me back. In the kindest possible way she told me I was immature, that I'd hurt her and she'd been wrong about me. She'd thought I was the kind of person who didn't care about society's conventions. She'd thought I was bigger than I am.

I often think about Elaine, imagine what could have been if I'd been braver. We could still be lounging on her holey rugs, drinking lapsang souchong and reading the Sunday papers. Sometimes I Google her but she doesn't have much of a 'web presence'. The only thing I once came up with was a poetry competition she'd won with the poem about the foxes. I keep the website in my Favourites. It's still there. I used to feel a tiny connection to her when I looked at it. Like I was touching her through the ether.

'Nameplates.' I place the plastic Toblerone-shaped holders on Phil's desk. He immediately reduces whatever he was looking at on the Internet.

'Nice one, mate.' He scrutinises them. 'Hang about, aren't we supposed to put Mr or Mrs in front of everyone's names? People's titles … Jen?'

Jenny turns round from her prissy long-nailed typing. 'Yes. We are.' Her pert little mouth, smothered in pink grease, smiles at me. 'Sor*ree*.'

'I suppose you want me to do them again?'

'If you wouldn't mind, mate.'

I do mind, you bastard. I bloody do mind. Who gives a toss whether some tedious captain of industry gets called Mr or not? Why all this pandering to archaic conventions? What does it matter?

'OK, Phil. Will do.'

I take the new nameplates in to Phil, who nods slowly in satisfaction as if I'm a naughty schoolboy who has finally realised the error of his ways. Jenny is sitting straight-backed, bolt upright, still tapping away as if butter wouldn't melt in her mouth. I know your secret, you dirty cow. I know what you get up to at night, right here, on that very desk.

Back at my desk I finish a poem I've been working on for a few days. In a sudden fit of impatience with myself, I send it to Grace along with this message:

—sorry for the long delay. ive had a lot going on at home, been having a bit of a bad time but im back now. are you still up for meeting up?

She doesn't reply. It's been weeks since I told her I was too busy to meet up, weeks of angst and indecision. She's obviously pissed off with me. Her last email made that clear. Ironic that she thought I must have a girlfriend or a wife. In her mind I must be some kind of Lothario. The thought almost makes me laugh. Thinking about Elaine, about what I threw away because I wasn't brave enough, has made me decide that I need to go for it with Grace. I will meet her and hopefully she will understand why I pretended to be someone else and hopefully she won't mind too much and hopefully …

Sometime later, I remember I've got to hand-deliver Lord Kilpatrick's letter. I walk down the stairs and do a whole circuit of the Principal Floor, going from the red Lords zone into the green Commons zone and back again, dropping off the letter on the way. Nobody notices me, nobody stops me, there is no sign of Grace. I am just a man in a suit, a blameless worker doing a blameless bit of work. Something strange happens to the wallpaper as I walk: at the edges of my field of vision the stylised flowers and leaves sway and grow, a bit like those fractals you can get as screensavers. When I stop and examine the pattern it remains static. I keep my eyes on the carpet as I walk on in case it moves again.

On the corridor outside Bishops Bar, I stand looking out over Peers' Court, through the diamond-shaped panes of a leaded window. People pass below, checking their phones, hurrying towards meetings, dawdling back from lunch, lighting fags. No one looks up. No one knows they are being watched. And then, below me, comes Grace, clutching a folder across her chest. She's walking, walking with a work purpose, like me. Only she's walking with Brett. His hair looks like it has been varnished: it's that dark and neat. Grace is wearing a short tartan skirt. Her legs look gorgeous. Brett must have noticed them. He can't not have, unless he's gay, which I suspect, despite his neatness, he's not. They are talking. I can't hear what they're saying but I can tell they are genuinely enjoying each other's company. Though they're not touching, something in the way they suddenly laugh and look at each other is intimate. They don't look like colleagues any more. Something has changed since I saw them together in Portcullis House. I know, I just know, that they have become – I can hardly bring myself to use the nauseating word – *lovers*. I follow their progress across the courtyard until they disappear under a stone arch, at either side of which squats a gargoyle with its tongue out.

I stand at the window for a long time, not seeing anything beyond my own furious thoughts.

'Everything OK, sir?' asks a security guard, padding past with his hands behind his back.

I look at him. He looks kind. An old fellow with a white beard and a plump red face, like Father Christmas. He looks comfortable, at ease with himself. I expect he's got a nice wife at home somewhere like Hornchurch and they live a simple, modest life, knowing their place, not expecting much, happy with their lot. A bit like my mum and dad. I've got an urge to tell him all my troubles. I want him to tell me not to worry, that it's all going to be all right.

'Everything all right?'

'Yes, fine, thanks.' I hurry on. By the time I near my office I'm practically running. I've got to try and recall my last message to her. But the recall function only allows you to pull back unread emails and I get a bounce-back saying she's read mine. Two minutes later this appears:

—I'm kind of busy myself these days so I'm not sure I'm up for meeting any more.

I crash my fists onto the keyboard.

33

I've got out of the habit of talking. The last person I spoke to was my mum, a couple of days ago. She was worried about me. 'We haven't seen you in ages. Why don't you come round? I went round to your flat last Saturday and you weren't there. Where were you?' Probably sitting on the roof of the House, which is where I've been spending a lot of time since Parliament dissolved and the weather's been hot.

My nerves are like the high E string on my guitar. Other people's cheeriness is a slap in the face. Thankfully, at the moment, with dissolution, there's hardly anyone around but back when I started feeling this way, it was like being trapped behind a glass wall. I looked at the builders laughing and smoking in the courtyards and the servers grinning in the canteen and I wondered if they were just too thick to understand the pointlessness of life, but then I noticed even the clever people – the Members and the Lords, the researchers and the clerks – they were always laughing too. It's like other people are a different species of human from me.

This strung-out feeling must have started one day but I can't remember when, the same way you can never pinpoint exactly when a headache starts. It must have been a few weeks ago, since before the dissolution, because for a few weeks I was working while I felt like this. I can't remember whether I was feeling like this when I was going for jogs in the committee rooms. I definitely wasn't feeling right then, but I wasn't feeling as bad as this. Seeing Grace and Brett in the courtyard was probably it. I kept picturing them in other happy scenes: walking hand in hand along the South Bank, sitting outside cafés and nice bars, bicycling along country lanes, waking up in each other's arms bathed in sunlight; all those clichés from romantic comedies. Her email telling me she was too busy to meet confirmed what I suspected when I saw them in the courtyard. She was obviously too busy with him.

One evening before the House dissolved, Phil came in at quarter past six. I was still at my computer. 'Just knocking off now,' he said.

I nodded. He hung around in the doorway and I thought for a minute I saw genuine concern in his face. 'Don't work too hard, mate,' he said, before disappearing with Jenny, who had been hovering in the background. My misery must have become obvious, even to them.

The whole night I lie awake. The whole night, every night. This isn't just ordinary insomnia, the kind I've had on and off for years. This is full blown, wide-eyed, teeth-gritted, staring into the abyss insomnia. Sometimes I get my guitar out of the cupboard and strum it a bit, but I'm scared of making too much noise. It's been so long since I practised and I could use this insomnia for something worthwhile. All I want is nothingness but my brain won't switch off: it goes round and round, turning over every single embarrassing, sad, humiliating, nasty thing that has ever happened to me. Insomnia is so lonely. Every night the rest of the world seems to be asleep apart from me. Whenever I look at the white digital numbers on the clock I get more and more panicky. There's less and less time left to have a good night's sleep. Even if I get to sleep by 4 a.m., which I never do, I will only have had half the recommended amount of sleep. I am going to be exhausted tomorrow. The nature of time begins to seem strange: we are expected to sleep for eight hours, which is the same amount of time as a standard working day. Eight hours when you're asleep passes in a flash. Eight hours when you're lying awake seems like a week. I try and read *Kitchen Venom*, the book Grace was reading when I saw her in the canteen. I ordered a second-hand copy off Amazon. It's about a gay hunchback clerk and is set in the House of Commons. The author used to work here and was sacked for writing it, according to my Googlings, though I don't remember hearing anything about this at the time. It captures the atmosphere of the House really well but I find it hard to follow the plot because the panic in my head is filling my eyes. A couple of times I email Grace, desperate to reach out to someone. I feel I've plummeted so far down I've got nothing left to lose. But her out-of-office message bounces back and then I remember, of course: I shouldn't be at work either. Yet again I flick through her few public Facebook pictures. They are the same ones as before and, thankfully, none of them include Brett Beamish. I check out her Twitter but she hasn't tweeted anything since the last time I looked at it and I'm pleased to see she's not following Brett.

Now, at night, I persecute myself: over and over, I look back on my life and come to the conclusion that I've never been happy, I've always been like this, I'm always going to be like this, I'm never going to be different, I'm always going to be me. *I'm always going to be me.* I can't imagine when it's going to end. I can't remember not feeling like this. I am trapped in me and I don't even get a break from myself at night. It's like I'm stuck in one never-ending day.

The Boots near the Tube only sells herbal sleeping pills over the counter. They don't work. I am way beyond wimpy flower remedies. I need to bring out the big guns: the hardcore knock-out medication, but I can't go and see my doctor for a prescription.

It's been months since I got on the Tube.

I'm getting through a lot more own-brand whisky from the Tesco Metro. Sipping it calms me a bit and although I am tempted to drink myself into unconsciousness every night, I try to hold back from going down that rocky road.

Throughout the dissolution the weather is fantastic. It's the wrong weather for how I'm feeling: by rights it should be cold and rainy. The sunshine is an insult, like other people's happiness. The news is full of the forthcoming election. It feels very distant from me, as if it's happening in another country. Polling day comes and goes. Obviously, I don't go and vote. Even if I could get to the polling station, I'm not inclined to vote for any of the parties. None of them speak for me or to me. Nobody speaks to me.

Predictably, there's no change of Government. Even if there had been it would make no difference to me. I've been in this place for two previous general elections and my job has always remained the same; the Members might change in actuality but they don't change in spirit and, in any case, being in the Lords, things change even less; Peers die and are replaced by new Peers but they're all the same old farts ultimately. The Establishment perpetuates itself in its own image.

The hot weather does slow down my thoughts a bit when I'm lying on the roof, which is a relief, but, still, I often stand for ages on the parapet overlooking the inner courtyards and wonder what would happen if I threw myself over the edge. I worry one day I might actually do it, but the thought of the pain, my head cracking open like an egg on that hard stone floor, stops me for the moment.

oblivion like soft velvet
comforting as sleep

pulled over me like a blanket
to stop ~~the caged bird, caged budgie, caged parrot~~ my caged brain's cheeps

silence the ~~twitter~~ chatter of my brain
succumb to gravity
hope i pass out before the pain
and stop ~~being me~~ the agony of being

I write various poems in this vein and Google *painless suicide* but reading these nutty websites, most of which are written by American crackpots, makes me feel sick. They don't have any quick answers and half of them suggest I just ring 911. If there was some way I could just be painlessly switched off … I now understand why people take heroin … I wander around the corridors. The light in them is soupy and season-less. It could be any time of day. I try not to look too closely at the wallpaper in case the pattern starts growing again. The folderols and furbelows of Pugin's designs running over everything everywhere seems oppressive and obsessive, grotesque rather than beautiful, the product of a hyperactive mind on the edge of a mental breakdown, which is what I feel I'm on the edge of, or maybe I've actually tripped over the edge. I'm terrified I'm going to end up in a loony bin like Pugin. Except I've got nothing to show for myself, unlike Pugin, who at least racked up some impressive architectural achievements in his short life, as well getting married three times. No one notices me as I wander, not even the security guards. I've become one of the ghosts of this place. I want to be found, I want someone to ask me what's wrong and help me. I want to be rescued. I want Grace to rescue me.

34

—No, I'm not ignoring you. I just haven't been at work.

My whole body jolts. An email from Grace. Her tone so casual it's as if we are continuing our conversation from before, as if no time has elapsed at all. The email she is responding to was sent to her ages ago, sometime during dissolution, and just had a message in the subject line: 'are you ignoring me??'.

—i know, i forgot when I sent that email, I reply. i got your out of office thing. are you still very busy then?

—Not particularly.

—pleased to be back?

—What do you think?

—what did you do while you were away?

—Not much.

—are you cross with me or something?

—No. Why do you ask?

—all these short answers. you sound grumpy.

—Sorry. I'm just not in a great mood.

—i know how you feel. although im feeling better since you got back in touch.

—That's nice. Look, are we actually going to meet? Stop all this beating about the bush.

—OK.

—When?

Sweat is prickling on my forehead. My stomach is churning. She's right: we should stop beating about the bush. We should go for it. What will be will be (although, obviously, I do hate that phrase, along with 'Everything happens for a reason'. No it doesn't. Most occurrences are completely random and senseless.)

—how about tmr eve? I reply. but theres something I need to tell you first.

35

So many things to organise: flowers, food, champagne, haircut. Ideally, I'd get my suit dry-cleaned but there isn't time and even if there was it would take me a lot of psyching up to leave the House and go to the dry-cleaners'. Annoying that there isn't one in the House – you'd think it might be a useful thing for the Members and Lords to have. I'm going to have to wear my other suit, which isn't as good a fit as my usual suit, but is reasonably clean and doesn't look too bad. Luckily, I can go to the hairdresser's on the ground floor of the House, get food and champagne from the Terrace Cafeteria and the gift shop, and the flower lady can do the flowers. For thirty quid – a silly amount, but Grace is worth it – she makes up a really nice bunch of lilies and roses. I have no idea about flowers so I ask the flower lady to pick the kind of things most women like.

'Haircut,' states Phil, when I come back from lunch freshly shorn.

'Haircut.'

I keep the rest of my preparations secret from him and Jenny else they'd only ask a load of questions. So I stash the champagne in my desk drawer until they've gone home and then I put it in the communal fridge. After they've gone I buy the sandwiches and snacks and that's when I also freshen up in the shower down the corridor. Once dressed, I assess myself in the steamed-up mirror. I don't look as good as Dan Sheridan, obviously, but I reckon I look just about passable. I look as good as I can.

Up on the roof – both mine and Grace's favourite place in the

House – it's a beautiful warm evening, the perfect evening for romance to blossom. Once I've laid everything out to my satisfaction, I have to have quite a few swigs of Dutch courage. Six thirty I've arranged to meet Grace, which hasn't given me much time to prepare, but perhaps that's better than waiting around for longer and getting all worked up. I run through conversations in my head, explanations about why I don't look like Dan Sheridan. Nothing sounds particularly convincing. I am praying that she's kind, that she'll understand. I wonder if I should have told her everything last night via email, rather than just that I work here.

Big Ben sounds the half-hour. I arrange myself in a casual pose on the little wall that borders the roof. As the huge minute hand ticks to 6.31, then 6.32, I grow more and more tense. At 6.33, the door to the roof is flung open. I freeze. There she is. Grace Ambrose. The woman I love.

Part Three

January, a year later

36

'How do you plead?'

Brett took a deep breath, looked straight at the judge and, in as firm a voice as possible, said, 'Not guilty.'

He couldn't believe it was finally happening. The trial. For six months he had been preparing for it and, now, here he was in the Old Bailey, with every eye in the courtroom trained upon him. He stood with his shoulders thrown back and a deliberately mild expression on his face. He was wearing his Paul Smith suit and his Armani tie but neither were making him feel as lucky as they usually did. Despite what he hoped was an outward appearance of calm, his heart felt like a frog in a kettle and he kept having to sneakily wipe his hands on his trousers, they were so clammy. Sweat prickled in the armpits of his freshly pressed shirt. It was like being at the most terrifying interview in the world.

The prosecution lawyer was an uptight old fart called Mr Greenslade. He started making his case, telling the jury what a scumbag Brett was, in a voice that sounded like his nose was bunged up with snot. Brett wanted to shout 'Wrong!' after every point he made. He had not jealously started a fight with the victim because he was on a date with his ex-girlfriend. He had not struck the first blow. He had not pushed the victim over the edge of the roof of the House of Commons. These were all total lies. All he could do was cling to the truth: Grace had texted him to come up to the roof urgently to help her; the victim had been aggressive towards him; the victim had thrown the first punch and he had hit back in self-defence. The fall had been a terrible accident.

'After the victim fell, Mr Beamish did not raise the alarm, call the police or do any of the things you might expect him to do in such an event. Instead, he ran away from the scene of the crime. He insisted that Miss Ambrose come with him and they went back to his flat. It was only after Miss Ambrose informed the police the following day that any connection was made between Mr Beamish and the incident.'

Brett's gaze briefly dropped. This was the part of the prosecution's case that would be most difficult to fight. Running away had been wrong. It had been weak. Uncharacteristically weak. He wasn't proud of how he'd behaved later that evening either. Crying like a sap in front of Grace, begging her to stay, letting her see how crap his life really was behind all the bullshit. He shouldn't have made her come home with him. It hadn't made any difference to things: he hadn't persuaded her not to go to the police. Given that she had ended up betraying him anyway, it hadn't been necessary for her to see the truth behind the façade.

The most shame came from the feeling that he had let himself down. He hadn't behaved like the B-Man ought to. The *B-Man*? Who was he kidding? Still, the situation had ruined his reputation as … as what? … Right now, he couldn't remember what his reputation was or had been. It was a lightweight thing that had been torn apart through no fault of his own. If he thought about it too much, it brought tears to his eyes, so he blocked it out, like the fear. If anything, he was also the victim.

While Mr Greenslade went on in his pernickety roundabout way, Brett thought back to the day after the accident. As soon as he'd woken and found Grace gone, he knew what she was planning to do. He tried her mobile but she didn't pick up. It was 7 a.m. He reckoned she would go into work first, check out the scenario before going to the police. If he got there before her, accosted her before she had a chance, he might be able to persuade her not to. Just after 7.30 he jumped on the Victoria Line, feeling rougher than a badger's arse. The whisky he'd drunk to calm his nerves the night before had been like brake fluid. The palm of his right hand had a gash in the middle, covered in a bloodstained bandage. He couldn't remember bandaging himself up. Maybe Grace had done it. His other hand was grazed. He kept both clenched.

Everything appeared to be normal as he walked along the colonnade and up to the office. No sign of 'Reuben's' accident, no sign that anything terrible had happened the night before, although he didn't dare check the courtyard where he must have fallen.

No one was around but, given it was only 8 a.m., that wasn't unusual. He fired up his computer and scrolled vacantly through his emails. He stood up and flicked through the papers on the sideboard without taking anything in. He sat back down. With shaky hands he fumbled for his phone and tried calling Grace again. No answer. A message flashed up on the annunciator: THE THREAT LEVEL REMAINS SEVERE. In a daze, he switched it to the news, half fearing Reuben's fall would be the next item. He was back at his desk again, in a state of suspended animation, when three cops walked in.

'Are you Brett Beamish?'

'Yes?'

'We've had a report that you were involved in an incident last night.'

Brett's mind blanked. For once he had no idea what to say.

'A man fell off the roof of the House last night. We'd like to talk to you in connection with this incident.'

Brett's first thought was: do not say anything. Anything he said might be taken down in evidence against him.

'I … are you arresting me?'

'Yes, we are, Mr Beamish,' said one of the cops. He stated the charge and added, 'It would be best if you came quietly. You do not have to say anything. But it may harm your defence if you do not mention when questioned something which you later rely on in court. Anything you do say may be given in evidence.' *Against you*, Brett finished in his head.

He stood up and another cop surged towards him with a pair of handcuffs.

Being led through the corridors of his workplace in handcuffs had to be one of the most humiliating experiences of his life. Luckily, he didn't recognise any of the gaping bystanders. They were mainly cleaners and builders. Thank God, for once, for the slacker's start time of his own department.

Waiting six hours in a police cell that smelt like the toilet in the middle of it was also shameful. So was arguing with two half-witted bozos that he did not push anybody off the roof. The duty solicitor at the police station had been useless. Brendan Mullarkey. Joke name. Joke bloke. Couldn't organise a root in a brothel with a fistful of twenties, let alone how to get him off a jail term, but hopefully the barrister he was going to instruct was as good as he claimed. Her name was Jane Bond. Another joke name. They'd sound like a right bunch of clowns when it came to court. 'Jane's excellent,' said Mullarkey. 'A real high-flyer. Very, very sharp.'

And there was Jane now, looking amazingly hot even in her wig and gown. Except that, actually, her hotness only crossed his mind briefly as he was too shit-scared to think about anything except for getting through the trial. Getting through it and winning it. He tried to catch her eye, hoping for a reassuring smile, but she was making notes while Mr Greenslade droned on. Grace was due on soon as a prosecution witness and Jane was preparing to demolish her.

37

The Old Bailey took Grace back to her first day at the House of Commons. It took her back to her first impression of every institution she had ever encountered: school; university; Hugo's club. The imposing entrance, buzzing with people who looked like they already knew the rules. The public, self-conscious walk through them. The palaver of the airport-style security check. The fear of committing a faux pas, of appearing implausible and incompetent. Extraordinary that everyone – criminals, victims, witnesses, lawyers and jurors – appeared to use the same entrance. Surely they should have designed it better. Perhaps the Victorians or the Edwardians or whoever had built it relied on everyone knowing their place and not having a Jerry Springer-style fight in the lobby.

That she should have a key role in events at such an iconic building was also extraordinary. Though she was terrified, her ego swelled with the import of it all. The same feeling as at her granddad's funeral, walking behind the coffin, everyone watching as she took her place in the front pew. Then and now, her pride was tempered by guilt at revelling in the pomp of the occasion. She was wearing a new trouser suit, the first she had ever owned, in the hope it would lend her some gravitas. She wondered why she'd never bought one before – it might have helped her get promoted. Though it made her look somewhat butch, that was preferable to looking girlish or sexy. For once in her life she definitely did not want to look sexy.

After explaining herself and exposing the contents of her bag, the witness service was called to escort her to the waiting room.

She wished she had taken up her parents' offer to accompany her but, at the time, she had dreaded them knowing any more gory details than was necessary and thought it might look wimpish: like turning up at secondary school holding your mum's hand. Covertly, she observed the other people milling about. Some of the men, despite their respectable suits, crackled with suppressed violence. Their faces were etched with the tension of vicious lives, although she'd been told by the witness service that most defendants at the Bailey were accused of such serious crimes they were on remand, and so wouldn't be hanging around the public areas of the court. Even though these people looked like criminals, it didn't mean they were criminals. After all, Brett looked as clean-cut as a toothpaste advert and he had been accused of a crime.

A small middle-aged Asian woman appeared. She introduced herself as Kiranjit and escorted Grace up a series of marble steps and through several double doors to a hot modern corridor. Grace strode with fake confidence. In her new suit she wondered if passers-by thought she was a lawyer. She strained to think of small talk when Kiranjit's chit-chat about her journey petered out but nothing came to mind, the same way she could never think of anything to say to the witnesses she escorted to committee evidence sessions. Weird to be in the opposite role: for once a main player rather than a spear-carrier.

They arrived at a room furnished with an assortment of sofas and coffee tables piled with old magazines. The view from the window was a brick wall. A television stood in the corner. *This Morning* was on with the sound turned down. A girl in her late teens with hair scraped into a tight ponytail was curled on one sofa, chewing her nails. A shaven-headed man with a tattoo of flames creeping up his neck was sitting squarely on another sofa, snapping through the pages of *Hello!* Grace wondered what they'd witnessed; it was like guessing other people's illnesses at the doctor's.

While she waited she replayed, yet again, the post-fall events. The dying scream. Brett propelling her out of the House, ignoring her protests. Any moment she had expected a siren to sound and armed police to jump out from behind the statues of the lion and unicorn, but the policeman at the entrance barely gave them a second glance as they tumbled through the revolving doors. Within minutes they were side by side on the Jubilee Line and she was staring at her terrified reflection in the blackness of the opposite window. Brett kept his bloodied right hand in his pocket and attempted to hide his battered face by leaning against the glass panel at the end of the row of seats. His bruises were blooming but nobody raised an eyebrow. Thank God for the anonymity of the Tube, for the indifference of Londoners. The fracas they had left behind was, no doubt, horrifying: ambulances rushing to the scene, police helicopters hovering overhead, security guards swarming over the blood and gore like flies on shit.

Less than an hour later they were sitting on Brett's bed. Brett's single bed. Under the bare overhead bulb. In his shoebox of a bedsit. It was shockingly grim. Not in any way the sleek bachelor pad she had expected. Although his belongings were neatly organised, a miasma of grime hung over the place, the sort of grime that no amount of cleaning could expunge. Amazing that he always emerged looking so pristine. Amazing that he put up with such inhumanely cramped conditions. You could pretty much cook a meal and do the washing up from underneath his duvet. It was as small and cheerless as a prison cell. Which was where he could end up if things didn't go his way.

'What are you going to do?' she had asked.

Brett was sitting, head bowed, at the pillow end, feet planted on the floor, one set of knuckles grinding his forehead, in the attitude of Rodin's Thinker.

'Brett, tell me, what are you going to do?'

'Shut up. Can't you see I'm trying to think?'

Grace laughed – a short, metallic sound, tinged with hysteria.

'What's so fucking funny?' His head whiplashed round.

'Nothing.' Grace began to cry again. 'I think we should go to the police. We've run away from the scene of a crime. Somebody has died. Reuben's died. Brett, Reuben is dead. I can't believe it, you …' Her voice rose and a strange sensation expanded inside her: she was running out of breath; her throat was constricting; she was about to suffocate …

'Will you fucking keep your voice down.' Brett grabbed her wrists. 'The walls are really thin: the other tenants will hear.'

'Do you mean your flatmate? Your fucking "religious flatmate"?' Grace tried to shake her wrists free. 'Get off me. I'm going.'

'No, no, don't go.' Brett's voice swerved on a knife-edge from harsh to soft. 'Please, Grace, I'm sorry. Don't go. I need you to stay. I need you to help me. Please. I need you to help me work out what to do.' He loosened his grip but her eyes were still caught in his glare and she realised that, far from being angry, Brett was scared. He was not a monster. He had a conscience. He felt bad.

'I didn't mean to do it. I didn't mean him to go over the edge. You know I didn't mean that. I didn't know he was going to trip. I didn't push him. He came towards me, I moved out the way and then he tripped. You know that; you saw. Grace, tell me you saw. You saw it was an accident, didn't you?'

Grace nodded but she wasn't sure what she had seen. The accident … the *incident* – this word cooled the horror – the incident had happened so fast, had been such a mess of blood and glass and contorted limbs that she couldn't piece it together chronologically. Brett now had his head out of the window and was sucking on a cigarette. That he was even smoking shocked Grace. Smoking and drinking hard liquor: wordlessly, he had bought a half-bottle of cheap whisky along with the cigarettes on the march between Highbury and Islington Station and his flat. As if these were the standard props for a crisis. He had no glasses, just two chipped mugs. She saw why he hadn't wanted her to come to his flat before: it was the complete antithesis of his image. Had she known his home life was even more dilapidated than hers she would have felt more bonded to him, but now it seemed pathetic of him to care about his crap flat. So he didn't have as much money as he liked to make out? So he pretty much lived in a kitchen? So what? He poured them both three fingers of whisky without asking if she wanted it. She took one gasping sip and set her mug on the draining board.

'Smoke?' He chucked the packet onto the bed.

She shook her head. 'You can have my whisky too.' She indicated her mug. He poured it into his own and took another long swig.

'I think we should go to the police,' said Grace, as slowly and calmly as she could. 'I'll tell them I saw what happened and that it was an accident.'

Brett sat back on the bed and tapped his ash into her empty cup. 'If we go to the cops, it's gonna be the end of everything. They're not gonna believe it was an accident. They'll arrest me. I'll end up in jail.' He looked at her. His voice was thick and indistinct. 'I'm gonna lose everything. Everything I've got, I'm gonna lose. My whole career. Everything I've built up. My dad'll go mental ...'

'What does your dad matter?' Grace snapped. 'Someone has died and you're worrying about your career and what you're going to say to your dad?' She stood up. She had to get out. He didn't care about Reuben, he only cared about himself. He was a monster. He was going to drag her down with him.

'You're not going, are you? I'm sorry, I'm sorry. I know that sounded stupid. You don't know what my dad's like though. All this, all my bloody great career, all my success ...' He spat 'career' and 'success' like curses but didn't finish the sentence. His head flopped forwards and his shoulders began to judder. She was unsure whether to comfort him or pretend she hadn't noticed. So this was what it was like when a person like Brett cried. Neatly, silently, with heart-wrenching decorousness. Was it an act? He was astute enough to know that she was the kind of girl to be touched by men's tears. She watched him and decided, act or not, for the moment she would go along with him, give herself time to think what to do next. She slid beside him and put her arm around his shoulders. 'Don't cry, Brett. Please don't cry. Look, why don't you go to bed? It's late. We'll think what to do in the morning. Come on, let's lie down. Come on.' Easing his legs onto the bed, she untied his shoes. He was drunker than she had realised. The half-bottle was almost empty. The whisky had loosened his emotions. He was probably too drunk to dissemble. He slumped onto his side and lay with his legs drawn up and his face towards the wall. She pulled the duvet up and balanced beside him on the remaining sliver of bed. Her phone told her it was nearly one in the morning. They had been worrying over what to do for more than four hours.

Brett fell asleep. The whisky must have knocked him out but, as she lay listening to his slow, regular breaths, it struck her there was something indecent about his ability to sleep so easily, drunk or not. What had happened and what might happen next churned through her head. Reuben's scream. His presence, then his absence. The empty space on the roof where he had been. The mangled mess in the courtyard below that she hadn't seen but could well imagine. Mourners around a grave flashed into her mind. A coffin being lowered into the ground. Bells tolling. At four in the morning she sat up. There was a suspicion of dawn beyond the thin curtains. The sparse furnishings were tinged with grey significance: the four immaculate pairs of shoes lined up below the precisely arranged clothes rail, the tiny desk empty except for a square-edged stack of *Men's Health*s, the packet of Andrex squirrelled away from the other tenants, the lack of books, the lack of pictures, the lack of anything to denote what kind of person slept here. The lack.

Grace extricated herself from beneath the duvet. Carrying her high-heeled sandals, she slipped out of the bedsit. The hallway was silent, the other tenants asleep. She and Brett had heard some of them return home, joking with each other in their angry-sounding language. According to Brett they worked and slept in shifts, taking turns to sleep in the same beds. Theirs were grim lives, up until now divided by no more than a thin wall from Brett's in aspiration, opportunity and hope. 'Some of them are cleaners. They clean offices in the City. I think the others are builders,' he told her.

'Do they know where you work?'

'No. We never talk.'

As she tiptoed down to the piss-reeking communal lobby she feared bumping into one or another of them as they returned from a night shift, but the stairwell was empty and so was the street outside, save for a fox rooting among the bins. The fox stared at her before slinking between the bars of an iron fence and disappearing into some undergrowth. It looked as nervy as she felt.

She walked most of the way home as it seemed safer than hanging around for a night bus and her phone had died so she couldn't get an Uber. Her mind was so strung out she barely noticed the blisters from her sandals, although by the time she got to Stroud Green Road she took them off and braved the pavements with bare feet. Dawn was rising thin and high with the promise of heat later. The streets were busier than she expected with shift workers, street cleaners, taxis, long-distance lorries, even a milk float trundling down her own road: a reassuringly old-fashioned sight. Once home she resolved to sleep until seven and head early into work, where she would go straight to the Serjeant at Arms's office and inform whoever was there what she and Brett had witnessed. They would fetch the police. She would say it was an accident. It *was* an accident, Brett was right. They wouldn't arrest him. He hadn't intended to hurt Reuben. He'd been acting in self-defence. She would make sure they knew. She would tell them everything, right from the beginning. They would be kind, she was sure, to a nice young woman who had witnessed something so terrible and come forward so honourably. The prospect of unburdening herself calmed her a little but she still only expected to doze. Within ten minutes of stripping off her dress and lying down, she was fast asleep. Her phone, plugged in next to her, woke her at 7 a.m.: *Brett B Mob.* The words and the blue glow pulsed through her drowsy confusion. By force of habit she almost picked it up: she never let a phone ring unanswered. But a prescience of Brett's anger stopped her. He would attempt to dissuade her from going to the police. She turned the phone off and flung on the first reasonably secretarial outfit from the pile of clean clothes she had not yet got round to putting away. She needed to get to work before Brett. He was probably there now, upright as a folded ironing board in front of his computer screen, as if nothing untoward had happened. She had to get to the Serjeant's office before he had a chance to stop her.

*

'On 6 July at approximately 6.15 p.m. I went up to the roof of the House of Commons where I had arranged to meet the victim …' Grace skimmed the police statement, which Kiranjit had given to her. The bland, measured text sounded like someone else. And, thinking back to her panic at the time that these words had been transcribed, she hadn't felt like herself. If she hadn't been so pressurised by the black and white viewpoints of the policemen, she would have come up with something more nuanced.

The door rattled and she jumped to attention again. Kiranjit poked her head around the door. 'Grace? They're ready for you in Court One.'

It was like last call at a theatre. As she followed Kiranjit down the corridor, she silently mouthed her lines to herself: answers to the questions she was expecting. They passed through a vast marble hall with a domed roof decorated with vaguely religious murals of figures in robes. Black-cloaked barristers swooped about purposefully. RIGHT LIVES BY LAW AND LAW SUBSISTS BY POWER, boomed a slogan beneath one of the murals. The atmosphere was like Central Lobby only more forbidding. With the faintest flourish, Kiranjit opened a heavy door and Grace emerged, blinking, into the bright lights of the courtroom.

Like the Chamber of the House, it was far more cramped than she had expected. Here were the other players, all far too close for comfort: the judge, the defence and the prosecution with their robes and their wigs; the judge with the biggest wig of all. The other barrister was a surprisingly young, very attractive black woman. Among the white, middle-aged, greying men, she was like a flower in full bloom, although her beauty was somewhat obscured by her wig. This was obviously Brett's barrister. What a trump card for Brett to get a lawyer who didn't look like a lawyer. Her charisma effortlessly eclipsed the prosecution lawyer, Mr Greenslade, a thin, tense-looking man in his fifties, who was slumped next to Brett's lawyer, his nose buried in a handkerchief. His wig blended seamlessly into his wiry grey hair.

In the middle of the court was a large glass-fronted wooden pen: the dock. Inside, like a mannequin in a shop window, was Brett, wearing a suit so crisp it probably crackled when he walked. A woman in a shapeless navy jumper sat beside him. At least Grace presumed she was a woman: her solid cliff of a bosom was the only sign of femininity. She caught Brett's gaze swishing towards her and away again before they could make proper eye contact.

The whole Shakespearean cast seemed to be holding its breath. Since the interview with the police, her mind had repeatedly flashed forward to this scene, to the moment she would take the witness stand and answer questions posed by a man in a wig. That moment had come. She was spotlit and about to screw up her lines. Her mouth was dry and the middle of her stomach, just below her heart, felt as if it was being clenched by a cold hand.

Kiranjit passed her over to an usher, who led her into the witness box and proffered a Bible and a laminated card printed with the words 'I swear by almighty God that the evidence I shall give shall be the truth, the whole truth and nothing but the truth.' Her stage fright abated. At least her first few lines would be scripted. As she read them out, her voice gathering in strength, she found she knew the words off by heart even though she had never spoken them before. Like the Lord's Prayer, they were ingrained in her: a part of Britain's collective consciousness that she was able to access without effort.

When she had finished the oath, the courtroom breathed again. Mr Greenslade rose abruptly, stuffed his handkerchief into his sleeve and said, 'Would you please clearly state your name for the court?'

As she stated her name, Grace surveyed the chorus of jurors and the gallery, from which Hugo peered down, his eyes owlish behind his half-moon specs. At the back of the court was a plump woman with a grey perm and a bald man with eyes magnified by large spectacles. They were a small, unworldly couple, a bewildered huddle of beige raingear: Reuben's parents. Next to them was Reuben … or rather Gavin – she kept forgetting to correct herself. The grey plastic handle of his crutch was hooked over the back of the bench in front. Even apart from its sad purpose, it was an ugly, depressing object. He did not meet her eye.

38

'Grace Felicity Ambrose.'

She blushes when she says her name, like she's embarrassed by it. I don't know why, seeing as it is her real name, unlike Reuben Swift, which I now feel completely ashamed about, especially given the mileage Beamish's lawyer got out of it during my evidence, insinuating that not only was I an amoral liar, stealing a dead man's identity, I was also an unstable fantasist and, thus, an unreliable witness. Her cross-questioning was completely humiliating.

Grace Ambrose is still a lovely name, even though I'm far from finding her lovely any more. It still reminds me of rice pudding and heaven like I once told her. Now I know her middle name perhaps I should insert a new line in the poem I wrote about her name: i once thought it felicitous that i met you. now i know it was just bad luck.

'Miss Ambrose. Would you like to give us your account of the events leading up to the incident on the evening in question, the evening of the sixth of July last year?' Greenslade sounds as if his nose is literally plugged with two corks made of snot. I'm furious with him for having a cold and he's making a right bollocks of this whole trial as far as I can tell so far.

Grace glances at the jury. They look like a bunch of half-wits if you ask me. I hope they're properly following the whole thing.

'On the evening in question ...' she says, as if she's mimicking Greenslade, 'on the evening of the sixth of July last year, I had been invited to have supper on the roof of the House of Commons by Mr Swift ... sorry, Mr Smith ...'

I wince. I wonder if she misremembered my name deliberately. Her voice sounds really posh, posher than I remember it, but perhaps she's putting it on because we're in such a grand place. I think I probably tried to speak a bit more properly when I was giving evidence. She's wearing a really unflattering suit, completely different from her usual gear; I suppose she wants to be taken seriously.

The last time I saw her, I was in hospital. St Thomas'. Just across the river from the House. Within earshot of Big Ben. When I first came round from the coma I thought I was still in my office.

She'd come in behind Patrycja, my favourite nurse, carrying a paper bag in both hands, her knuckles white and eyes wide.

'Hello … is it OK …?' Her voice was quavery.

If I hadn't been shackled by splints and hoists and drips and Christ knows what other medical palaver, I would've jumped out of bed and tried to escape. But I was shackled and, in any case, I couldn't walk at that point.

'I will leave you both alone,' said Patrycja.

'Grapes.' She placed the paper bag on my bedside table.

I stared at her. Her expression was set to 'sad smiley': forehead crumpled, eyes wide, lips pressed together and pulled down. I didn't know what to say. I felt like I was on display, horribly exposed, like a medical exhibit. Why had she turned up anyway? Did she think I would be pleased to see her? I wasn't going to make it easy for her. I said nothing. I waited for her to talk.

'Bit of a cliché, I know, but I thought perhaps actually grapes are what you feel like when you're ill. I've got you some chocolate too. More of a treat really than grapes.' She got a posh box of chocs out of her bag – Green & Black's – organic, Fair Trade, 70 per cent cocoa. To be honest, I prefer Cadbury's. Her hands were shaking and I realised from this and her wittering that she was nervous. 'I hope you don't mind me coming to visit you. I came a few days ago but you were asleep. I didn't know whether you'd want to see me really … I'm so sorry about what happened … really really sorry … but thank God you're all right … well …' She glanced at the clothes-horse thing that was keeping the blankets off my legs. Obviously 'all right' was overstating it a bit. I let her monologue run its course, enjoying the sight of her getting more and more uncomfortable and her gradual understanding that, actually, no, I didn't want to see her really and, yes, I did mind her coming to visit me.

'Sorry …' She gathered up her bags. 'This was a mistake. I shouldn't have come. Stupid of me …'

'Why did you come?'

'To see how you are, of course. I was worried about you. It's been a nightmare.'

'It hasn't exactly been a picnic for me.'

'No, no, of course not. It must be awful. I am … I really am so sorry.'

'Why do you keep saying sorry?'

'I …' She looked at me, scared. 'I'm just sorry about what's happened. And … I want you to get better.' She stood up.

'Stay.' This came out a bit commanding so I added, more softly, 'Grace, I'd like you to stay … I don't blame you for anything.'

Her shoulders slumped and she sat back down. Actually what I said was not true. I did blame her for getting Brett to come up to the roof. I blamed her for not being the girl I thought she was. I blamed her for being like all the other girls who don't like me. I still do.

We talked about being in hospital – me being in it, that is, as she had never been in one as a patient and medical stuff clearly both intrigued and freaked her out. She kept looking over her shoulder at the other poor sods in the ward and I knew she was wondering what was wrong with them but thought it rude to ask. I let her look under the clothes horse at my legs, which were all skewered with external fixation pins, like spit-roasted meat. She clapped her hand to her mouth, as if she was about to be sick. Admittedly, the external fixations were like some sort of medieval torture device. 'You are going to be able to—'

'Walk again?' I offered, as she didn't seem able to get the words out. 'Yeah, they say I will but it's going to be a long time. A lot of physio and stuff. I might always have a limp.'

She apologised again and muttered some guff about how lucky I was to survive, the miracle of it all, the fact I'd fallen onto a lower roof rather than the ground, the rolls of fibreglass lagging left out by the builders that had broken my fall. Then she looked around nervously, as if she thought someone was eavesdropping. 'I guess you haven't heard.'

'Heard what?'

'About Brett.'

'What?'

'He's been arrested. Charged with GBH.'

'Bloody hell.' I tried not to smile. 'What, is he in prison?'

'No, he's on bail pending trial.'

'Blimey.'

'The police are waiting for you to be well enough to speak to them.' Grace's eyes were lowered to her twisting hands. I knew she wanted something from me, something she was finding difficult to say.

'Is he still at work?' I asked.

'No, of course not. They couldn't have someone on bail coming into the House, bringing it into disrepute.' She said 'disrepute' like she was mocking the House and its prissy morals and I knew immediately that she felt sorry for Brett, as sorry as she did for me, if not sorrier. 'They've suspended him until the trial. On full pay, but, still … he's beside himself …' She was embarrassed to say his name in front of me. She looked out of the window.

'Are you still having a thing with him?'

She jerked to attention. 'No, of course not.'

'But you were.'

Her forehead crumples in puzzlement. 'How do you know?'

'It was obvious.'

She looked out of the window again. 'We are not having a thing any more and it was hardly anything anyway. It was over by the time of … by the evening we met.' She couldn't look at me. She was still a pretty girl but the way I felt about her had changed. Like some sense was knocked into me when I hit that pile of lagging. I felt distant from her. There was no connection any more. I prodded around inside myself for the way I used to feel but it was like trying to find a bruise that's healed. She was just a superficially charming, slightly twee indie girl that I once mistook for someone deep and, despite the muzziness in my head, I knew she wanted me to help Brett, to tell the police that he did nothing, that it was an accident. I wondered if, even though she claimed they weren't together, he had put her up to it. I still wonder.

I said nothing. I didn't tell her what I was going to do. Mainly because I didn't know. All I could think about was the immediate future: one day at a time. Concentrating on getting physically well. It was almost a relief after worrying about my mental state non-stop for months on end. Apparently the police had come in a few days after I emerged from the coma but I was too off my head on morphine to give them any sensible answers about what had happened. The truth was, I couldn't really remember. But the more Grace went on, the more I got a better idea of what I would do.

'I'm a witness, you know,' she said. 'For the prosecution.'

'What do you mean?'

'A witness for your side.'

Surely she was on Brett's side? My head was too woolly with morphine for complicated legal stuff.

'I'm a witness against Brett. I went to the police. I told them what I'd seen. I thought it was the right thing to do. Now I bloody well wish I hadn't …'

She wanted me to ask her why but I didn't. I didn't make it easy for her.

'I had to give a statement,' she said, after a pause. 'I didn't realise they'd end up arresting Brett. I'm so bloody naive. I thought it was an accident. I didn't know he was going to be accused of GBH.'

'He punched me quite a few times.' I stared at her hard but her eyes were on her hands.

'You did punch Brett first … quite a few times …'

She didn't look up again, so she didn't see my amazement that she had come to visit me while I was crocked up on a trauma ward and implied it was my fault that Brett had been charged with GBH.

'Brett's in a bad way,' she went on. 'So I hear.'

There was another pause.

'He's not allowed to talk to me,' she explained. 'But I've heard that he doesn't know what to do with himself. He's one of those people who's completely lost without work. And he's absolutely terrified that he's going to end up in prison. Not surprising he's terrified to be honest …'

I said nothing. I let her babble on. My silence spoke volumes. Or at least I hoped it did. *Brett's in a bad way?* She must be having a laugh. Look at me: half crippled; almost a bloody raspberry. I let her leave without the answers she wanted.

*

Greenslade is still asking Grace about the evening of my fall. I glance at my mum and she squeezes my hand.

Grace is saying: 'Obviously, as soon as I saw he was a different person from the pictures he'd sent, I began to feel … uneasy. So I texted Brett and asked him to come up to the roof.'

'What did you write in your text?'

'Something like: "Am on roof. Urgent. Need your help. Please rescue me from mad date."'

Some of the jury smirk. Greenslade purses his lips. This is not helping my case. She's supposed to be on my side.

'Please continue, Miss Ambrose.'

'We talked for a bit, Reub— sorry, Gavin, and I. At that point I still thought he was called Reuben Swift.' She swallowed. 'This was what he called himself during our email conversations before we met …'

Mr Greenslade is now wringing his hands together underneath his robe as if he's trying to keep warm. I wish he'd take charge. Get her to shut up about Reuben Swift.

'I asked him why he had sent me pictures of someone else, and he said, "Why do you think?" I think he thought we'd built up enough of a bond over email that I would overlook the fact he'd pretended to be someone else. Then, when I was checking my phone to see if Brett had texted back, he put his hand on my knee …'

I can't look at her. My ears are burning. I can't look at my parents either.

'Carry on, Miss Ambrose.'

'This felt like a … like an invasion of my space so I got up and said I was going to leave.' She pauses. Mr Greenslade nods for her to carry on. 'He begged me not to leave and at that moment Brett turned up …'

'And then what happened?'

'Gavin demanded to know what Brett was doing there. He was beginning to get cross. He told Brett that he'd invited me up there, and it was his private place. I tried to leave, but Gavin shoved me behind him, tried to stop me from leaving ...'

She's a bloody liar. I want to stand up and shout out. She's committing contempt of court or perjury – I'm not sure which but definitely one of them.

'Then there was a bit of a scuffle.'

'A scuffle? How did this "scuffle" start?'

'I can't remember exactly.'

'You seem to have remembered everything else. Surely you must remember this. Who touched whom first?'

'Brett touched Gavin's arm but it was hardly anything. He just grabbed his arm quite lightly after Gavin had shoved me out the way and said, "Don't touch her." And then Gavin went ballistic—'

'When you say "ballistic" ...?'

'He went totally mad. He shouted, "What are you going to do about it?" and then he punched Brett in the face.'

'In your statement to the police, you said Mr Beamish punched Mr Smith a number of times. Is this correct?'

'It was self-defence. They both hit each other. It all happened really fast. But Mr Beamish was definitely trying to defend himself. They ended up wrestling on the floor. I was trying to pull them apart but I got knocked over. The next thing I knew they were both on their feet. Then Mr Smith suddenly lunged towards Mr Beamish but Mr Beamish stepped to the side to avoid being hit again and that was when Mr Smith fell over the edge. It was an accident.'

In the corner of my eye I sense a slumping in Brett's posture and a grateful exhalation of breath. I can't believe Grace is doing this to me. I can't believe she's protecting Beamish over me. I'm the victim. Why should that bastard get off scot-free? He's got away with everything his whole life. I can feel my parents looking at me but I can't look back in case their worried faces make me cry.

'M'lord, I have finished my questions.' Greenslade sits down, pulls out his handkerchief and blows his nose like a trumpet. I despair of him. Perhaps he's a CPS lawyer because he's not good enough to work in defence.

A note is passed from the clerk to the judge via the usher in a way that reminds me of the forelock-tugging meal that's made of delivering messages to the Chairman in committee meetings. Lots of things remind me of the House actually: the decor of oak, brass and green leather; the layout; and the strict rules imposed by a load of middle-class, middle-aged white men in horsehair wigs and black gowns. The judge, plonked on his throne, like the Speaker or the Archbishop of Canterbury. Strange how the institutions of the Establishment mimic each other. Or maybe it isn't strange: parliaments, courtrooms and churches, they're all designed to inspire awe and obedience. The powers themselves haven't been fully separated but the house of each power is designed to separate its occupants into their rightful places: the leaders, the accused, the accusers, the spectators, the worshippers.

The jury does not fill me with confidence: twelve completely average-looking people, with expressions as vacant as if watching daytime TV. When I was giving evidence I found it impossible to read what they were making of me. The same goes for what they make of Grace. If anything, most of them seem bored. When the judge announces the court is not going to adjourn, one sighs loudly. Only a couple have a spark of intelligence in their eyes. I don't think ordinary people ought to be allowed to judge complicated moral and legal arguments.

*

You don't even need to hear Brett's lawyer speak to see that, unlike Greenslade, she's as sharp as a knife, in total command. She stands with her robes draped regally around her, like the image of a statue on a coin. A very good-looking woman: typical that Beamish would end up with her.

'Miss Ambrose, why do you think Mr Smith got so angry when Mr Beamish appeared on the roof of the House of Commons?' Her voice is cool, verging on sarcastic. Grace is visibly squirming. I sneak a glance at Brett and his profile looks self-satisfied – it's his usual expression, to be honest – as if he's internally congratulating himself on his lawyer's performance.

Grace's answer is so definite it's like a punch.

'He was jealous.'

'Why do you think he was jealous?'

'He was jealous that Brett and I had had a relationship and that Brett had interrupted what he thought was his first date with me.'

I want to hide under the bench. I wish my parents weren't here. I wish I hadn't stayed to watch the rest of the trial but if I get up and leave now everyone will look at me.

'What was your relationship with Mr Smith?'

'We didn't really have a relationship. I mean, we knew each other but not very well. Only via email. As I've already said, he pretended to be someone else for the whole time we were emailing. I didn't know his real name. I didn't even know he worked in the House until just before we met up.'

'Were you friends?'

'No, I wouldn't say we were friends. I had no idea who he really was.'

The bottom of my stomach is sucked away.

Brett's lawyer asks about 'the nature' of 'our connection', how we got to know each other and, without any hesitation whatsoever, without any heart, Grace tells the court everything about us, from my first email to my last; from my fake photos to the songs I sent her to the silent phone messages she believes I left on her voicemail. She goes on about how she was sure I had followed her around the House, makes out I was some kind of frightening loony.

She doesn't look at me once but several of the jurors do. They stare at me like I'm a piece of shit. I look at my hands and I listen. Hearing it straight from Grace makes me feel like a piece of shit. I am a piece of shit. I am so stupid. I blew everything.

I've lost track of the questioning but then one makes my heart jolt.

'Did you know that your security pass was found in the drawer of Mr Smith's desk during the police investigation?'

'No.' I can see the cogs whirring in her mind, memories reeling back. 'I remember losing it but I got the pass office to issue me a new one. I didn't realise Mr Smith had taken it.'

How I wish I hadn't found it now. Everything started with that pass.

'He had your pass but he did not hand it back to the pass office.' Miss Bond stares pointedly at the jury and turns back to Grace. 'Did you know that Mr Smith was living in his office?'

Grace recoils. 'No. I didn't know that.' I stare at the floor. All this has already been dragged out of me when I gave evidence. My every private shame is being held up to the light. This lawyer is destroying me.

'Mr Smith had been living in his office for nearly a year, as far as we can gather. He had a flat in Essex but he chose, for reasons of his own, to live in his office.'

For reasons of his own. Because I was terrified of leaving the building. Why doesn't she tell Grace that? She dragged it all out of me during my evidence. How when I moved in my neighbours took an instant dislike to me; they thought I was up myself because I had bought my flat and had a job and they were council tenants on benefits. A rowdy family of mum, step-dad, two thuggish teenage sons and two thuggish Rottweilers. I used to hear them shouting at each other, endless arguments, the dogs barking non-stop because they weren't walked enough, thumping techno at all hours. There were so many shady-looking people coming in and out of their flat I was sure they were dealing drugs. When I knocked on their door and asked very politely if they could turn the music down one night as I had to get up early for work, they told me to fuck off and turned it up even louder. This went on for several nights. I complained to the council, who sent an officer round. After that the bullying started for real: dog shit and lit matches through my letter box, threats to set their dogs on me and name-calling whenever they saw me on the stairs – 'faggot', 'batty boy' and the worst: 'paedo', which they even graffitied on my front door. Presumably because I was a single man, living alone, who kept himself to himself. In their eyes a weirdo. But maybe I was a weirdo in everyone's eyes. Other people in the block began looking at me strangely. Either they had seen the graffiti before I had a chance to paint over it or my neighbours had been spreading rumours. I stayed at the office later and later. Eventually I stopped going home. The House was the only place I felt safe.

'I didn't know where he lived,' Grace is saying. 'As I explained, I didn't even know he worked at the House until just before we met.'

'Did you know that this lipstick was also found in his desk drawer?' Miss Bond holds up a clear plastic bag containing a black and gold tube. With sharp-nailed fingers she extracts it from the bag, uncaps it and twists it up so everyone in the court can see the bright-red stick of colour. 'Cherries in the Snow by Revlon.'

She passes the uncapped lipstick to the clerk, who passes it to Grace, who examines it with puzzled amazement.

'What colour lipstick do you usually wear, Miss Ambrose?'

'This is my lipstick,' says Grace. 'I'm almost 100 per cent certain this is my lipstick. I used to keep one in my desk at work and it went missing round about the time I was communicating with Mr Smith. I remember I had to buy another one.'

'Where do you think Mr Smith got this lipstick from?'

'I think he must have taken it from my desk at some point … some point when no one was in the office.'

'Why do you think he took this lipstick?'

The judge coughs. 'Miss Bond, how can Miss Ambrose know what was going through the defendant's mind?'

Good point, old boy, good point.

But Grace pipes up: 'I think he probably wanted a memento of me. I think he was … sort of … obsessed with me.' She looks down briefly as if embarrassed by how conceited this sounds. 'I didn't realise it at the time but I think he was stalking me.'

The lipstick is returned to Miss Bond. She casts a long triumphant stare around the courtroom, slowly twists the lipstick back, recaps it and places it with cruel daintiness on the lectern in front of her.

'Did Mr Smith ever express suicidal thoughts to you?'

Her question is so throwaway and sudden I can tell Grace is caught off balance, the same way I am. She didn't ask about this during my evidence. Grace shakes her head, her forehead crumpled with shock.

'Please answer the question, Miss Ambrose.'

'No. I don't have any reason to believe this.'

'During the investigation his computer was searched and it

was found that he had looked at suicide websites.'

'I don't know about this.'

'Did he ever send you this poem?' Miss Bond holds the printout at arm's length from the top and reads from it like a town crier with a scroll. This whole public humiliation is unbearable. It's like I'm being forced to take off all my clothes in front of everyone.

'"Oblivion like soft velvet / comforting as sleep / pulled over me like a blanket / to stop my caged brain's cheeps / silence the chatter of my brain / succumb to gravity / hope I pass out before the pain / and stop the agony of being."'

The words sound ridiculous in her deadpan voice.

My mum makes a bleating squeaking sound. Everyone's eyes dart towards her, including mine. She's sobbing into her hanky. Dad's arm is around her. I don't know what to do. I'm simultaneously frozen and on fire. Mum and Dad don't know how to deal with the way the world is now. This is too much for them. They don't need to know my innermost thoughts; no one does, but especially not them. They're innocents, even more innocent than me. They can't handle harsh, worldly people like Brett and Miss Bond, and I can imagine what they think of Grace: that she's a scarlet woman, an icy temptress who turned my head with her sophisticated, middle-class ways. They think I should've stuck with our own kind: a good, solid working-class girl with her feet on the ground. Not put my head above the parapet. If only a good, solid girl had come to my rescue. I want to protect Mum and Dad from her scorn: *I wouldn't say we were friends … I think he was stalking me.* I want to protect them more than I want to protect myself. Grace must sound so aloof to them, so superior, her mouth full of cold marbles. I don't know how they're ever going to get over this and, for the first time since this whole process started, I feel guilty, guilty for putting them through it.

'Do you think, given Mr Smith's obvious instability and suicidal ideation, that the fall was, in fact, an attempt to realise that ideation?'

My mum sobs again and I lean over and squeeze her hand, which is clenched around her damp hanky. Everyone apart from Miss Bond turns to stare at us and I feel like telling them to fuck off. Miss Bond carries on. She's merciless. To her, I'm a loser. She'd never bother with a man like me. She thinks Grace is a loser too.

Grace shakes her head. 'No, his fall was not a suicide attempt. It was an accident.'

Miss Bond nods at Grace. To the judge, she says, 'M'lord, I have no more questions.' She sits with a dramatic waft of her robe, like a parachutist coming down to land.

The judge turns to Grace. 'We will now have a break for lunch. You are free to leave the court or, if you wish, you can come back and listen to the rest of the proceedings from the back.'

Grace whispers to the usher and he leads her from the witness box and out of a door at the back of the court. Her face is white and she keeps her head down. I wonder if she'll come back.

The court rises, the judge shuffles out and Greenslade comes over and tells us we can have lunch inside the Old Bailey if we want – there's a café – or we can go out. We decide to go to a café round the corner, for fear of bumping into Grace or Brett, but it's full of City types, shouting into iPhones. Me, Mum and Dad so obviously don't look like we work round here that I expect everyone knows we're at a trial. That's if anyone is even paying any attention to us, which they're not.

'I should've made a packed lunch,' says Mum, as we sit squeezed on tall spindly chairs between a load of overconfident, overpaid people, and tuck into our overpriced sandwiches.

I'm relieved it's too loud to talk as none of us know what to say to each other. The trial is the elephant in the room, too big to mention, and I don't want to set Mum off again. Her face is blotchy from crying and she keeps peering at me worriedly, like she thinks I'm about to go bananas.

'Oh!' she says suddenly, looking past me, her eyes expanding from worried to completely petrified. I glance over my shoulder. Brett is at the counter choosing what to have in his sandwich. He ignores us and makes a big show of looking as casual as possible: hands in pockets, big smile to the girl layering up ham and salad – 'hold the mayo', ostentatious tip clattering into the cup of loose change by the till. I wonder if he spotted us before or after he came in, if this is some sort of dare to himself or a challenge to us.

Like frightened rabbits, we stop chewing and stare blankly in front of us. Someone leaves, so there is a chair nearby. I can barely breathe for fear that Brett is going to come and sit on it but that's a challenge too much even for him and I hear him ask for the sandwich 'to go'. He walks past the window without looking in. For a moment only half a metre and a sheet of glass separate us.

'The bloody cheek,' says Mum, as the defendant – or, in my mind, the guilty – ambles out of sight. Dad and I mumble in agreement.

Without saying anything to each other, we go back at the last possible moment to minimise the risk of seeing him again. Mum's peering at me once more.

'You're not feeling like that any more, are you, Gav?' she asks, as we cross the street. She doesn't need to explain herself. I shake my head and put my free hand, the one that's not holding my stick, on her shoulder. I suppose that was Grace's one concession towards helping me: stating that my fall was not a suicide attempt.

Grace is hunched alone on a bench on the other side of the dock from where we were sitting. I might have known she'd come back to watch the rest. Curiosity has got the better of both of us. As we file past, Mum and Dad bumbling in front and me behind them dragging my bad leg, I accidentally catch her eye and she presses her lips together in an apologetic smile. I get a lot of pitying looks when people see my stick: pity mixed with relief that they don't need one. At least I'm not in a wheelchair. I realise Grace feels bad. For the first time, I consider the situation from her viewpoint and I see she's been caught between Brett and me. I wonder why she's here alone, why she's brought no one with her. She looks completely miserable.

We take our seats and I hang my stick on the back of the bench in front. The way she told the court my fall was an accident – so determined and definite – I realise I've been an idiot. I shouldn't have pressed charges. I should have let it go. None of this incriminating stuff about me would've come out. The lyrics of 'Silk Skin Paws' by Wire run through my mind – 'I shift the blame to the worm in the bottle, I shift the blame to anyone standing before me' – and I wonder if I am the worm in the bottle or if Grace is or even Brett, but I don't have time to think too much because Brett is now in the witness box. He's standing in this very confident upright way, like an off-duty footballer, and he's staring right at his lawyer like they've got some special relationship. I bet he's shagging her. And I bet he intimidated Grace into giving evidence that helped him out. The way she talked about him at the hospital that day, I knew he'd been working on her, making her feel sorry for him. He doesn't look like a broken man – not as broken as me, at least. He fitted right in among all those City wankers in the café. His voice rings out as if he's giving a PowerPoint presentation. I remember him in the Debate announcing to Grace that he'd got her a 'latte to go' and how I hated him at first sight.

39

'... and then he punched me right in the face. So, naturally, I defended myself,' said Brett. He kept his eyes on Jane, let the rest of the courtroom fade out. He enunciated clearly and kept his voice at an assertive but not aggressive mid-level.

'How many times did Mr Smith punch you?'

'I would say ten times. It's hard to be precise as it all happened so fast. But, yes, ten times approximately.'

'Could you describe what else happened?'

'He kicked me. Then he wrestled me to the ground. There was a bottle of champagne he'd brought up for his picnic with Miss Ambrose, and he fell on it and it broke. There was champagne and glass everywhere. We both got cut. I could also smell alcohol on his breath. He'd been drinking.' Brett had been rehearsing this for months but it still came out stilted.

'What was your relationship with Mr Smith prior to this incident?'

'I had no relationship with him. I had no idea who he was.'

'Why was he hitting you?'

'He seemed to be angry about me coming up there to the roof, interrupting his picnic with Miss Ambrose. He said the roof was his private place and that I shouldn't have come barging up there.'

The questions and answers danced smoothly back and forth between them. They were a good double act. Jane was the kind of person he could work with. He had a lot of confidence in her. Not so much confidence to stop him from nearly shitting himself just before the trial began but, still, she was a damn sight more impressive than the CPS's lame brief.

*

His first meeting with Jane had been kind of humiliating. Her office was in the Temple, in Five Paper Buildings, the chambers of QCs Jonathan Simons and Hilary Truelove. When he first walked in he had been surprised she was black but he hoped he had hidden it, then blushed at the worry he might not have, which he was sure immediately made his surprise obvious. Christ, she would think he was racist. Why shouldn't she be black? Why was he surprised? Perhaps because he had pictured the Temple as being even more white than the House of Commons. Hell, even the name – the Temple – sounded so ancient and Establishment. It was, literally, like going into some sort of mall made of buildings that looked like churches. There were even more men wafting round in wigs and black robes than you got in the Palace.

Subliminally, he had also assumed that all female lawyers looked like Nadine. At first sight the only thing Jane had in common with Nadine was that she was very good-looking and even though she was wearing a demure grey skirt suit, it couldn't hide her absolute killer body.

'Pleased to meet you, Miss Bond,' he'd said, when they shook hands over her leather-topped desk. 'Great name you've got there. Bond, Jane Bond. I won't say "shaken, not stirred": guess you must get that all the time.'

Jane Bond's sticky painted lips stretched into a smile but her eyes assessed him coolly. 'Yes. If I had a pound for every time someone's said that to me, I wouldn't have to do this job. And you did just say it.'

He grimaced. He was losing his touch. He'd been out of action too long. Mind you, her attitude was kind of charmless, considering he was a potential client. 'Perhaps Mr Mullarkey should've passed me on to Miss Truelove then.'

'Hilary Truelove is a man. And he's a silk so you wouldn't have been passed on to him, in any case … not on legal aid.'

So, this chick was a ball-breaker. Making out like he was some kind of charity case. These days there always seemed to be some chick breaking his balls: Nadine, Grace, they were all the same …

'*Anyway …*' She indicated a stiff-backed wooden chair on the other side of her desk. Brett sat down and she lowered herself into her own large ergonomic chair with ballerina poise, pulling her knees in their pencil skirt to one side. 'I've got the brief from Brendan … so how about you fill me in on the situation from your point of view, Mr Beamish?'

Brett filled her in on the situation from start to finish. Jane wrote notes in a blue foolscap exercise book in small, tight writing. She was wearing a gold cross on a chain, which dangled in the tempting shadows of her open blouse. The blouse was buttoned up to one inch above the middle of her breasts. Nothing was on show apart from the soft skin of her throat but there was something very projecting about her bust, even though it was small and covered by her suit jacket. Brett tried to focus on the fast movement of her pen nib. Sometimes he glanced out of the window, which overlooked the Thames. Sometimes he looked around her office. It was in one of the turrets of Five Paper Buildings, up ten flights of stairs. Leather-bound copies of *Halsbury's Laws of England* lined the shelves and piles of papers tied up with pink ribbon were stacked on the desk and floor. There was a marble fireplace and old-style glass lanterns overhead which let out a weak yellow light. Apart from her chair, the furniture was all really old-school, not unlike his office in the House – she even had the same green and brass table lamp as him. Except, unlike him, she was grand enough not to have to share her office with anyone else. It was weird to be the other side of a desk, for someone else to be the expert. This was what it meant to be emasculated.

The case was going to need a lot of investigation into Gavin's past, she told him. 'If he comes across on the stand as you've described then you've got a good run on this,' she said, after hearing the few titbits about Gavin's weirdness that Brett had gleaned from Grace the night of the accident.

'Obviously, if you can get any other information about him that might assist me, that would be very welcome.'

'I'll get as much dirt as I can.'

Jane nodded. 'Any information would be helpful.'

'I'll give you whatever you need, Miss Bond.'

She looked up at this, fleetingly held his gaze, and smiled.

'You can call me Jane.'

He smoothed his tie. The B-Man charm wasn't all gone.

'Am I going to win this?'

'We don't talk about winning in the criminal court, Mr Beamish. This is about justice, not winners and losers. I always do everything I can to get the best result for my clients.'

'Call me Brett ... It's about winners and losers to me, Jane. And the best result will be me winning this case.'

'We don't talk about winning because in the eyes of the court there is a victim.'

'I'm the victim in this situation, seriously.'

She consulted her notes. 'I understand how you feel, Brett, and, like I said, I'll do everything I can to get you the best result.' She looked up and stared straight at him. 'I will tell you that I've never had an innocent client go down.' Her sudden smile had a glint of cheekiness and he felt a wash of relief. He had confidence in this chick. He guessed it was against some sort of lawyerly protocol to speak of winning outright, but it was clear that she was the sort who gave a good fight. A girl after his own heart. In different circumstances he might have asked her out for a drink.

'I love your perfume,' he said, as she ushered him out of her office.

'Right.' She frowned at him as if he'd overstepped some sort of mark. 'Thank you.'

'How long've you been working here?'

'Five years. I was called to the Bar five years ago. This is where I did my pupillage and now I'm a tenant.'

'Right.' Brett only vaguely understood what she was on about. Suddenly he saw himself as she probably did: just another moronic brawler, getting into trouble over some worthless girl. She probably had a rich boyfriend who'd never been in trouble with the cops. Some fellow lawyer, or perhaps a banker, who had bought her that very delicious, very expensive-smelling perfume.

'Would you like my card?' He pulled his snakeskin case out, remembering as he handed his card over that none of the contact details were relevant any more, apart from his mobile number, which she already had. There'd be no point her ringing his office, unless she wanted to speak to Grace. When he got to the bottom of Five Paper Buildings, he felt really low in more ways than one. Through a ground-floor window, he glimpsed some lawyers, laughing and joking, with their feet on their desks. No doubt they all had their names hand-painted on the wooden sign outside the main door in Times New Roman, along with Miss Jane Bond. One of them caught him staring and, as he turned and scurried down the steps, he was sure he heard another gale of laughter.

He'd done his best to dig the dirt on Gavin via Grace. It had taken a month to persuade her to meet up with him. That meeting – on a bench near the Peter Pan statue in Kensington Gardens last summer – was the last time they had seen each other before the trial. Kensington Gardens had been the most neutral place he could think of: unconnected to either of them, far from CCTV cameras and anyone they might bump into. He had felt like a secret agent. If it wasn't for the life-and-death seriousness of it all he might have enjoyed the scenario.

‘We shouldn’t be doing this.’ Grace had kept glancing over her shoulder, as if they were being watched. ‘You know: the police—’

‘I know: they’ve told you not to talk to me. I’m not supposed to talk to you either.’

It was the first time they had seen each other since the accident. Grace was looking summery in a denim miniskirt, the sexiness of which was almost cancelled out by the Birkenstocks on her feet, although she had avoided looking like a total lesbian by going down the kooky route and painting her toenails blue. Why couldn’t she just do classic colours? Like Jane Bond, for example. Jane’s nails were always immaculately manicured with red or pink polish. Nadine had once said that girls who wore ‘funky’ clothes and make-up were trying too hard. She was right. Hadn’t anyone ever told Grace that class and femininity were what decent blokes liked? Still, she obviously suited anxiety and heat because her face was possibly thinner and definitely tanner; in fact, she was thinner overall, verging on svelte. Even her thighs looked less chunky. Somehow this distracted him from his rage. He’d forgotten how he had once found her quite attractive. It was also a relief to be with someone who knew everything, with whom he didn’t have to maintain total vigilance. Comforting. A memory of them grappling on a bed in the Travelodge popped into his mind but he shoved it away. Although he had occasional lewd imaginings about Jane Bond, his sex drive had basically gone right out the window. Lately, he wasn’t even sure he’d be able to perform to his usual high standards if called upon to do so. Anyway, they were taking enough risks just meeting up and, unless he blew the loan his dad had given him to help fight the trial, the only hotel he could afford right now would not be chic.

‘You look well,’ he said.

‘Thank you.’ She eyed him like he was being inappropriate. ‘So do you … look well, I mean.’

'Cheers. Appreciated … What've you been up to?'

'Not much. Went to see my parents.'

'Not been on holiday?'

'I don't have enough money. Unlike you, Brett, I am only a Band C committee assistant. I don't get paid enough to go on holiday … not anywhere good, anyway.'

'Oh, OK. Look, shall I just quit the small talk? I was only being polite.'

Grace looked both ashamed and affronted. 'Sorry. It's just I feel really worried about us meeting up like this. In person.' She glanced over each shoulder again but no one was around, except a woman in a burqa slowly pushing a pram. 'You know, we are being illegal.'

'Woo-hooh, *illegal* …' Brett made a spooked face. 'What, you think that lady over there is some sort of undercover operative, got a mike in the stroller, maybe a few sticks of gelignite—?'

'Keep your voice down. She might hear. Actually, I did read something about Al Qaeda terrorists escaping from somewhere disguised in burqas … or maybe they disguised themselves in burqas before they bombed somewhere … I can't remember—'

'Grace. Chill. Nobody is monitoring us. The cops know people are gonna meet up and talk. They can't keep track of everyone on bail. Look, I know you are the centre of the world of Grace but in the bigger picture no one gives a rat's fat arse about you or me, so can you just get over this paranoia? Given what's happened, I think it's fair enough to meet up.' He didn't need to spell it out: *you owe me, Grace. Big time.* The meeting had got off on the wrong foot. The plan had been to gently butter her up, then tangentially dig for dirt. Too long in the weird dead zone of suspension from work, he was losing his touch when it came to interpersonal relations – *the ability to persuade and influence key stakeholders in a convincing and diplomatic style.* The last six weeks had deskilled him.

'OK, then, what is it you want to talk about, Brett? I am not talking about the case. You're probably right the police haven't got time to monitor every Tom, Dick and Harry but it is completely illegal for you to intimidate a witness.'

Grace's surprising bluntness was frustrating but sort of admirable. He'd always thought of her as a pushover. He softened his expression as much as possible. 'Grace, I'm really sorry if I'm intimidating you—'

'—You're not intimidating me. I'm just saying it's illegal to intimidate a witness or influence a witness's statement in court. I've got a witness care officer. She told me that. There's laws in place to protect me.'

'Yeah, yeah, I know the whole deal … OK …' Brett sighed, as if pent up with a million things he wanted to say but couldn't. The way to play it was with heart-rending sincerity:

'Grace, I just needed to see you. It's too weird not to, after everything that's gone down. It's been really hard. I can't talk to anyone …'

Grace scuffed the parched grass beneath her feet. 'I realise it must be hard for you … I'm sorry …'

He ignored this. What good were apologies? She'd apologised before, and now she didn't even sound convincing. He had to get info. Subtly. Or maybe not so subtly.

'You know they've upped the charge?'

'What?' She swung round, eyes wide.

'The charge. It's now GBH with intent. I found out at my plea hearing. Gavin's spoken to the police.'

'Oh my God …'

'Yeah. He told them that I intended to hurt him, that I pushed him on purpose.'

'Oh my God …'

'Yeah. But you know I didn't, right? You know it was an accident. Right?'

Grace glanced over her shoulder again. A man in red shorts and a white vest ran by. To him they were an ordinary couple, enjoying a blameless but slightly tense evening in the park. An ordinary couple with ordinary-couple problems. The guy was probably running off his own worries. When he was out of earshot, Grace hissed, 'We're not supposed to talk about this, Brett. What if someone finds out?'

'No one's going to find out unless you or I tell somebody. And I'm not going to tell. Are you?'

Grace shook her head. He turned his most sincere gaze onto Grace. Sincerity, like patience, did not come naturally. But, actually, he did feel pretty sincere all of a sudden. 'I'm fucking terrified, Grace. I could get life for this.'

'Life!'

'Yes, the maximum term for GBH with intent is life. My brief says I'm looking at six years if I plead guilty or it could be up to ten years if I plead not guilty and they convict me. I'm shitting myself so much I'm even thinking about pleading guilty to get a shorter sentence.'

'No! You can't do that! God … I can't believe he's done this.' Grace chewed on her thumbnail. 'He's made a terrible situation even worse. I can't believe it.'

Suddenly directness as well as sincerity seemed the best way forward. After all, why wouldn't he be curious about his accuser? 'What's Gavin like?'

'I don't know. I hardly know him. I only met him that one time on the roof.'

'Is that all?' This loser had derailed his entire life and she barely knew him?

'Oh, and once the other week in hospital.'

'Hang on, you went to see him in hospital?'

'Yes.'

He stared at her in astonishment. She jutted her jaw. 'I felt like I wanted to see him, after everything that's happened. Same reason you wanted to see me, I suppose.'

Brett doubted this. She had no ulterior motive for seeing Gavin, except, perhaps, guilt. Guilt was one of her main motivators. He'd sussed that out about her. It was the main reason she'd agreed to meet him.

'How'd it go? Was he pleased to see you?'

'No, not really, not surprisingly.'

'Right.'

'He's in a bad way.'

Brett fought back the temptation to say 'good'. 'I'm sorry to hear that,' he murmured.

'He's going to be able to walk again though, thank God.'

'Yeah, that's a relief.'

'Although he might always need to use a stick.'

'I see …' Brett examined his nails for non-existent dirt. He needed to get back to the point of this meeting. 'So, anyway, most of your relationship with this guy was conducted online?'

'We didn't have a "relationship", Brett.' Grace glowered. 'We were never even friends, not properly. We just emailed each other for a while. I didn't even know his real name or that he worked in the House. He pretended to be someone else. Reuben Swift. Made out he was some sort of musician, some sort of singer-songwriter, when he was just a shit poet. I know it sounds really stupid but I think …' She looked at her blue toenails.

'—Think what? Tell me.'

'… I think he was in love with me or thought he was in love with me, even though he didn't know me. The whole thing was completely mad. He was like a stalker. In fact, I would say he was a stalker.'

'Did you ever mention me to him, back then?'

Grace's gaze shifted to the side.

'Did you?'

'… Yes, maybe, but only briefly.'

'What did you say?'

'Nothing much. He asked about my colleagues and I just told him about you and Rosemary …'

'You never said we were having a thing?'

Grace winced. Hard to tell if she was wincing at the memory of their 'thing' or at his suspicion she might have told Gavin about it. 'No! Of course not. No, he just guessed somehow.'

Attention to detail had always been Brett's strong suit and, even though he'd been fucked up lately, his brain was suddenly firing on all cylinders. Piecing together the build-up to Gavin's fall was like drawing together the threads of the argument in a committee report. Brett had always been logical. If he hadn't favoured politics, he could have been a lawyer, he reckoned. The way Jane Bond's brain operated was similar to his own. From what Grace told him he could work out how Gavin had gone from jealous obsession to the edge of insanity and had literally tipped right over. Something that had been bobbing around in the back of his mind, something half forgotten, suddenly surfaced: he had seen Gavin before – in Portcullis House the first time he and Grace went for lunch together, and in the corridor one Friday when he'd been exploring the House. Gavin was the weirdo giving him daggers. Gavin already knew who he was. Gavin had been hating him for months before the accident.

Grace was now babbling with the nervousness of the guilty: '… When I went to visit him in hospital I told him you were in a bad way, that you were worried sick and you could end up in jail. I was hoping he'd tell the police it was an accident …' Clocking his dropped jaw, her eyes widened again as if her defenceless bunny act might be enough to ward off any anger. '… I know it probably sounds stupid of me, but I was hoping he would help you, that if he told the police it was an accident they'd drop the charge …'

Brett cradled his head in his hands. Yes, it bloody did sound stupid. It was stupid. Goddamn, Grace was naive. She had no idea how the world worked. She had no idea of the true vindictiveness and self-interest of most people. Couldn't she see that by appealing to Gavin's better nature she had screwed everything up for him even more? This was what happened when you hung out with people with a totally different world view.

Jane's questions ended and the CPS lawyer began his attack. Brett swatted away his questions easily. He'd been sitting through the trial long enough to see the guy was a jerk. Even the reporters kept laughing at his stupid outdated phrases. Brett was sure his laid-back Aussie accent was making a mockery of Greenslade's old-school BBC voice and he was pretty certain the court was more on his side than Gavin's, just because Greenslade was such an obvious prick. Plus, during the cross-questioning of his evidence, Gavin had come across like the loony tune he clearly was: pretending to be someone else – a dead man, for crying out loud, and living in his office because he was agoraphobic, which sounded like a bullshit phobia to Brett – how could you be scared of going outdoors? In any scenario Brett would have hated the guy. He was the kind of bloke who would've been picked last during sports. Even the way he'd been nibbling his sandwich in that café at lunchtime had been irritating, as was the way he now sat hunched up at the back with his folks; all of them with faces like slapped arses. Brett's own dad would tell Gavin to 'swallow a bag of concrete and harden the fuck up'.

He hadn't planned on telling his parents anything unless he ended up in jail, but when the story broke in the *Daily Mail*, he let them know in case they found out via some stickybeak

English mate who had read it. Predictably, Dad had gone apeshit and, after crowbarring the full story out of him, shouted, 'Brett, you're an idiot. I told you: never mix business and pleasure. If you had listened to me and taken my advice, you wouldn't be in this bloody mess. I'm totally disappointed in you. I can't believe my own son is a fucking criminal.'

'I'm not a criminal, Dad. There hasn't been a trial yet. There is such a thing as innocent until proven guilty. You might have heard of it.'

'Don't be sarcastic with me. You're a bloody idiot—'

He had heard the sound of the phone being wrenched out of Dad's hand, and Mum came on the line: 'You know your father, Brett, he's just worried. He always gets angry when he's worried. He doesn't mean it. You know it's just his way. He wants the best for you. We both do … we're both so worried …'

He could practically hear her wringing her hands.

One good thing Dad had done was transfer five grand into his bank account – 'A loan, right, 'cos a decent brief, who's gonna get you off, is not gonna be cheap. Soon as you sort yourself out, you can pay it right back.' He didn't know about legal aid and Brett wasn't about to tell him. Apart from buying him a suit for a job interview when he graduated from uni, it was the first time Dad had given him any money since he'd left home. Dad was the toughest bastard he'd ever met and he'd never wanted to be indebted to him, but, fuck it, the loan would get rid of his credit card debts and buy him some time if the House stopped paying him while he was suspended.

Only one of Greenslade's questions really rattled him. It was the one he had been bracing himself for: 'Would you like to tell the court what you did immediately after Mr Smith fell off the roof of the House of Commons?'

'What I did?'

'Yes.'

'I was with Miss Ambrose.'

'I know. But I want to know what you did immediately after Mr Smith fell.'

Brett shifted a little on the stand. 'I went back to my flat, with Miss Ambrose.'

'And then what did you do?'

'Spent the night at my flat.'

'Who with?'

'With Grace. Miss Ambrose. Asleep. Nothing sexual occurred.' The word 'sexual' buzzed in the hush of the courtroom as if lit up with neon. Brett caught one of the reporters glancing over towards Grace, who was sitting on her own on a bench on the other side of the dock from Gavin. Her face was dead white, like she was about to puke.

Jane looked ready to spring up and make an objection but the judge patted the air in a calming gesture.

'Did you go to the police?' asked Greenslade.

This was the point that was hard to explain away. Brett could hear his blood pumping in his ears. 'No. I was going to, but the next day Miss Ambrose had already gone to them, and when I got into work I was arrested.'

'Your lordship, I have no further questions.'

As soon as Greenslade sat down, Jane stood up, like they were on a see-saw.

'Your lordship, I have one more piece of evidence to put before the court. A written character statement in support of my client from his manager at the House of Commons, Mr Hugo Llewellyn.' Brett peered up at the gallery, where Hugo was craning his neck to hear. His expression was rapt and appreciative and he was stroking his whiskers as if watching a thought-provoking piece of modern theatre.

'Please, go ahead, Miss Bond.'

'Thank you, m'lord.' She read from a piece of paper. '"It has been my pleasure to be acquainted with Mr Beamish since January last year, at which point he commenced work as an economic specialist for the Economic Scrutiny Committee, for which I am the clerk. He was on secondment from Her Majesty's Treasury and, indeed, I was the chair of the interviewing panel that appointed Mr Beamish to the post. He was the most impressive applicant by far for the job and his subsequent excellent work for the Committee bore out those notable first impressions manifestly …"' Hugo's prose style made Jane sound like a bad ventriloquist. '"Mr Beamish is assiduous, well-mannered, trustworthy and possesses a rigorous intellect, superb attention to detail and a truly Stakhanovite work ethic …"' Hugo now had his chin in his hand and was leaning over the edge of the gallery with the other hand cupped around his ear. His character reference was so OTT it sounded like he was taking the piss; yet again that old Commie work ethic thing. None of the jury would know what he was on about. '"His professionalism knows no bounds. In short, he is an ideal employee. I was shocked when I learned of his arrest. The crime with which he has been charged is utterly antithetical to his character. Mr Beamish was, and is, dedicated to his career. It is improbable that he would risk losing all the success he has achieved thus far by committing such a senseless act. I fully endorse the good character of this young man and would commend him to anyone as a rare example of integrity and honour amongst the youth of today."'

He owed Hugo a drink for this. *Integrity and honour*: thank God someone had noticed.

'Thank you, Miss Bond,' said the judge. 'And, now, may we have the closing speech from the prosecution?'

While Greenslade and Jane gave their closing speeches, Brett studied the jury. They didn't look up to the job. Most of them were staring into the middle distance with their mouths open. Surely juries should comprise experts, not ordinary people. Brett wondered why Hugo hadn't given the character statement in person. Perhaps he feared the press. Brett switched focus to the reporters, scribbling into their notebooks. Scruffy ratbags. Nosy, lazy bastards. He used to watch them during public evidence sessions with the Economic Scrutiny Committee, knowing that what most of them were writing down would be way off the mark. He wondered which filthy rags these guys worked for and how they'd write him up. Bloody parasites, feeding on other people's misery. Fuck, it was shameful. No wonder Hugo hadn't wanted to damage his rep by standing up in court. He wasn't such a dumb old bastard as he appeared. He knew which side his bread was buttered on.

The closing speeches were knotted with the same long-winded, old-style phrases as Hugo's – 'I invite you to consider', 'It would be your duty to', 'Let us note the fact', 'May I remind you', 'I am minded to note', 'Indeed', 'Furthermore', 'Moreover', 'Nonetheless'. Brett wished they'd hurry up, tell it straight, get the whole ordeal over and done with. He was feeling so tense, he could barely concentrate on what either Greenslade or Jane were saying. From the corner of his eye, he spotted the usher surreptitiously texting someone beneath the table. This seemed totally disrespectful. The judge looked bored too. Hopefully he wasn't too past it to get to grips with the case.

Once Greenslade and Jane had each given their two cents' worth, the judge gradually came to, a dinosaur rousing himself from an aeon of sleep. In a voice so monotonous he could have been reading the footy results, he began summing up. Despite the fact he looked like he was about to kick the bucket and he spoke so slowly Brett wondered if he was on tranquillisers, he had grasped the facts surprisingly well. Some jurors scribbled notes, although they might have just been doodling.

The judge rambled on, always using ten words where two would do. Finally he concluded: 'May I remind you that the test for a guilty verdict is beyond all reasonable doubt. If you have sufficient doubt that Mr Beamish committed this crime, you must find him not guilty.'

Brett stood with his head bowed, sending out thought waves of innocence to the jury.

The court was adjourned. It was 3.30. If the jurors reached a verdict by 4.30, which seemed unlikely, everyone would be sent home and their deliberations would recommence the following day. Another night of sleepless waiting. The waiting was worse than the possible punishment, like waiting to be sick when you were feeling nauseous. The jurors filed out with inappropriate haste, bumping up against each other. Brett wondered if this was because they'd already made up their minds. 'All rise,' announced the clerk. Everyone stood and waited for the judge to shuffle out. Brett turned to the dock officer, who was so butch she made him feel effeminate. She nodded and opened the door of the dock.

40

The good-looking reporter smiled at her as he left the courtroom, but Grace didn't smile back: the situation was not a smiling matter. The reporter was handsome in a raffish way, not half as clean-cut as Brett. Something ironic in his expression convinced Grace that he was the person who had sniggered when Mr Greenslade had asked her if she had been 'in drink' on the night of the incident. 'No, I was not "in drink",' she had replied, which provoked another snigger. While watching the rest of the trial from behind the reporters' bench she had studied him. He had nice hair: thick, wavy and dark, not dissimilar to Dan Sheridan's, in fact – the poor guy whose identity Gavin had stolen. At one point the reporter had glanced over his shoulder, sensing her gaze, and their eyes had met. She wondered which paper he worked for and how he was going to write up the trial; specifically, how would he write her up? Headlines slammed into her mind: SECRETARY REVEALS COMMONS SEX SECRETS. JEALOUS STALKER'S COMMONS SUICIDE BID. COMMONS LOVE TRIANGLE SUICIDE ATTEMPT.

Once the summing-up was over, she loitered in the courtroom with Kiranjit until Gavin and his family had gone. Gavin limped ahead of his parents, leaning heavily on his stick. Mr Smith laid a protective hand on Mrs Smith's solid beige back. They all stared straight ahead as they passed: Mrs Smith's face crushed, red and damp; Mr Smith's, rigid, pale and dry; Gavin blank. She pictured Mr and Mrs Smith eating dinner at a small Formica-topped table; plain, old-fashioned food – pork chops, boiled potatoes and peas. Silence would hang between them, only broken by the tinging of the carriage clock on the mantelpiece in the lounge and the occasional platitudes they murmured to each other. She thought about the name Gavin Smith. It made her think of Rich Tea biscuits on a rainy afternoon. A railway waiting room in a place like Crewe. A commemorative plate from the back of the *Sunday Times* magazine that had ended up in a PDSA charity shop. The name Gavin Smith was the polar opposite in style from Reuben Swift.

She wondered what Mr and Mrs Smith thought of her and Brett, whether they hated them or whether they were too humble for hatred. No doubt Gavin hated her, although, when she had caught his eye as they all filed back after lunch, she had glimpsed something – regret, perhaps – in his expression. She'd tried an apologetic smile but she wasn't sure he'd read it right. She wondered where he was living now, if he was back at his flat or staying at his parents'. That he had lived in the House for over a year was absolutely crazy. He was like the Hunchback of Notre Dame. Right down to falling off the roof of a huge Gothic building and surviving. Which made her like Esmeralda. The kindhearted gypsy girl, who got her handsome prince in the end. She was going by the Disney version, although she had a vague idea that in the original book Esmeralda was hanged and Quasimodo died of heartbreak. If she hadn't been so repelled by the thought of Gavin lurking around the House and spying on her, Grace would have admired him for his daring in living there, although it was daring born of desperation, which wasn't really daring at all. She wondered what had driven him to it, and how he'd managed not to get caught. In practical terms the House had everything you needed to live: food, washing facilities, and plenty of leather chaises longues to sleep on. It would be possible to use it literally like a house.

*

After ten minutes Kiranjit let her go. Brett would apparently leave after another half-hour. Everyone's exits were staggered to avoid awkward encounters outside. THE LAW OF THE WISE IS A FOUNTAIN OF LIFE, she read from the murals in the marble hall on the way out. LONDON SHALL HAVE ALL ITS ANCIENT RIGHTS. And, more puzzlingly: POISE THE CAUSE IN JUSTICE'S EQUAL SCALES.

Back home she wondered whether to text Brett a message of support. This was potentially his last night of freedom. In his place she'd be going mad, unable to eat or sleep or possibly even talk. Brett was made of sterner stuff but, even so, he was only human. Her memory was caught by his decorous weeping on the night of the accident. She imagined him perched on his neatly made bed, staring at the wall only three feet away. You did well today. Good luck for tmr. I'm thinking of you, she composed on her phone, but the dry impersonality of the medium seemed wrong, inadequate to the momentousness of the situation, so she abandoned the message. In any case, Brett might interpret it the wrong way: that she wanted to get back together.

She wished the situation could have been resolved without court. What had happened affected no one but themselves. They could have sorted things out between them. A picture of Brett and Gavin hugging each other, possibly in the middle of a big yurt, popped into her mind. Why did the great, clunking, expensive machinery of the legal system have to be involved? When it came to personal problems, it was, as with Parliament, like using a sledgehammer to crack a nut.

Just before midnight, as she was drifting into sleep, the beep of an incoming text jolted her awake. Her bedside table glowed in the phone's blue light. Thanks for today. BB

Good luck. I'll see you tmr, she texted back. She wasn't compelled to go into court again and although part of her wanted to hide from the world and stay in bed forever, she also wanted to know the verdict as soon as it was delivered.

The next day the court rose and sat like a church congregation as the judge entered and fumbled towards his throne. After only an hour of deliberation that morning, the jury had reached a verdict. Grace's heartbeat had gathered pace with every turn of the minute hand on the clock in the court's café. If the way she was feeling was anything to go by, Brett must be on the verge of a heart attack. She no longer had the protection of the witness waiting room and had to sit and watch the rest of the trial in the public gallery on a bench behind Gavin and his family, a few feet from Hugo, who kept trying to catch her eye.

The foreman of the jury was asked to stand, as was Brett. Brett planted himself ramrod straight as if facing a firing squad. His skin was waxen, with dark circles under his eyes. The unnerving assurance from the day before had drained away. The foreman, a heavyset man with a slow-witted face, hoisted himself up.

'Have you reached a verdict on which you are all agreed?' asked the clerk.

'Yes, we have,' nodded the foreman self-importantly.

'In respect of the count that he unlawfully and maliciously injured Gavin Smith with intent to cause him grievous bodily harm, do you find the defendant guilty or not guilty?'

The foreman consulted the paper in his hand as if he had forgotten the verdict already. 'Not guilty.'

The courtroom expelled a collective sigh, like air escaping from a balloon. Brett closed his eyes. Grace's heartbeat quickened then slowed. The foreman and the rest of the jury grinned towards Brett, who pressed his palms together and nodded as if bestowing a blessing. Colour had flooded back into his face. It is good, it is right what you have done, he seemed to be saying. Like acolytes, they had paid homage to his decency and he graciously accepted their dues.

Gavin's head was bent, his mother's and father's arms were around him but he remained immovable and unreactive to the cacophony of congratulations in the courtroom.

Grace wondered what would happen next. From the way Brett and Miss Bond were beaming at each other she suspected they'd be going for a celebratory drink to which she wouldn't be invited. The end of the trial ought to be marked in some way but she wasn't sure what was appropriate. She escaped from the public gallery before the others and hid for a while in the toilets, giving everyone time to leave the building. She felt strangely flat, in a no-man's-land of emotion. Her life could now continue, but she had no idea what to do next, both in the immediate future and beyond.

Outside the court no one was around. Or at least no one she recognised. A number of rough-looking families and smooth-looking lawyers were dotted about, smoking and chatting and shivering in the January cold. A few press photographers loitered on the other side of the road with big cameras but, thankfully, no one took her picture. She lingered like a wallflower at a party, feeling as if she ought to communicate with someone in some way. She needed to debrief, chew the fat, but with whom? As she made to leave, she caught Hugo ambling along the pavement on the other side of the road, hands in pockets and a golfing umbrella hooked over one wrist. He had a preoccupied but pleasant frown, as if wondering what drink he fancied to revive himself now the curtain had come down. She considered sneaking off in the opposite direction, even though it appeared he was heading the way she wanted to go but, before she got a chance, his fruity voice parped: 'Aha, there you are, my dear. I'm so glad I've caught up with you at last ...'

'Hi Hugo.'

'I just wanted to congratulate you on a most excellent performance yesterday. I don't think Brett would have done it without you.'

'Thank you. I'm sure your statement was a lot of help too.'

'Which way are you walking?'

'To the Tube. St Paul's.'

'May I accompany you? I'm not very good with the Underground. I usually drive into work but as I was coming here this morning I left the car at home – didn't think I'd be able to find anywhere to park. I'm sure you're far more *au fait* with public transport and can point me towards Westminster. Better go in and catch up, but do feel free to take the rest of the day off if you need to recover. I'm sure it's been very draining for you.'

There was no way to refuse his company. They walked at Hugo's trundling pace, him on the outside of the pavement, in case, as he explained, a carriage splashed her with mud. He pointed out locations that appeared in Dickens and did not mention the trial again.

Nearing St Paul's, Grace glimpsed Brett and Miss Bond sauntering towards a smart new restaurant down an alley off Paternoster Square. She felt relieved after all that she hadn't bumped into him. Hugo might be an unsatisfactory debrief partner but Brett wouldn't have been much better, seeing as he had other fish to fry. He and Miss Bond looked like boyfriend and girlfriend rather than a recently acquitted defendant and his 'brief', as he had proprietorially described her. She threw her head back and laughed at something he said as he held open the door into the restaurant's hard, shiny interior.

'Will Brett be allowed back to work now?' she asked Hugo, interrupting his rumination on Marshalsea Prison, where Dickens's father had been jailed for debt.

Hugo halted. A shrewd light sharpened his watery blue eyes. 'My dear, hasn't he told you?'

'No. What?'

'He's been offered a job at the Royal Bank of Scotland, contingent on … things going his way today.'

'Oh … right.'

'You remember he disappeared to RBS during the dissolution. I knew he was up to something. He's a very ambitious young man, is our Mr Beamish … Yes, his secondment with us is over, I'm afraid, and, given the way things have gone today, he's now free to take up his new job. Under the circumstances, I think it's probably for the best.'

'Yes, you're probably right.' Grace realised from the delicacy of Hugo's explanation that he thought she was disappointed, that she was pining after Brett and her testimony had been a coded declaration of love. She pointed Hugo towards the westbound platform of the Central Line and instructed him to change at Bond Street. She decided to take the eastbound line to Bank, even though she could have gone the same way as him. 'I suppose I'll see you at work tomorrow,' she said, hoping he might suggest she take another day off to recover.

'Indeed you will. New term, New Year, new broom and all that. Cheerio.' He raised his umbrella in cheerful salute.

41

Seven thirty, still in his office on the tenth floor of the RBS HQ, Brett was trying to figure out his new phone. It had so many more features than his previous phone that he kept accidentally bringing up the Internet when he didn't want it and sending texts twice or sending them before he'd finished so people got messages saying I am go or How or When are. He couldn't be arsed to read the instruction booklet and, in any case, he'd left it at home. His fantastic new home. One hundred square foot of clean, sharp lines with a 24-hour concierge on the ground floor, a gym and pool in the basement, a view of the Thames from the balcony and, best of all, a kitchen that was a totally separate room from the bedroom. Finally, he was in a pad that reflected exactly who he was. His neighbours were young professionals just like him. There would be no embarrassment about entertaining the ladies chez BB any more. Not that he'd entertained any ladies there yet. He'd had some hopes about Jane Bond but she had made it clear after his acquittal that they were nothing but necessary associates. It had been disappointing but, ultimately, fair enough: she didn't want him tainting her brand and, in the long run, if they had started a thing he would've always felt indebted to her and not fully in the driving seat, which wasn't really his scene. Plenty of eye candy in his new office anyway. The sweetest of which was Sabine, a beautiful asset manager from Paris who, as his dad would say, had 'legs right up to her bum'. He'd certainly like to manage her assets.

As it happened, it was Sabine's twenty-sixth birthday that day and she'd sent a group email inviting everyone for drinks at

Vertigo, a champagne bar on the forty-second floor of Tower 42, just round the corner. He was flattered to be invited, seeing as he was the new kid on the block, and, though he wasn't keen on tall buildings these days, despite the fact he now spent most of his life in places high above the plebs, he was hardly going to wuss out of Sabine's birthday because of vertigo. Kind of an insensitive name for a rooftop bar, come to think of it. He couldn't see a very small bar being called Claustrophobia or a big open-air bar named Agoraphobia. This reminded him of Gavin, which reminded him of Grace, which reminded him that he ought to contact her and say thanks. He'd been meaning to do this since the trial but everything had wound up so manic straight after and had carried on being so manic that he hadn't got round to it. Plus, he just couldn't work out the right words. Really, he just wanted to forget the whole episode. He'd landed on his feet and life was now sweet. After a little glitch – well, a major glitch – the B-Man was moving on up. The new job was a blast – hard work but, still, a blast – and though he'd started too late for this year's round of bonuses, he was told that come next Jan., he'd be raking it in.

Still, thanks were due to Grace. He'd do it right now. First he'd check Facebook. Actually – genius! – he'd friend her on Facebook: it would be a way of staying in touch without really being in touch. It would show he thought warmly of her without having to go into it all. Once she'd accepted his friend request he'd maybe send a more personal message. His fingers twitched into action.

Part Four

January, another year later

42

Grace and Rosemary settled into the downturn towards home time. The two hours between four and six o'clock were always painfully long, even more so than the other hours in the day, which were long enough. Time taunted them with the imminent prospect of freedom by slowing to the pace of dripping treacle. The light was already fading, the sky growing purplish over the yellow turrets of the Palace. Their office still overlooked other offices across a wide inner courtyard, where other people still also sat at desks in front of computers, bathed in epileptic fluorescence. It was cosy peering into warm, bright offices from the vantage of another warm, bright office. They were all so protected, not only by the stone and guns but by the sheer weight of tradition, the promise of their comfortable pensions and the knowledge that they could work here until their retirement and would never lose their jobs unless they did something truly terrible.

Hugo shuffled in on the woody, meandering strains of an oboe solo emanating from his office and asked if Grace wouldn't mind typing up a letter for the Chairman. '… I'll just dictate. It's to Elsie …'

'Elsie?'

'John Elsingham. Put his name and address in the top left—'

Grace typed *John Elsingham MP, House of Commons.*

'No! He's not a Member any more.'

'Oh. When did that happen?'

'For heaven's sake. At the last election. He's also a Lord now. Don't you read the papers, Miss Ambrose?'

Grace shrugged, deleted *MP*, repositioned the cursor, and typed *Lord.*

'He's still a Right Hon, by the way … capital R, small t, Hon with a capital H …'

'What does "Right Hon" mean, anyway?'

'It means Right Honourable, of course.'

'Yes, I know, but what does that mean?'

'It means you're a Privy Counsellor. Usually you are or you have once been a member of the Cabinet. The Lords of Her Majesty's Most Honourable Privy Council … Part of the inner circle …'

'Not necessarily right or honourable then?'

Hugo's beard twitched around his mouth. 'That, of course, is not for me to opine upon. Nor you, my dear. We are merely impartial servants to this great institution. Now, back to dear John … No, no, no, don't type it in – the Chairman can write "Dear John" himself …'

On the way back from the Chairman's office, she had to stop at the press gallery to deliver fifteen embargoed copies of the Committee's report on Financial Stability. The press gallery was where the Westminster-based political correspondents hung out. It was up a complicated series of stairs and corridors off the Principal Floor and Grace invariably got lost.

'Could someone point me towards the press gallery, please?' she asked, finding herself, as usual, accidentally walking into an office full of harassed-looking journalists. Various people looked up irritably and then one man stood and said, 'I was just going up there myself. Do you want to follow me?'

As their eyes met there was a frisson of recognition but Grace couldn't place him. He was a tall guy, quite good-looking, with dark, wavy hair.

'Have we met before?' he asked, as he ushered her out of the office.

'I'm not sure.' Grace studied him. 'You do look familiar. I

presume you're a journalist?'

'I'm afraid I am.'

'Have you been based at the House for a while?'

'About a year …' His forehead wrinkled in thought. 'Hold on … oh …'

The moment she saw the light dawning in his eyes, Grace remembered where she had seen him before. 'The Old Bailey,' she said. 'You were reporting on Brett's trial.' No point in being coy.

'The Old Bailey! Now I remember! That's right. God, how weird … I remember you. You were a witness, right?'

'That's right. For the prosecution.'

'Yeah, it's all coming back to me now. That poor bloke that fell off the roof. And your boyfriend was accused of pushing him.'

'Ex-boyfriend … Not that we were ever really …' Grace trailed off. She clutched the reports to her chest like a shield. They were now on the stairs leading up to a door that had *Press Gallery* painted on it in cream lettering.

'Sorry. Ex.' The man held the door open. 'But he got acquitted, right?'

'Yes.' Grace wished the man would shut up about the trial but he seemed to be delighted by the great coincidence of having reported on it and bumping into her again. She wondered which story he'd written. She'd looked them all up of course and pored over them in mortification, then tried to forget them immediately. The *Daily Mail* had described her as 'pretty, auburn-haired secretary, Grace Ambrose, 30', which had been gratifying if somewhat patronising. But this guy didn't look like he worked for the *Daily Mail*.

'You gave a very good performance, if I remember rightly.' The man grinned, as if paying her a compliment, although performing well at a trial hardly seemed like something to be that proud of. 'Sorry, I should introduce myself.' He held out his hand. 'Matt Gordon. I work for *The Guardian* … would you like me to take those?'

'Grace Ambrose. No, I'm fine. Thank you.' Awkwardly, she offered her right hand while still clinging on to the reports. His hand was firm and warm. He looked like a *Guardian* journalist: tie-less, jacket-less, an inexplicable but definite attitude of leftiness – it could have been the hair; he had undoubtedly lefty hair. His name rang no bells but she guessed he didn't write for the G2.

'Yes, I remember now: Grace Ambrose … Wonderful name you've got … Do you know what I thought when I saw you on the witness stand?'

'No.' Grace dropped her gaze. This was excruciating: this stranger knew all about the most embarrassing moment of her life so far.

'"Grace under pressure."'

'What?'

'"Grace under pressure." Hemingway's definition of courage. I thought it was very courageous of you. You don't often see that round here.' He gestured in the direction of the Chamber.

'Thanks.' Grace flicked her eyes away. His attention was so frank that she thought she might blush if she held his gaze. Was he flirting or did he just want a follow-up to his original story?

They were now in the press gallery at the row of leather-topped tables where committee reports, press notices and other newsworthy matters were laid. The last of the day's sun was streaming pink through the airborne dust onto the parquet floor. She placed her reports in the Economic Scrutiny Committee tray and made to leave.

'So you're still working here, then?'

'Yep. But I'm applying for jobs elsewhere. I've got an interview next week.' It suddenly seemed very important for him to know that her life wasn't defined by the House.

'Oh yes, doing what?'

'Editorial assistant. At a publisher's not far from here, actually. In Belgravia.'

'Very posh! Sounds great. So that's your real passion: books?'

Grace nodded. It had only recently occurred to her that this was what she wanted to do and, even though the job she was going for the following week sounded far more exhausting and responsible than being a Band C committee assistant, she actually felt, for the first time in years, excited by the prospect of a challenge.

'What about the guy who was acquitted – your ex – what was his name?'

'Brett Beamish. No, he's left, got another job.'

'Brett Beamish: that's right! It's all coming back to me.' Finally, he caught the pained look on Grace's face. 'Sorry, you probably don't want to go over it all again … especially not with a journalist …'

'… Not really.' Grace shifted a little further towards the door. 'I'd better go.'

Back in the office Rosemary opened her biscuit tin and offered Grace a chocolate chip cookie. 'Do you ever hear from Brett?' she asked.

Grace jumped, already nervy from the encounter with the journo guy. It was as if Rosemary could read her mind. 'No. Not really. Why?'

'I just wondered. He just popped into my head, that's all.'

'We're friends on Facebook. He updates his status a lot. Last I saw he was "Kicking back with a bottle or two of champers".'

'Really!'

'Might have been one of his little jokes.'

'Is he still at RBS?'

'Yeah. There was another status update that said he'd been promoted.'

'Well done him. Probably suits him more, that sort of go-getting environment. I always thought it was a bit slow-lane for him here. Bit sort of old-fashioned and traditional. Hugo said as much, didn't he? I expect all that business made him more determined than ever.'

'That business' was how Rosemary always referred to it. Grace noted she didn't ask about Gavin. Gavin was not on Facebook, as far as she could tell from her attempts to search for him. But then Gavin Smith was a common name. Googling him brought up 3,510,000 results. Top of the list was a professional poker player. It wasn't the Gavin Smith she knew. For a long while her Gavin Smith appeared to have no web presence, apart from the articles on the trial that contained his name, and the last she had heard of him was via HR, who sent a chirpy email informing her that he had taken voluntary redundancy. The implication was that he had been coerced into this rather than face a disciplinary hearing for the security regulations he had breached by misappropriating her pass and living in his office. She supposed he was back in Essex, back in his flat, wherever that was, although she wondered if he had found another job in a different part of the country, perhaps even a girlfriend. She felt a twinge of envy that Gavin had moved on, even though the poor guy deserved a new life. At least he was no longer hiding away in the great cosy edifice of the Palace. She knew only too well how easy it was to do that.

Only a month ago she had idly Googled him again. She'd tried various combinations of keywords – *Gavin Smith Essex, Gavin Smith House of Lords, Gavin Smith agoraphobia* – maybe he'd emerge on some sort of therapy chat room – and, extraordinarily, her Gavin Smith had come up on the website of Kill Your

Darlings Press, a small independent publishing company based in, of all the most un-Gavinish places, Stoke Newington. He'd published a slim volume of poetry entitled *in the Palace of red nightmares*. She knew it was slim because she'd ordered a copy and pored agog over the number of poems that were thinly veiled paeans – or perhaps elegies – to her. Some of them were obviously written in the first flush of obsession: 'eyes like blue skies … hair like the remains of the day …', 'lips like cherries in the snow, forbidden fruit I want to taste', '… a name like creamed rice, voice like crème fraîche / maybe even my name would sound divine in your mouth …' She cringed as she read them, feeling the dirty claustrophobia of unwanted sexual attention all over again. Some of the – presumably – later poems had a bitter edge – 'i fell head over the spires for you / there for the goddess of grace i went / no buts no ifs for me / because neither you nor he / were heavensent', 'cherry lips turned rotten / stomach turned on fruit / i should have forgotten' – and quite a few featured a recurring character called 'Plastic Man' or sometimes 'Man of Plastic', whom the narrator of the poem wanted to 'skewer on a turret's spike' or 'scythe down with the serjeant's sleek dark sword' or 'trample beneath the unicorn's hard stone hooves and be crushed between the lion's sharp stone teeth'. His Palace was an Alice in Wonderland phantasmagoria of gargoyles that sprang to life, enormously fat lords and floral wallpaper that started growing and 'grew so much it trapped the sleeping beauty in her office'. There were various political poems – one linking 9/11 with 7/7 called 'when arabic numerals turned american' and another conflating the damage caused to London on 7/7 with his own injuries – 'and we all limp on / nearly undone / but not quite / tunnelling our way / towards the light'. Another equated Plastic Man with the Prime Minister – 'smooth bland features / cast in the same bland mould / Men of Plastic / watch out with your blue-sky thinking / if you get too near the sun you'll melt.' The back cover said 'Gavin Smith was born and bred in Essex. He used to work at the House of Lords but doesn't any more.' Further Googling of *Gavin Smith poet* revealed that he'd read at various poetry nights around London, even as far afield as Brighton. She was quite impressed. There was an upcoming event at the Poetry Café in Covent Garden at which he was billed to read. She considered going, before catching herself: Gavin wouldn't want her there. The final poem in his collection featured a woman that she sensed was not her: 'a woman who listens to foxes and wishes she was one of them / because foxes, though cruel, are not as cruel as humans.' The collection was dedicated 'For Elaine' and, though his mum had looked like an Elaine, she was sure Gavin would never be so modern as to call his mother anything other than Mum. She hoped Elaine was bringing him more happiness than she ever had.

She spent the next half-hour Googling *Matt Gordon Guardian*. His byline photo came up with dozens of stories beneath. He looked nice: handsome, intelligent, not too clean-cut but not an out-and-out scruff – pretty sexy, actually. She wondered how old he was – early thirties, she reckoned. Older than her, in any case, with a well-established, impressive career. Plus he read books: well, he could quote Hemingway, at least. *Grace under pressure*. She liked that. She hadn't realised what she had done was courageous. She never thought of herself as brave, the complete opposite really. He was probably only trying to flatter her but, still …

She scrolled through his stories until there it was: COMMONS CLERK ACQUITTED ON SECRETARY'S EVIDENCE.

> Brett Beamish, a senior Commons clerk … Beamish's case was boosted by evidence from his ex-girlfriend, Grace

> Ambrose … Ambrose said: 'It was an accident' … Smith had started a fight with Beamish, a high-flying economics specialist, out of jealousy: 'He was jealous that Brett and I had had a relationship … I think he was sort of obsessed with me' … Smith had stalked Ambrose during the months preceding the incident. He had communicated with her via email under the pseudonym Reuben Swift, and, due to severe agoraphobia, had taken to sleeping in his office …

Poor Gavin. He came out of it looking like a nutter. Never mind her boosting Brett's case, the story had boosted Brett's then job by about three grades. 'High-flying economics specialist': he would've liked that.

'Chairman's draft finished at last,' announced Hugo, staggering into the office as if he'd just performed a back-breaking Herculean feat. Since Brett's departure he'd had to write all the briefs and reports himself, something he took every opportunity to moan about.

Grace printed the draft report out and took it to the photocopier. While the copier chugged out fifteen double-sided A4 stapled pages, she wondered about Matt Gordon, whether she would bump into him again before she got a new job and, if she did, whether he would ask her about the trial again. Typical: the only eligible man she'd ever come across in the House and his first impression of her was as a witness at her ex-boyfriend's trial. Not exactly a turn-on.

Returning to the office with her arms full of hot, crisp reports, she noticed a cream envelope in the post tray with her name handwritten on it and *Personal* in the top right-hand corner. A disciplinary warning from HR? A sacking letter? An anonymous note from Gavin, who had somehow sneaked back into the building? Her heart thumped as it always did when confronted with private correspondence at work.

She sliced the envelope open with a paperknife. There was a single sheet of cream paper inside with a green portcullis crest and a note written in a smooth, flowing hand.

Dear Grace
Hope you don't mind me writing to you like this. Wanted to catch you before you end up leaving the House. Sorry if I came across a bit insensitive earlier. I always make a fool of myself when I'm nervous. It was really nice to meet you and I was just wondering if you'd let me buy you dinner as a way of making it up to you? Somewhere away from 'the Westminster bubble'. Promise I won't mention anything about you-know-what. No worries if you're not up for it. Hope to hear from you soon and good luck with your interview next week.
Matt x

Grace stood smiling at the letter. Handwriting was so much more meaningful than texts and emails. Especially when your handwriting was as nice as his.

'Something interesting?' asked Rosemary.

'Yes, I think so,' said Grace. She slid back into her chair, trying not to smile too obviously, and looked again at the note from Matt. *Away from the Westminster bubble.* Yes, 'away' would be good. Selecting the nicest ballpoint from her penholder, she took out a compliments slip from the box on her desk and wrote her reply.

Dear Matt,
Thanks for the kind offer. Are you trying to put me under pressure?
Grace x

Outside, Big Ben agitated itself into striking the final hour of the working day. Inside, Grace felt as warm as freshly photocopied paper.

Acknowledgements

First off, I would like to thank my agent, Zoë Ross, and the team at Aardvark Bureau; in particular Emily Boyce, my editor.

I am very grateful to the following people, who helped with my research: Fiona Baigrie Hooper, Dale Jones, Natasha Jennings, Tanya Nash, His Honour Judge Peter Rook QC and, in particular, Siobhán Kelly, who gave me a great deal of her time. Any factual mistakes are all my own.

Thanks to Estelle Ana Baca, Nick Golding, John O'Donoghue, Harriet Paige and Tom Rebbeck, who read various drafts and gave excellent editorial advice, and to David Rose for his moral support.

Big shout out to Martha Sunarah Daïs (with yet another diaeresis and not an umlaut) and Catherine McNamara for help with the Australianisms.

I salute my colleagues and friends at the House of Commons, who are great and nothing like anyone in this novel.

In addition, I would like to thank the Arts Council for awarding me a grant, which helped fund the writing of this novel.

Finally, of course, much love to my extended family for their enduring support and to Martin and my best bud, Leah Sonnamara Rose.